Ben Tubbs Adventures

by

Richard Jefferies

Introduced by Andrew Rossabi

Petton Books
Foulsham, Norfolk

1 April 2016

The RICHARD JEFFERIES SOCIETY (Registered Charity No. 1042838) was founded in 1950 to promote appreciation and study of the writings of Richard Jefferies (1848–1887).

President   Andrew Rossabi

Secretary   Jean Saunders
                 The Old Mill
                 Foulsham
                 Norfolk NR20 5RB

Website   http://richardjefferiessociety.co.uk
email   info@richardjefferiessociety.co.uk

British Library Cataloguing in Publication Data.
A catalogue record for this book is available from the British Library.

ISBN: 978-0-9563751-7-9

Introduction by Andrew Rossabi ©

Typeset in Palatino Linotype.

Published by Petton Books, Norfolk, 1 April 2016.

Printed by Azimuth Print Ltd., Bristol.

Paper from forests that are managed to meet the social, economic and ecological needs of present and future generations.

Richard Jefferies on his fourteenth birthday
November 6, 1862
Photograph by J. G. Barrable, London

Notes on the text

Long before the Society had any plan to publish *Ben Tubbs Adventures* an unknown person typed a copy from the original manuscript. In doing so he or she improved the punctuation by adding commas and paragraphing Jefferies' text, which sometimes ran continuously over several pages. Mrs Frances Gay, Chairman of the Society, made a photocopy of the typescript 'running to 338 octavo pages… with the intention of sharing her fascination for this work with other members of the Society'.[1] However the transcriber made numerous errors, some serious, e.g. 'refectory' for 'refractory' (p.14), 'impossible' for 'possible' (p.77), 'setting' for 'dawning' (p.148), 'tidied' for 'tided' (p.156). Phrases, even sentences, were omitted in places. All this made necessary a laborious collation of the transcript with Jefferies' original. We have made further minor changes to the punctuation, to make the text easier to read, whilst spelling errors have been corrected.

Acknowledgements

The Richard Jefferies Society offer their sincere thanks to Andrew Rossabi for his masterly and learned introduction, for checking the typescript against the original manuscript held at the British Library and for adding footnotes. Jean Saunders is thanked for keying in the text and for producing the book; Peter Robins for proof-reading it. The initial prompt to produce the book came from Raymond Morse who held an incomplete type-written version of the story.

---

[1] *RJS* Annual Report 1974/5, p.3.

Abbreviations used in the footnotes

AF   *Amaryllis at the Fair* [1887] (London: Quartet Books, 1980).

AP   *The Amateur Poacher* [1879] (London etc.: Thomas Nelson & Sons [1911]).

B   *Bevis* [1882], Edited with an Introduction by Peter Hunt, The World's Classics (Oxford and New York: OUP, 1989).

BT   *Ben Tubbs Adventures*. Introduced by Andrew Rossabi (Foulsham, Norfolk: Petton Books, 1 April 2016).

E   Walter Besant, *The Eulogy of Richard Jefferies* [1888] (London: Chatto & Windus, 1889).

GH   *The Gamekeeper at Home* and *The Amateur Poacher* [1878, 1879], With an Introduction by David Ascoli, The World's Classics (no. 516) (London: Oxford University Press, 1948).

LP   Samuel J. Looker and Crichton Porteous, *Richard Jefferies, Man of the Fields, A Biography and Letters* (London: John Baker, 1965).

MM   George Miller and Hugoe Matthews, *Richard Jefferies, A bibliographical study* (Aldershot: Scolar Press, 1993).

MT   Hugoe Matthews and Phyllis Treitel, *The Forward Life of Richard Jefferies, A chronological study* (Oxford: Petton Books, 1994).

NB   *The Nature Diaries and Note-Books of Richard Jefferies*, edited with an introduction and notes by Samuel J. Looker (London: The Grey Walls Press Ltd., 1948).

OA   *The Open Air* [1885] (London: Chatto & Windus, 1904).

RHH   *Restless Human Hearts* [1875]. Introduced by Andrew Rossabi (Longcot, Oxon: Petton Books, 2008).

RJS   *Richard Jefferies' Letters to Aunt Ellen*. Introduced by The Richard Jefferies Society (Faringdon: Petton Books, 6 November 2009).

RJS   The Richard Jefferies Society.

SH   *The Story of My Heart, My Autobiography* [1883], (London: Quartet Books, 1979).

T   Edward Thomas, *Richard Jefferies* [1909], With an Introduction and Bibliography by Roland Gant (London: Faber and Faber, 1978).

TF   *The Toilers of the Field* [1892] (London: Longmans, Green, and Co., 1894).

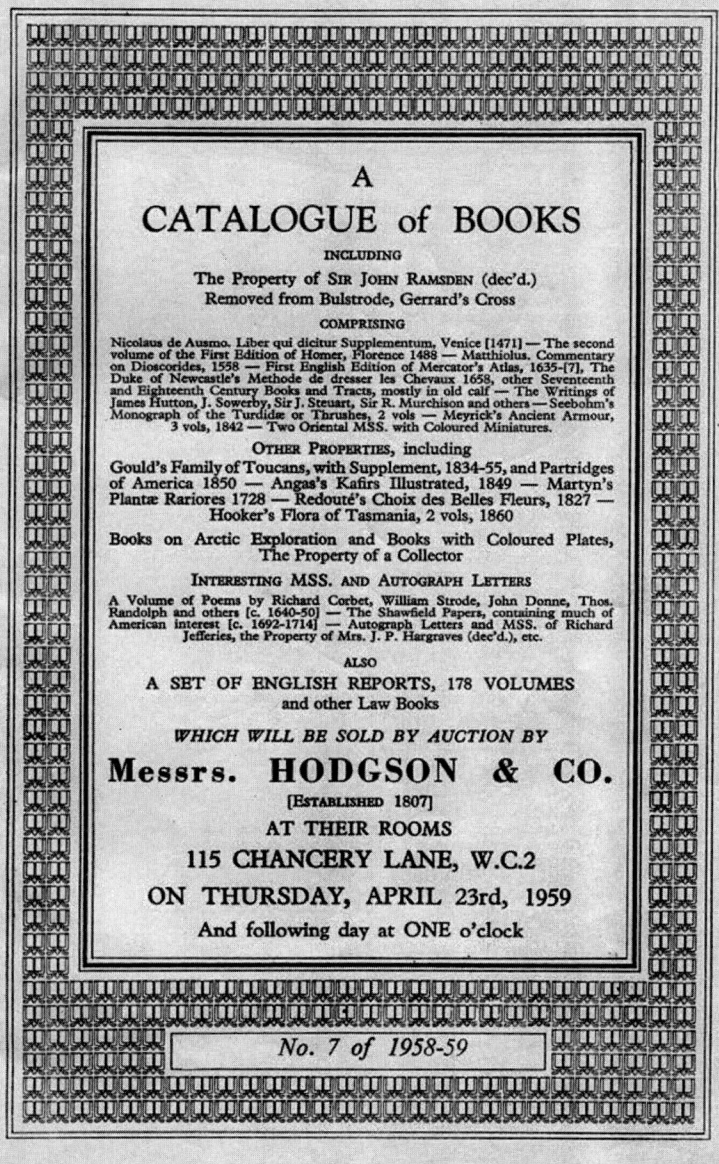

The auction catalogue that listed the sale of the manuscript for 'Ben Tubbs Adventures' – Lot 579.

Friday, April 24th, 1959

MSS. and LETTERS of RICHARD JEFFERIES.

THE PROPERTY OF MRS. J. P. HARGRAVES (decd.)
niece of Richard Jefferies.

Sold by Order of the Executors.

[margin annotation: "Hargrave his daughter — not his niece"]

578 Jefferies (Richard) Thirteen autograph Letters, signed "Richard" to his aunt Mrs. Harrild (some extracts of which appear in Edward Thomas's "Richard Jefferies," 1909) written from Coate, and Snodshill near Swindon, the first in 1860 when 12 years old, the last in 1871, describing his life at Coate Farm and his early experiences as a journalist with "The North Wilts Herald," also 5 A.Ll.s. (not complete) (18)

579 Jefferies (Richard) Original (apparently unpublished) MS. of a Story for Boys, entitled "*Ben Tubbs Adventures, by R. Jefferies,*" *closely written in an early hand (approximately 30,000 words) on about 59 pp. of a 4to exercisebook*

¶¶ *It is the story of a young rascal of 15, his wild experiences at school, from which he ran away; he boarded a ship at Bristol to cross the Atlantic, was shipwrecked and picked up by a slave ship, landed at New Orleans, watched the sale of slaves, passed through Texas, was captured by Indians, escaped, and with a Mexican arrived at S. Miguel, California; there he fortuitously met with friends and eventually found his way home.*

580 —— MS. copy of a Sermon on " 12 Luke 52v " *written on 13 small slips of paper* [1867], with MS. notes and fragments, a letter from New Zealand " *to the unknown Author of the " Gamekeeper at Home,"* 1879, etc., in 3 envelopes

581 —— A.L.s. from Smith, Elder and Co., sending him copies of " The Gamekeeper at Home " and enclosing a cheque for £75 for the Copyright, 24 June, 1878, with the agreement to publish " Greene Ferne Farme," 1 p., fol., 1879 (3)

582 —— Agreements with Longmans to publish " Story of my Heart," *signed by Publisher and Author* 10 August 1883, and for " Field and Hedgerow," 25 October 1888 (2)

583 —— Agreement with Sampson Low, Marston, Searle and Rivington to publish " Bevis," with conditions as to profits from the 3-volume edition and rights to print in America, *signed by Publisher and Author,* Jan. 23, 1882 (1)

584 —— Agreement with Sampson Low to publish " Amaryllis at the Fair " offering to advance £50 representing " *a Sale of Two Thousand Copies," signed by Publisher and Author,* 3rd December 1886 (1)

Samuel Looker's hand-written correction in the margin.

vi

Introduction

Andrew Rossabi

The manuscript of *Ben Tubbs Adventures* remained unpublished during Jefferies' lifetime. It was stored in the oak chest where he kept his papers. After his death in 1887 and that of his widow Jessie in 1926 both the chest and its contents came into the possession of their daughter, Mrs Phyllis Hargrave. Phyllis died at the end of 1958 and in April 1959 her cousin Christine Billing, who had lived with her at Seaford, put the *Ben Tubbs* manuscript and various other items up for sale with Hodgson's the auctioneers.[2] The sale was held at their rooms in Chancery Lane on 23 and 24 April. In its issue of 29 May, under 'Notes on Sales', the *Times Literary Supplement* reported that the manuscript had fetched £320.

The amount was almost certainly beyond the purse of Samuel Looker at that time and the buyer was more probably Colonel H.L. Bradfer-Lawrence, a noted antiquarian and collector who had already bought Looker's Jefferies manuscripts.[3] After his death in 1965 his executors deposited most of his collection of medieval western manuscripts, together with his substantial collection of manuscripts and printed books by Jefferies, on long-term loan to the Fitzwilliam Museum, Cambridge. The collection was then acquired by the antiquarian booksellers Bernard Quaritch, the founder of whose firm Jefferies dubbed 'that giant of the modern auction-room' in *Amaryllis*.[4] It was later dispersed among the British Library, Leeds University Library, Tokyo, and private collectors.

---

[2] Miss Billing presented the oak chest and Jefferies' writing-table to the Coate Museum in 1960.

[3] Colonel H.L. Bradfer-Lawrence (1887-1965) was educated in King's Lynn and worked as a Land Agent in Norfolk. He was a keen antiquary from his early years. He wrote 'The Merchants of Lynn' (1927) and 'Castle Rising' (1929). In 1935 he moved to Yorkshire on becoming managing-director of Hammonds Bradford Brewery. His interest in Richard Jefferies began early in the Second World War and he had virtually completed his collection by 1950. On Bradfer-Lawrence as book-collector see A.S.G. Edwards, *The Book Collector*, Vol. 53 no.1 (Spring 2004).

[4] *AF*, pp.45-6.

The British Library acquired the Jefferies manuscripts (including *Ben Tubbs Adventures*), letters and notebooks in May 1975, while the books in Bradfer-Lawrence's collection, including many rare and valuable first editions, were sold in July 1980 by G.M. & R.C. Davis, a Wiltshire firm specializing in Jefferies, who issued a 12-page catalogue, with a short preface about the collection, in a limited edition of 250 copies.

Professor Alain Delattre of Poitiers University claimed to have 'discovered' *Ben Tubbs Adventures*, both in 'The Jefferies Saga' and in his lecture 'John Richard Jefferies, His Worst and His Best',[5] where he called attention to the flagrant racism of the scenes aboard the slave-ship *Lopez*. Thus, apropos Looker and Porteous's statement that at the age of twenty-one James Jefferies 'decided he wanted to see more of the world, and, probably in London, joined a ship bound for America',[6] Delattre pertinently asked, 'Why London?'.

> If we had to make a guess, we would choose Bristol, because in John-Richard's first novel, or rather long short story, *Ben Tubbs Adventures*, which we alone of all critics have read after we discovered it, the hero embarks there. [7]

However, Delattre did not explain precisely what he meant by 'discovering' *Ben Tubbs*. Did he mean he was the first to unearth the manuscript in the Fitzwilliam Museum, read it, and bring it to the Society's attention? If so, it would have been sometime between 1962, when he first visited Wiltshire, and 1975, when at a *RJS* meeting held on 6 January the Secretary Cyril Wright gave a brief history of the novel, which he said was written in 1865/6, when Jefferies was 17. Mr Wright then gave a chapter-by-chapter synopsis, interspersed with readings by Mrs E.M. Thompson and Mr C.G. Couzens. He described *Ben Tubbs* as 'a schoolboy thriller', spoke of 'hair-raising if improbable adventures' and called the work 'a lively, extravagant, uninhibited piece of authorship'.[8]

oooOOOooo

---

[5] Professor Alain A. Delattre, 'John Richard Jefferies: his Worst and his Best,' lecture given at the Centenary Weekend held in the Swindon Arts Centre on Sunday, 2 August 1987. (*RJS Talks & Articles*, No. 62).

[6] LP, p.9.

[7] Delattre, 'The Jefferies Saga, Or The Man Who Died Twice', undated typescript, 135pp, p.51.

[8] *RJS* Annual Report 1974/5, *op. cit.*

Ben Tubbs Adventures[9] is Richard Jefferies' first extant book-length work. Neither Besant nor Thomas mentions the novel, nor do Looker and Porteous, and its existence remained unknown until 1959. That Looker does not mention it is surprising, since he certainly knew of its existence, having a copy of the Hodgson sale catalogue, on which he wrote to correct its description of Mrs Phyllis Hargrave as 'Hargraves' and 'niece of Richard Jefferies'.

Looker had befriended Mrs Hargrave, corresponded with her and often visited her at her home in the hamlet of Cox Hill near Perranporth. A devoted collector of Jefferies' manuscripts, letters and notebooks, he must surely have been aware of the unpublished novel even before the Hodgson sale. Yet he makes no mention of it, either in *Man of the Fields*, his biography of Jefferies seen through the press by his friend Crichton Porteous and published in 1965, some six years after the emergence of *Ben Tubbs*, or elsewhere. A possible explanation for Looker's silence is that Mrs Hargrave had expressed her wish for the manuscript to remain unpublished, and nothing said of it, because she feared exposure of a juvenile work of such inferior quality might damage her father's reputation.

We do not know when *Ben Tubbs* was written. Matthews and Treitel propose a date of c.1864 on the basis of the 'neat, tight scrip[t],' which is 'clearly early' and resembles the handwriting of the letters of that period. They remark the work's obvious parallels with Jefferies' abortive march to Moscow and subsequent attempt to reach America, 'but whether it was written before or after… has not yet been determined'. [10]

It seems more likely that Jefferies composed the novel after, in 1865 or 1866, at some time during the interval between the Moscow escapade and his joining the staff of the *North Wilts Herald* in March 1866. He probably wrote it in the room of the farmhouse attic that had been reserved for his use as a concession to his literary bent, perhaps, if in winter or early spring, with numbed fingers like Amaryllis sketching white wild violets in the garret at Coombe Oaks.

oooOOOooo

---

[9] MM, D24, p.739; MT, pp.14-15.
[10] MT, p.14.

Jefferies ran away on 11 November 1864, a few days after his sixteenth birthday.[11] He had a companion in his eighteen-year-old friend and first cousin James (Jimmy) Cox, who lived with his widowed mother on a neighbouring farm across the road at Snodshill. Cox worked as a clerical assistant in the G.W.R. works at Swindon.[12]

The boys planned to march to Moscow, but once across the Channel found themselves handicapped by their inadequate French and reached no further than Picardy. They returned to England, then, rather than go home, where they perhaps feared parental retribution, travelled to Liverpool after seeing a newspaper advertisement for a cheap crossing to America. The tales of Jefferies' father, who had worked his passage as a young man, were a likely spur. At Liverpool, however, they discovered the tickets did not include the cost of meals and bedding.

---

[11] E, p.50. No report of the incident has been found in the local newspapers, and it would be interesting to know the informant from whom Besant had the date of 11 November 1864.

[12] Clinton Masseck cites a letter from Cox in which he says that it was his idea to make the journey on foot; that Jefferies planned to tell the story of their travels in a book; and that from Moscow the boys intended to continue to Siberia, cross the Bering Strait to Alaska, and so reach America by the back door, so to speak. (*Richard Jefferies: Étude d'une personnalité* (Paris: Émile Larose, 1913), footnote pp.113-4.)

Cox was born at Snodshill on 11 October 1846. In 1880, at the age of thirty-four, after his mother sold the family farm and moved to the vicinity of London, he emigrated to New Zealand. There he kept an extensive diary covering the years 1888-1925. He worked first as an agricultural labourer, then as a fibre-washer in a flaxmill. Unemployed during the depression years of the 1890s he became a tramp, until he found work again as a jobbing labourer. He died in 1925, some years after recovering from major surgery for cancer.

See the article on Cox by social historian Miles Fairburn in *Dictionary of New Zealand Biography*, vol. 3, 1996, from which the above is taken; Fairburn's *Nearly Out of Heart and Hope*, a book about Cox based on his diaries (Auckland University Press, 1995), reviewed by Mark Daniel in *RJS Journal* No.5 (Spring 1996), pp.33-4; the talk given on 2 December 1996 by Lady Treitel, then Hon. Sec. of the RJS, summarized in *RJS Autumn Newsletter* 1996-7 (pp.6-7) and reviewed by Matt Holland in the Swindon *Evening Advertiser* (3 December 1996).

During a two-month tour of New Zealand in the winter 2009-10 John Price, Chairman of the RJS, visited some of the places associated with Cox as reported in *RJS Spring Newsletter* 2010 (pp.5-6).

The characters of Mark in *Bevis* and Orion in *The Amateur Poacher* are thought to have been based chiefly on Jefferies' brother Harry but in part on Jimmy Cox.

When they tried to raise the necessary money by pawning their watches they were detained by the police and sent back to Swindon in disgrace.

A decade later Jefferies drew on the adventure, which lasted about a fortnight, for an episode in his early novel *Restless Human Hearts* (1875), whose title is perhaps significant in the context.

Victor and Francis are the orphaned sons of deceased widower Charles Knoyle. Their uncle, wealthy banker Horton Knoyle, husband of *femme fatale* Carlotta, acts as their trustee and guardian. He has sent them to a tutorial establishment run by an aged clergyman in a remote corner of Sussex, where they chafe under the strict regime.

Victor is twenty-two, Francis twenty-one. Between the brothers there exists 'the strongest affection and friendship.'[13] Victor is 'turbulent and restless', Francis 'milder and feebler, more easily made good.' Victor overcomes Francis's scruples and persuades him to join him in 'a month or two of "lark" in France'. They wait until their next quarter's allowance comes, then bolt. They go first to London, and thence start via Dover for Paris. On the train they fall in with some cardsharps and lose most of the £40 with which they set out. Francis is for remorsefully returning home. Victor will hear of no such thing. He is made of sterner stuff: 'he had started to see France, and see France he would.'[14]

When they try to pawn their watches in Dover, they are seized by two plain-clothes detectives on suspicion of being involved in a recent jewel robbery. Released after questioning, they raise £5 on their watches, and, the last steamer gone, hire a sailing boat in which they cross the Channel 'sick as dogs', arriving at Calais at one in the morning. They sleep in a cabaret, where the chambermaid laughs in their faces when they complain of the narrowness of the bed, and next morning set off along the poplar-lined road to Paris. Tired and hungry, they are invited by a peasant into his cottage.

> They asked for dinner; he took them in; they found the soup admirable, and the good man grateful for the five-franc piece they gave him. Had it been an English labourer's cottage they would have starved on sour cheese and bread. Here they feasted on delicious soup, and set out strong and refreshed.[15]

---

[13] *RHH*, p.65.
[14] *ibid.*
[15] *ibid.*, p.66.

However, they lose their way and stumble across a large house, an establishment that turns out to be a home for the illegitimate children of the English aristocracy. After spending the night there, they return to Calais and thence to the tutor's with sixpence left in their pockets.

Jefferies was writing fiction, yet behind the episode it is possible to discern reality in shadowy outline. Victor is based on James Cox, the instigator of the exploit; Francis on the more timid and conscience-stricken Jefferies. Certain details tally with the facts: the escapade takes place in 'late autumn', around Michaelmas; the boys are arrested when they try to pawn their watches; a peasant offers them hospitality, inviting them into his cottage and serving them a delicious soup.

Jefferies referred to the latter in the first of his letters to *The Times*, where he compared the Wiltshire labourer's monotonous diet of bread, cheese and bacon unfavourably with the soups he had enjoyed in Picardy:

> Vegetables are his [the Wiltshire labourer's] luxuries, and a large garden, therefore, is the greatest blessing he can have. He eats huge onions raw; he has no idea of flavouring his food with them, nor of making those savoury and inviting messes or vegetable soups at which the French peasantry are so clever. In Picardy I have often dined in a peasant's cottage, and thoroughly enjoyed the excellent soup he puts upon the table for his ordinary meal. To dine in an English labourer's cottage would be impossible.[16]

At the same time much has been altered or omitted. According to Besant[17] Jefferies, not his friend, was the scheme's originator. In the novel there is no mention of the attempted crossing to America. Victor and Francis are appreciably older than Cox and Jefferies. They try to pawn their watches in Dover, not Liverpool. And so on. But on one point at least the fiction stuck to the truth: the expedition ended in ignominious failure.

However, there is no mention of it in *Ben Tubbs Adventures*, save the general idea of two boys running away (from school, not home) and working their passage to America.

oooOOOooo

---

[16] 'The Wiltshire Labourer,' *The Times*, 14 November 1872, p.8. Collected in *The Toilers of the Field*, where for the passage cited see pp.212-3.
[17] E, p.50.

To return to the date of composition. While *Ben Tubbs* is clearly an early work, the jaunty assurance of the writing, the ironically inflated, mock-pompous style with deliberate use of ponderous Latinisms for humorous effect, the detachment of the narrative persona, suggest at least the possibility that the novel was written later than supposed.

If we look for internal evidence, Finnikin's exhaustion and feverish thirst in Chapter 12[18] may be a reminiscence of Jefferies' illnesses of 1867 and 1868; they certainly went into the account of Noel Brandon's fever in *Restless Human Hearts*.[19]

Again, during the violent storm in the same chapter,[20] reminiscent of that in *Bevis* before the mock battle of Pharsalia, Finnikin sees a meteor.[21] In a letter published in the *Astronomical Register* of March 1871,[22] Jefferies reported witnessing one night a meteor that lit up the surrounding landscape. There is no certainty that the passage in *Ben Tubbs* was inspired by the memory, Jefferies had seen meteors before, but it is at least possible.

At first sight the prairie fire in Chapter 12 might also seem to support a later date of composition. In *The Amateur Poacher* the first-person narrator refers to his friend Orion (Jefferies' brother Harry in reality, called Orion after the mighty hunter of Greek legend) with the comment:

> The last I heard of him he had just ridden through a prairie fire, and says the people out there think nothing of it.[23]

Following the enforced sale of the Coate farm in 1877, Harry had emigrated to Texas in c.1878. Therefore, if his account of a prairie fire in a letter home suggested that in *Ben Tubbs*, we would have a *terminus post quem* of 1878. However, this is clearly much too late for what gives every sign of being a juvenile work, probably composed, as said, in the late 1860s.

oooOOOooo

---

[18] *BT*, p.140.
[19] *RHH*, p.228f.
[20] *BT*, p.141.
[21] *ibid.*, p.141.
[22] 'A Brilliant Meteor', *Astronomical Register*, Vol. IX, No. 99, March 1871, pp.65-6. Credit for the letter's discovery belongs to Dr Rebeccca Welshman.
[23] *AP*, p.11.

Divided into thirteen chapters, *Ben Tubbs Adventures* is nearly 70,000 words in extent, and penned in a brown-to-maroon stiff-backed exercise-book [size 7¼" x 8¾"] with black spine, now held in the Manuscripts Room of the British Library.[24] A white label pasted to the front cover bears the legend, written in the same black ink as the text:

BEN TUBBS
ADVENTURES
BY
R. JEFFERIES

The bottom right-hand corner of the cover is missing: otherwise, apart from loose stitching, the exercise book is well preserved. The book has 124 unlined pages, of which 120 are filled.

The hand is a neat, tight, mostly right-sloping copperplate. Punctuation (viz. title)[25] and spelling are sometimes uncertain. Misspellings include 'reccomend,' 'seperation,' 'cuboard,' 'partizans,' 'obsequeous,' 'dissappointment,' 'praire' and 'stedfastly'.

It is not clear whether Jefferies wrote the work solely for personal amusement and the entertainment of family and friends, or intended it for publication. However, the lack of corrections indicates that the manuscript was probably a fair copy, made perhaps with the intention of submitting the work to a newspaper or book publisher. The copy may have been carried out at the behest of Aunt Ellen, who complained of her nephew's illegible hand.[26]

A novel of voyage and adventure, *Ben Tubbs Adventures* was Jefferies' first essay in a genre to which he was temperamentally drawn. It looks forward to the tale 'Who Shall Win?', the novels *The Rise of Maximin*, *Bevis*, and *After London*, and was probably influenced by the greatest quest story of them all, Homer's *Odyssey*, one of Jefferies' favourite

---

[24] BL Add. MS 58826.
[25] See 'A Note on the Text', above p.1.
[26] In a letter to Aunt Ellen on *North Wilts Herald* notepaper dated 5 December 1866 Jefferies acknowledged his hand was difficult to read, adding 'It is very odd that altho' I can read it myself with ease all others seem more or less puzzled' (*RJL*, p.26). Thomas (p.56) records that the *Herald*'s staff once signed a round robin against Jefferies' handwriting.

books as a boy, to which, in Pope's translation, perhaps with Flaxman's illustrations, his father introduced him at an early age.[27]

The eponymous hero is a fifteen-year-old rascal living with his widowed mother 'in an obscure village in the S.W. of England'.[28] Lacking paternal discipline the boy has run wild and become virtually unmanageable. Ben's pranks include dressing up as a ghost and scaring the life out of the local parson. At her wits' end, patience exhausted, the mother finally packs him off to boarding-school, a Dotheboys Hall from which, after being bullied by the other boys and publicly flogged for truancy by the headmaster Dr Smales, he runs away with a friend called Ned Snicks.

The boys plan to go to California and turn gold-diggers. Funded by the lucky find of a purse on the road, they walk to the Bristol docks, where they board a ship and work their passage to America.

A fortnight into the voyage a storm blows up and the ship goes under. The two boys are the sole survivors. The *Lopez*, an American slaver commanded by Captain Tinglum and carrying 200 or 300 blacks in her hold, picks them up. After a brush with a British frigate the *Lopez* safely reaches New Orleans. Accompanied by first mate Martin Finnikin, a short thickset Irish-American whose flat nose is 'much like a frying-pan,'[29] the boys ride on mustangs across the vast Texan prairies. During the journey they encounter wolves, Comanche on the warpath, a prairie fire, stampeding buffalo, a meteorite and other perils, before being rescued in Mexico by Ned's father and taken back to England.

oooOOOooo

---

[27] 'It was my father and not the schoolmaster who introduced me to Homer—without him I should never have appreciated the *Odyssey*.' (Letter to George Bentley from The Downs, Crowborough, Sussex, dated 12 June [1886]).

Bevis makes repeated reference to the *Odyssey*; it is one of the boy's favourite books. As a war-song on the eve of the mock battle of Pharsalia Bevis reads aloud the passage where Ulysses slays the suitors with his great bow, marching up and down the room, his own bow in hand, and stamping his feet the while. When he is pushed over the edge of the quarry in the fight with Ted, and is stuck on the hurdle that breaks his fall, his first thought is, what would Ulysses have done in such an extremity?

In *The Amateur Poacher* (p.21) the narrator says that 'Ulysses was ever my pattern and model, that man of infinite patience and resource'.

[28] *BT*, p.1.

[29] *ibid.*, p.71.

Fanny Hall recalled that as a youth her cousin was

> fond of shutting himself up at the top of the house near the 'cheese-room,' where he spent much of his time in the production of blood-curdling romances.[30]

Ben Tubbs, like many first novels, reflects the young author's taste in reading. At the Sign of the Saracen inn, where Ben and his mother stay the night during their coach journey to Dr Smales's Academy, the boy

> sat up to a late hour reading a musty novel which he had found. It was a tragic tale full of ghosts and mysterious rhymes, trapdoors, dank dungeons, secret passages, awful tortures and Heaven knows what else... He was soon ankle deep in atrocious murders and other dismalities. He was very fond of reading or rather devouring tales of adventure or anything of that description.[31]

This sounds very much like a Gothic or sensation novel.

---

[30] 'Jefferies Luckett' [Fanny Catherine Hall], 'The Forbears of Richard Jefferies', *Country Life*, 14 March 1908, vol. 23, [pp.373-6], p.376.

[31] *BT*, p.18 and pp.19-20. In *The Amateur Poacher* (p.12) the narrator pores over the Gothic tale *Koenigsmark the Robbber*. The full title was *Koenigsmark the Robber, Or, The Terror of Bohemia; in which is introduced Stella, or, The Maniac of the Wood, An Affecting Tale* (sometimes given as *'A Pathetick Tale'*). The book belonged to a sub-genre of Gothic fiction known as the *Räuberroman*, the robber- or bandit-novel. Its author Rudolf Erich Raspe was best known for a collection of tall stories published in English as *The Surprising Adventures of Baron Münchhausen* (1785).

Koenigsmark der Räuber, oder Der Schrecken aus Böhmen followed in 1790. The first English translation (or rather adaptation) by Victor Jules Sarret (whose name, confusingly, is often given as H.J. Sarrett) was published as a chapbook by James Williams in 1801. A pirated edition of 1808 purported to be by 'The Monk', i.e. M.G. Lewis, aka 'Monk' Lewis, one of the main purveyors of the Gothic fiction that enjoyed a vogue at the end of the eighteenth and beginning of the nineteenth century.

Recounted by Baron Münchhausen, *Koenigsmark the Robber* tells the story of a bandit leader so invincible he is believed to be a warlock. The tale's many fantastic elements include

> an enormous yellow-eyed spider, a wolf who changes into a peasant and disappears amid a cloud of sulphur, and a ghost who sheds three ominous drops of boiling blood.

(Edith Birkhead, *The Tale of Terror, A Study of the Gothic Romance* (The Floating Press, 2012), p.77. Ms Birkhead, misled by the title page, wrongly attributes the tale to 'Monk' Lewis.)

However, the main influence on *Ben Tubbs* and some of Jefferies' early work was Fenimore Cooper (1789-1851), the American author of popular historical romances of frontier and Native American life. Cooper is not much read nowadays but he has been called the first major American novelist, and by the time of his death was generally considered the 'national' novelist, whose work best embodied the values of the young country.

Jefferies had been introduced to Cooper's work by Edward Fentiman, principal of Fentiman's Academy, one of the Swindon schools he attended. Fentiman

> had himself been a boy, and had set up wigwams and raged on the warpath, and he lent Fenimore Cooper's 'Leather-stocking' tales to Jefferies, and thus helped him to the notion of camping out and playing at Indians on the shores of the reservoir and on Hodson Ground. [32]

The 'Leatherstocking Tales' comprised five novels: *The Pioneers* (1823), *The Last of the Mohicans* (1826), *The Prairie* (1827), *The Pathfinder* (1840), and *The Deerslayer* (1841). One can imagine that the titles themselves induced a frisson in the young Jefferies, who, as *Bevis* makes clear, was a highly adventurous lad imbued with the spirit of exploration.

The novels featured Natty [Nathaniel] Bumppo, alias Leatherstocking, alias Hawkeye, a frontier scout and backwoodsman thought to have been based in part on the legendary Daniel Boone. Bumppo is a

---

[32] T, p.37. Masseck (pp.40-1) cites a letter from Mr Fentiman's daughter, from whom Thomas clearly had his information (a Miss W.M. Fentiman is listed in his acknowledgments page, x).

The relevant passage of Miss Fentiman's letter reads: 'A little later [i.e. after the Misses Cowell's] he attended Mr Fenteman's [sic] school in Devises [sic] Road in Swindon where "he received an ordinary education in English, French, Latin, mathematics, etc.... My father never spoke of Jefferies as an exceptional boy, said he was very quiet, dreamy and reserved, which made him unpopular with the other boys. He was passionately fond of reading and devoured insatiably the tales of Fenimore Cooper, chiefly *The Leather Stocking* [sic], that his father [sic; but '*son*' in the French is probably a misprint for '*mon*'] had lent him and that gave Jefferies the idea of camping out and playing Red Indians in the woods near Hodson and Burderob [sic]."' [translation from the French by the author]

Miss Fentiman told an acquaintance that Jefferies later wrote to her father to thank him for his help and encouragement. (Mrs. M.E. Bayley, letter dated 9 May 1952 in the *Swindon Evening Advertiser*, cutting held in the Richard Jefferies Collection, Swindon Public Library)

rough but sterling character who opposes the march of progress. He embodies many of the values Jefferies admired.

Fenimore Cooper's stories celebrated self-reliance and self-sufficiency, the ability to live alone in the wilderness, woodcraft, skills and values akin to those implicitly lauded in *Bevis*. His novels expressed a love of the virgin forests and prairies of the American West. The third 'Leatherstocking' tale was entitled *The Prairie* (1827), and, apart from forest, the vast prairies of Kansas and Texas form the chief landscapes of *Ben Tubbs*. The novel is full of the outback, frontier spirit. The Martin Finnikin character has something in common with Bumppo, and might have stepped straight from the pages of a Cooper novel.

oooOOOooo

Jefferies wrote *Ben Tubbs Adventures* perhaps in part as compensatory fantasy for the failed voyage to America. Phyllis Treitel has shown how large a place the continent held in his imagination.[33] He saw America as 'a land of adventure and romance'.[34] His work contains many admiring references to the enterprise of its people.

'Who Will Win?, one of Jefferies' earliest tales, subtitled 'Or, American Adventure', is set in the Deep South during the Civil War. The protagonist's uncle Jerome Bourton 'had been a fine specimen of the rover in his youth; had traversed the American continent, rifle in hand', and 'his tales of daring' had implanted 'a wild wish to visit the new world in his nephew's breast'.[35] Here we probably have an oblique autobiographical reference to the tales of Jefferies' father.

James Jefferies, as said, had worked his passage to America as a young man. Our sources differ over the year. James himself recalled:

> I been in America—New York State on the Hudson for near Two Years, when I was about sixteen.[36]

---

[33] Phyllis Treitel, 'The Other Side: Visions of America', *RJS Journal*, No.2 (Spring 1993), pp.25-29.
[34] *ibid.*, p.25.
[35] 'Who Will Win? Or, American Adventure', first published as a serial in six parts in the *North Wilts Herald* between 25 August and 29 September 1866, was later collected by Grace Toplis in *The Early Fiction of Richard Jefferies* (1896), where the above quote appears on p.93.
   The Bourton character has much in common with Finnikin.
[36] J.L. Jefferies, letter to A.T. Rake, 21 November 1896. BL Add. MS 58822A.

James was born in 1816, so he would have left in 1832 or 1833. However, a marginal note pencilled in his father's copy of Nelson's *Festivals and Fasts* reads 'James left for America 1835'.[37] Fanny Hall, on the other hand, followed by Edward Thomas, gives the year as 1837. Thomas says

> He is said to have worked his passage out to America in 1837, and there, in Canada, and up the Hudson river, he stayed a year or two, and moved about a good deal, working, I have heard, as a farm labourer.[38]

It seems that James returned reluctantly to England to take over the running of the smallholding at Coate, his father having threatened that 'unless he came back, the farm… would go to an elder sister's husband'.[39]

James often reminisced about his youthful adventures in America and it may be supposed that his sons hung eagerly on his tales. In *Amaryllis at the Fair* the eponymous teenage heroine gets her father, Farmer Iden, who is clearly based on James,

> to tell her stories of the deep snow in the United States, and the thick ice, sawn with saws, or, his fancy roaming on, of the broad and beautiful Hudson River, the river he had so admired in his youth, the river the poets will sing some day; or of his clinging aloft at night in the gale on the banks of Newfoundland, for he had done duty as a sailor.[40]

Jefferies was planning to visit America about the time his father came up to London for the Great Agricultural Show at Kilburn in the summer of 1879. James stayed with his son at Surbiton for some weeks, and later recalled:

> Has [sic] he intended making tour there [America] then he took down all I could tell him and I very soon after had a letter from him & a Book

---

[37] Our thanks to Jean Saunders for bringing the fact to our attention. John Jefferies' copy of *Nelson's Festivals: A Companion for the Festivals and Fasts of the Church of England with Collects and Prayers for each solemnity* by Robert Nelson (London, 1773, 23rd edition), owned by Andrew Lewis, is currently on loan to the Coate Museum.
[38] T, pp.25-6.
[39] Jefferies Luckett, *op.cit.*, p.375.
[40] *AF*, p.97.

of Walt Whitmans [*Leaves of Grass*] and the pages marked w[h]ere I had described. I have that letter & book still.[41]

In the event Jefferies never went to America, and the haunting sense of failure over 'the road not taken'—[42] may have been in mind when, his romantic love of the sea stirred by the sight of the yard arms and masts of the clippers rising above the roofs at the Bermondsey docks, he wrote:

> Hardly any of us but have thought, Some day I will go on a long voyage; but the years go by, and still we have not sailed.[43]

However, as said, his younger brother did go. After the enforced sale of the Coate farm in 1877, Harry emigrated to Texas in c.1878 and married at Richmond, Virginia, in 1884.

Treitel believes the enthusiasm for America evinced in Harry's letters home may have fired his brother with a desire to make 'a visit of two or three months.'[44] Family and work commitments may explain why he never did.[45] America thus became a '"lost domain" or land of longing', halfway between real and ideal, the nearest place on earth to the elusive 'Other Side,' the phantasmagoric country of the fable recounted in *Bevis*.

Jefferies' son Henry maintained the family connection with the North American continent by emigrating to Canada and joining the merchant navy.

In *The Amateur Poacher* the boys determine to visit Calypso's isle in a leaky old punt. They take their gun and

> the Indian bow, scooped out inside in a curious way, and covered with strange designs or coloured hieroglyphics: it had been brought home by one of our people years before. There was but one man in the place who could bend that bow effectually; so that though we valued it highly we could not use it.[46]

Perhaps James was 'the one of our people', who had brought the bow back as a souvenir. A passage in *Bevis* testifies to the fascination that esoteric scripts and hieroglyphs held for the boy.

---

[41] J.L. Jefferies, *op.cit.*
[42] Title of the first poem in Robert Frost's collection *Mountain Interval* (New York: Henry Holt and Son, 1916).
[43] 'Red Roofs of London', *OA*, p.228.
[44] Treitel; *op.cit.*, p.26.
[45] *ibid.*, pp.26-7.
[46] *AP*, pp.29-30.

Again, Bevis and Mark name the brook down which they pole their raft the New Mississippi, and christen the blue boat they rig with sail the *Pinta*, the name of Columbus's craft.

An American snap-shooter puts in an abrupt appearance towards the end of the novel. The episode, largely disconnected from the rest, seems based on reality: father and son may have witnessed such a demonstration of shooting skill during James's visit to Surbiton.[47] It was another example of the can-do spirit of the Americans.

The dining-room clock at Coombe Oaks, the farmhouse in *Amaryllis at the Fair*, is American: it is described as having 'a loud and distinct tick'.[48]

William Morris, editor of the *Swindon Advertiser*, with whom Jefferies is said to have been friendly, and who lent books to the youth, may also have infected him with an enthusiasm for America. A passage on the Niagara Falls in his history of Swindon shows that Morris had visited the continent.

Part of America's attraction for Jefferies was that it was a still virgin land not 'used up' like Europe: it offered the chance of exploring the unknown. Some of its allure comes out in the portrait of Finnikin, first mate of the *Lopez*:

> His had been a roving, lawless, wild life. At one time he had been an hunter ranging over the boundless prairies and woods of Mexico and Texas, later a miner in California and later still a sailor... He still remembered how free he had been when chasing the buffalo on his brave mustang, still wished to be flinging the circling lasso, still thought of his unerring rifle. In the hurry and bustle of the day these thoughts were never uppermost but in the still, dark hours of the night they came over him with irresistible force, and at such times Finnikin would arise and walk the deck. Finnikin's was not a poetical or romantic disposition; he well knew that in the eyes of the world he now held a much higher position than as a half-clad wild hunter. He was now fast verging on fifty and, as each year flew swiftly on, he

---

[47] W.J. Keith ('Notes on *Bevis*', p.13) writes: 'In the *RJS Annual Report* for 1978, Mark Daniel records an advertisement in *The Times* on 23 October 1879 for Dr Carver, champion rifle shot of the world, performing at the Canterbury Theatre of Varieties (Westminster Bridge Road). Reference is made to "the patent shooting recently exhibited" in "The Squire and the Land" (*The Old House at Coate*, p.166).'
[48] *AF*, p.17.

lamented the days gone by and resolved that each voyage should be his last.⁴⁹

The passage offers a foretaste of the coda to *The Amateur Poacher*, the pages beginning

There could be no greater pleasure to me than to wander with a matchlock through one of the great forests or wild tracts that still remain in England.⁵⁰

All this to show the deep and lasting fascination that America held for Jefferies, both as adult and boy, and to explain why the continent occupies such a prominent place in his earliest surviving fiction.

oooOOOooo

Ben Tubbs Adventures is a juvenile work whose early date would be apparent from its feebleness, if for no other reason. The novel will have some value for scholars interested in tracing the development of Jefferies' oeuvre but as literature *Ben Tubbs* is largely worthless and its exhumation will do little to enhance his reputation.

True, there are redeeming features: Jefferies shows a youthful facility for yarn spinning, while the narrative voice has an engaging geniality and exuberance, with hints of a sly, mischievous, tongue-in-cheek humour. The ironically pompous tone serves as narrative keynote. A man is not named Abe but 'denominated Abe'. Characters do not fall asleep but 'enter the regions of Morpheus'. The frequent use of the archaism 'quoth' is in like vein.

Otherwise, however, this very early fiction displays little sign of promise. The faults are patent. Chief among them are the weakness of the plot, the lack of any overarching story, the episodic nature of the narrative. There is no central idea or point. *Ben Tubbs* is uncertain what it wants to be. The novel starts out as a light comedy of manners and morals, with some boisterous satire of authority figures such as parents, parsons and schoolmasters. Then, shortly before the mid-way mark, the story changes tack and becomes a *Boys' Own Paper* adventure with voyage across the Atlantic and crossing of the American continent. Then

---

⁴⁹ *BT*, p.92.
⁵⁰ *AP*, p.273f.

at the end the novel abruptly turns full circle and returns to domestic comedy, as the youthful hero is welcomed home by his mother.

The comedy often descends into farce: Mrs Tubbs collides with Ben on the stairs and both tumble to the bottom; Parson Snobbs, taking to his heels at the sight of Ben dressed up as a ghost, runs headlong into a gatepost and knocks himself out.

Another motif from which Jefferies seeks to milk humour is the characters' habit of snoring, which becomes almost a running gag. Another trait rather insisted upon for comic effect is Ben's gargantuan appetite.[51]

The closing pages take us back to the world of silent movie slapstick, with maid Sarah ending up on her backside in the coal box after being hit in the eye by an orange thrown by Ben, drunk on the wine he is allowed to celebrate his return.[52]

Another problem is implausibility. Ben and his friends cross most of the American continent, from New Orleans to Mexico, on foot or on horse, but apparently without the aid of a map. Nothing is said to identify where the characters are at any moment, no places are named until the last chapter, where we suddenly hear of San Miguel and the 'dreary tenantless town of Christobal',[53] the Rio Bravo del Norte,[54] Rio Gila and Rio Colorado, as if Jefferies has looked up an atlas. Whatever his feelings about the continent, he fails to evoke America (or Mexico) with any particularity.

The arrival of Ned's father and his coincidental meeting with the party acts as a providential *deus ex machina* to get the boys back to England and the novel over and done with. His sudden appearance beggars belief.

The characterization is thin. Apart from the autobiographical Ben none of the characters are realized in any depth. They remain ciphers. Ned is a shadowy replica of Ben, as Mark of Bevis. Jefferies tries to give some weight to Finnikin, the most substantial character after the hero, but he is little more than a larger-than-life stage Irish-American,

---

[51] e.g. *BT*, p.126.
[52] *ibid.*, p.158.
[53] *ibid.*, p.143.
[54] The name given in Mexico to the river known in the United States as the Rio Grande.

composed of a few mannerisms, his pipe, his 'waals', 'kalkilate's, 'present-ly's and 'neow's.

We are reminded of an observation made by Cyril Connolly. After remarking that great novelists such as Tolstoy and Proust can create characters who 'behave unlike themselves, dare to be false to type', he continues

> But weaker novelists can only sling a few traits on to the characters they are depicting and then hold them there. 'You can't miss So-and-so,' they explain, 'he stammers and now look, here he comes—"What's your name?" "S-s-s-so-and-s-s-s-so." There you see, what did I tell you!⁵⁵

So with Finnikin and his interminable 'waal's. The Mexican Don Luis is recognizable by his sardonic demonic laugh, insisted upon *ad nauseam*. As if that weren't enough, the Jose character too has 'a short low demoniacal laugh'.⁵⁶

Among other faults must be counted the phonetic speech of several characters. Sam the orator's is excruciating.⁵⁷ Similarly one more 'waal', 'kalkilate' or 'neow' out of Finnikin, and the reader is ready to scream Violet Elizabeth Botts fashion. Even the Mexican Don Luis says 'waal', in case we have forgotten we're in America. What little authenticity such dialogue has does not compensate for its difficulty in decipherment. In general Jefferies cannot create dialogue that will dramatize a situation or forward the action. It is one of his principal weaknesses as a novelist.

The determined humour soon becomes wearing; the story is long-winded; the writing verbose and in places banal, cliché-ridden. Bullets 'speed upon their errand of death'.⁵⁸

Redundancy is a recurring fault. The characters make 'a long, tedious, monotonous journey in which they met with no incident worth recording'.⁵⁹ On the same page Ned's father assumes 'a most sorrowful, dolorous tone'. One recalls the prolixity of Frank Richards's Billy Bunter stories, where the author was paid by the word and spun his tales out to inordinate length by the insertion of superfluous adjectives.

---

⁵⁵ Cyril Connolly, *Enemies of Promise* [1938] (Harmondsworth: Penguin Books, 1961), p.65.
⁵⁶ *BT*, p.146.
⁵⁷ e.g., *ibid.*, pp.42-43.
⁵⁸ *ibid.*, p.111.
⁵⁹ *ibid.*, p.155.

At other times the writing is laboured. Jefferies goes into unnecessary and tedious detail in the account of Finnikin and the boys crossing a river on horseback.[60] The action scenes[61] recalled the adventure stories ('ripping yarns') in the *Hotspur* and *Wizard* comics of the writer's misspent youth. The prairie fire is described in rather breathless and melodramatic fashion.

Another feature of *Ben Tubbs* is the vein of cynicism, common to all of Jefferies' early fiction. The Mexican Jose, for example, soon changes his tune and is all politeness once he learns he will be paid for acting as guide to the party.[62]

For the modern reader, however, the chief stumbling block is not the poor quality of *Ben Tubbs* but its overt racism, to which Professor Delattre was the first to call attention. True, Jefferies displays a prejudice widespread, almost endemic, in Britain of this period; writes for comic effect; merely presents a caricature, a stereotype. Again, there is a passage where he makes plain the appalling conditions in which the slaves are held and the cruelty of the crew.[63] The same is true of the auction of the slaves held on the *Lopez*'s arrival in New Orleans.[64] It can be argued that Jefferies here shows some sympathy for the plight of the slaves. However, that sympathy is contradicted by his generally contemptuous tone and treatment of the blacks as figures of fun. The reader feels Jefferies' sympathy does not run deep and is largely window-dressing.

The slaves are referred to variously as niggers, black beetles, cockroaches, admittedly in jest, but a jest in singularly poor taste. They are portrayed as simple-minded children who roll their eyeballs to show the whites; who are at the mercy of their emotions, which they cannot control; and who sing 'in their own unintelligible gibberish'.[65] It is unpleasant to read Jefferies' attempts to milk comedy from their wretched situation.

---

[60] *ibid.*, pp.109-110.
[61] *ibid.*, pp.132-3.
[62] *ibid.*, p.145.
[63] *ibid.*, pp.76-77.
[64] *ibid.*, pp.93-94.
[65] *ibid.*, p.92. See George Miller, 'Was Jefferies a Racist?' (No. VI in his 'Discoveries' series, *RJS Annual Report* 2009-2010, pp.18-20), a measured response to the charge brought by Alain Delattre in his centenary lecture 'John Richard Jefferies: his Worst and his Best'.

Rather an unhealthy attention is given to scenes of corporal punishment, both at Dr Smales's Academy[66] and later aboard the *Lopez*. Blackee the cook, who addresses Finnikin as 'massa', is at once coward and sadistic bully, lovingly fingering a cane before chastising the blacks hiding under the dresser. Indeed Jefferies seems to have something of a fetish about caning. There is a distinct whiff of sado-masochism in the beating episode, behind a comic veneer again reminiscent of the Bunter stories:

> Then did fearful groans, awful yells, frenzied shouts of laughter, numerous whacks, quantities of wops, innumerable smacks make the air of that apartment in such a state of vibration that Ned was fain to show the white feather, that is, to evacuate the room.[67]

'To evacuate the room' is typical of the style.

Trouble is, it becomes obvious from his treatment of them that Jefferies does indeed regard the blacks as beetles: they are insects, not human beings at all. He dehumanizes, depersonalizes, other characters as well, but here the process is seen at its most extreme.

Though at one point he refers to 'the savage'[68] Jefferies' attitude to the Comanche is conspicuously less racist than to the black. He admires their skill as riders, likening them to Centaurs. Indeed Ben is fascinated: he watches them in the forest 'with a continuous stare, his whole soul peering from his eyes'[69] and later 'with untiring interest'.[70]

Perhaps the reason for the fascination is that the Comanche live in close harmony with nature. There is a hint of the Noble Savage, of romantic idealism, in Jefferies' attitude. It is akin to his interest in gipsies or 'gips'. Perhaps if he could have seen the black slaves on their native soil in Africa he would have shown them more respect.

oooOOOooo

That said, the report is by no means wholly unfavourable. In general the book has an engaging gusto, the writing an engaging *riant* quality; the satire is genial. The novel improved on a second reading, when we were more alert to the irony of the narrative voice.

---

[66] *ibid.*, p.44f.
[67] *ibid.*, p. 78.
[68] *ibid.*, p.121.
[69] *ibid.*, p.104.
[70] *ibid.*, p.104.

There is already something of Bevis in Ben: no Little Lord Fauntleroy but a mischievous prankster: wilful, spoiled, defiant, destructive, impulsive, reckless, easily bored, but also plucky, proud, and imaginative. Ben resembles Bevis above all in his adventurousness and courage. To climb down the crater of an extinct volcano suspended on a rope, he 'summoned up courage, of which article he had a considerable quantity'.[71] Self-praise perhaps, but Ben is a brave lad, of that we feel sure.

Amid the capers of the early chapters Jefferies strikes one or two serious notes. He shows an interest in child rearing when he inveighs against 'tales of bogies and other nursery fictions calculated to render darkness terrible,' suggesting he may have been himself frightened by such stories. Ben is brave because he hasn't been terrified in infancy by such tales:

> It is greatly to be desired that all children like him should be exempted from such superstitions as are often impressed upon them by the stupidity of nurses who, to save themselves a little trouble, invent all sorts of rubbish.[72]

Again, even if the language is conventional, a description of the dawn has a solemnity that stands out against the prevailing skittish, ebullient tone:

> Now certain rosy streaks of light conjoined with the fact that the stars looked precious dim and warned the travellers that day was approaching. Suddenly the sun cleared the summit of a hill and shot his beams in all directions causing the dew to glitter with a lustrous light; the birds woke up and the stars went out.[73]

There are several descriptions of the dawn,[74] and Ben's spirits always rise when he gazes upon 'the glorious luminary' as he almost invariably terms it in this juvenile fiction.[75] Jefferies pays much attention to the sky, particularly by night.[76]

---

[71] *ibid.*, p.152.
[72] *ibid.*, p.18.
[73] *ibid.*, p.51.
[74] e.g. *ibid.*, p.137.
[75] e.g., *ibid.*, pp.120, 124, 128, 151.
[76] e.g. *ibid.*, pp.113, 119-120.

Likewise the sea, with which the sky is often conjoined, inspires several lyrical passages, such as the description of the ship out on open water after leaving Bristol docks:

> Now they were upon the great broad waters of the Severn, the men were sent above, the white canvas sails were unfurled and the ship with a joyous bound sprung on her way to the shores of the New World.[77]

The phrase 'with a joyous bound' nicely encapsulates Jefferies' delight in sailing, manifest in Chapter XX of *Bevis*,[78] and his lively interest in all to do with ships and the sea. The picture of the *Lopez* is likewise charged with feeling:

> To the eye of an observer at a distance nothing could have been more beautiful and soul-inspiring than the fine lines, raking masts and immense spread of snow-white canvas which bore the "Lopez" swiftly onwards.[79]

Jefferies knows the nautical terms 'all standing' and 'cat's-paw', and the correct names for the parts of a ship, including the sails. The extent of his knowledge suggests that he had often pored over the entry on ships in his copy of Hall's Encyclopaedia, an oracle much consulted by the boy, as *Bevis* makes clear.[80]

---

[77] *ibid.*, p.64.
[78] Chapter XX, p.176f.
[79] *BT*, p.76. The passage recalls the three ships of the line Jefferies saw under full sail when he and a boatman rowed six miles 'straight out to sea', as he reported in a letter to his Aunt Ellen during his sojourn at Hastings in 1870 (*RJL*, pp.72-3). They rowed alongside the huge ships and one cannot but think of Turner's magnificent watercolour 'A First Rate Taking in Stores' (1818), currently on display (until 10 April 2016) at the Cecil Higgins Art Gallery in Bedford.
[80] In his memoir of his father Harold states that the ancient encyclopaedia consulted by Bevis was 'the old Hall's encyclopaedia,' which 'contained many interesting articles, particularly a long one on the building of the old three-deckers and other vessels'. (Richard Harold Jefferies, 'Memories of Richard Jefferies,' *Worthing Cavalcade* (1944), p.20)

The encyclopaedia 'did not quite reach to the days of glorious Nelson' (*B*, p.192), so it was probably published in the eighteenth century and may have come from John Jefferies' library.

The British Library catalogue lists *The New Royal Encyclopaedia; or, Complete Modern Dictionary of Arts and Sciences, on a New and Improved plan. Containing a… Display of the Whole Theory and Practice of the Liberal and Mechanical Arts, etc.*, by William Henry Hall, published in three volumes in London in 1788.

An amusing send-up of the devices of the novel looks forward to the authorial asides in *The Dewy Morn* and *Amaryllis at the Fair*:

> In this cook's shop we will, for the present time leave them [Ben and Ned] and using the well-known and equally well-used privilege of writers, put on a pair of imaginative seven-leagued boots and after a few preliminary skips, hop with one gigantic bound from the New World to the Old, and alighting in the parlour of Mrs Smales remain there in the form of some persevering smoke which will not go up the chimney.[81]

The scene where Ben and Ned find difficulty in lighting a fire to cook the rabbit they have found in a snare anticipates Bevis and Mark's castaway existence on New Formosa. Jefferies adds a humorous touch: the boys finally get a fire going but have forgotten that a rabbit needs to be skinned before it can be cooked. The scene of them bolting their meal at the inn is likewise well observed and amusing.

There are moments of narrative tension: for example, the sudden appearance of the Indian on the forest path as Ben keeps watch one night.[82] The storm-at-sea in Chapter 6 is powerful, if melodramatic; the brush of the *Lopez* with the British frigate exciting, as is the episode of Ben pursued by a party of twenty yelling Comanche.[83]

The best thing in the book is the description of the American prairies, and the sense of space and freedom they convey, even if the description of a river valley perhaps suggests the Wiltshire downs rather than Texas:

> Far beneath him he could see the winding blue river clothed on each side by a narrow strip of wood succeeded by the boundless rolling prairie extending to the far off horizon.[84]

The article 'on the building of the old three-deckers and other vessels' is found in the second volume under 'Treatise on Naval Affairs', in the sub-section 'Naval Architecture'.

When unable to get the *Pinta*, the boat he and Mark have rigged out with sail, to tack properly, Bevis consults the encyclopaedia, but it does not help. 'What you really want to know is never in a book, and no one can tell you.' (*B*, p.193)

[81] *BT*, p.94.
[82] *ibid.*, p.103.
[83] *ibid.*, p.120f.
[84] *ibid.*, p.123.

There is a powerful sense of adventure as Ben crosses the prairie and heads west toward the sinking sun. The sun is the central image in Jefferies' work.

A nice touch: dreaming he is being scalped by a Comanche, Ben wakes to find gold-prospector Pierre tugging at his hair.[85]

The ending is typical of Jefferies' early novels: all in a rush, a buffalo stampede conveniently disposing of superfluous characters.

oooOOOooo

If largely wish-fulfilment fantasy the book has some biographical interest, and at least raises interesting questions.

Was the teenage Jefferies wild and unmanageable like Ben, portrayed as rascal, scamp, prankster? He doesn't go to school till he is fifteen. Quizzing the boy on his arrival to ascertain the extent of his knowledge Dr Smales finds him 'woefully backward'.[86]

Was Dr Smales's Academy based on a real school? The precise detail at several points in the narrative suggests Jefferies may have been drawing on memory. The school, 'a large square heavy looking building',[87] has about 150 boy pupils. The playground is enclosed on three sides by a high wall, on the other by the house.[88] A large shed serves as gymnasium. The boys are allowed out of school on Saturdays.

Fictional accounts of schooldays are almost invariably autobiographical, and certainly the chapter reads as if based on personal experience, if modified. There is, for example, no evidence that Jefferies ever attended a boarding school.

Again, is it legitimate to find a clue that Jefferies and Jimmy Cox in effect ran away from home on their abortive trip to Moscow, when we read that after running away from school both Ben and Ned 'felt some slight twinges of conscience for having left them [their parents] in such an abrupt manner'?[89] Besant is unequivocal: 'The boys ran away.'[90]

---

[85] *ibid.*, p.129.
[86] *ibid.*, p.23.
[87] *ibid.*, p.21.
[88] *ibid.*, p.25.
[89] *ibid.*, p.67.
[90] E, p.50.

The confident use of Latinate words like 'instanter'[91] and 'cachinnation' indicates Jefferies had received a middle-class education. Although he uses such words ironically, for humorous effect, their frequency suggests they had been drummed into him at school, and that the education Jefferies received was designed to turn pupils into middle-class Pooterish clerks.

Again, we have perhaps a clue to Jefferies' religious feelings, particularly his attitude to Christianity, in the scene where Ben is *in extremis*, sheer cliff ahead, party of yelling Comanche behind:

> Ben knew but little of Christianity beyond the name, he had but seldom bowed the knee, never had he trusted in God, never offered up a prayer in the real sense of the word. But now with death beneath, and worse than death behind, a sense of dependency came over him and he mentally prayed the Great Maker of the Universe to deliver him.[92]

There is a parallel here with utterances Jefferies made during his first serious illnesses of 1867 and 1868, when he was 'on the edge of the grave'[93] and told his aunt that for the first time he found consolation in the Bible.[94]

It took Jefferies a long time to find his métier: in a career spanning twenty-one years (1866-87) it was not until 1878 that he turned to nature and the countryside as his proper subject. There are few anticipations of the nature writer in *Ben Tubbs*. However, the episode of Ben and Ned's truancy includes a description of birds and a sunset.[95] Despite clichéd phrases such as 'feathered tribe' and 'the vault of heaven', and the would-be humorous tone, the passage shows some detail and sensitivity, however slight, in the observation. Later, in America, Ben and Ned are stilled at one point by the majesty of nature,[96] a scene anticipating that in *Bevis* where the boys sit in silence listening to the

---

[91] *BT*, p.20.
[92] *ibid.*, p.121.
[93] T, p.58.
[94] Letter to Aunt Ellen dated 28 August 1868. 'I never found my Bible a consolation before, but I have during the last two or three days, for its promises are full of mercy, and I have found it true, for I have prayed earnestly and God has answered me...' (*RJL*, p.60)
[95] *BT*, p.35.
[96] *ibid.*, p.118.

music of water pouring over a hatch.⁹⁷ Ben has one or two such moments of deeper appreciation of natural beauty:

> The path widened again and to his great joy, at about a mile ahead, he saw that the cliffs went down and gave place to the rolling prairie, whose tall grass—such is the power of fancy—he would have sworn he saw waving. At this joyful sight his heart expanded and he uttered an exclamation of thankfulness.⁹⁸

Again, we learn that Ben 'delighted in shooting and was already tolerably expert with his rifle'.⁹⁹ The shooting of the deer is described with some elaboration.¹⁰⁰

The writing is sometimes careless of repetition, with words repeated in the same sentence. 'The next moment another fearful yell smote upon his affrighted ear'¹⁰¹ is typical of some of the prose. But in general the fluency and confidence of the narrative are impressive enough.

oooOOOooo

For all its faults *Ben Tubbs* has one claim to distinction. It is unique in dealing with a particular school: Dr Smales's Academy is the only such institution described at any length in Jefferies' work.¹⁰² Jefferies wrote much about education and learning but surprisingly says next to nothing about his schooldays. The goose-girl parable in *Restless Human Hearts* shows his hostility to Gradgrind rote-learning. The essay 'The Pigeons at the British Museum' and passages in *The Story of My Heart* make clear that though an avid reader, particularly in his youth, he did not regard books as the fount of all wisdom.

In *Bevis*, where Jefferies imaginatively recreated large tracts of his boyhood and where it might be thought that there would be some reference, if only oblique, there is not a whisper of school. Instead the novel celebrates the type of outdoor education in which Jefferies believed: true knowledge comes from living outdoors, in the open air, in

---

⁹⁷ *B*, pp.22-3.
⁹⁸ *BT*, pp.122-123.
⁹⁹ *ibid.*, p.102.
¹⁰⁰ *ibid.*, pp.110-111.
¹⁰¹ *ibid.*, p.121.
¹⁰² Unless we include the deserted grammar school depicted at the end of Chapter IV of *Wild Life in a Southern County* and again in 'An Extinct Race' (in *The Toilers of the Field)*. The school was situated in Bishopstone, a village beneath the scarp of the downs near the Wilts-Berks border.

close contact with nature, in the company of wind and sun, and the learning is largely unconscious.[103] The boys learn from experience, by their mistakes, they in effect teach themselves with minimal parental guidance.

In *Restless Human Hearts* and again in *The Story of My Heart* Jefferies complains that there is no education of the heart and the soul as there is of the intellect. He thought the former by far the most important. In the autobiography, which traces the history of his spiritual and intellectual development, he records how 'the last traces and relics of superstitions and traditions acquired compulsorily in childhood' fell away from his mind like dead leaves.[104]

Often in his work he emphasizes the evils, or at least limitations, of book-learning, and the importance of unlearning. He wanted some 'alchemy of the imagination' to inform the works of scientists and philosophers. In 'Nature and Books', trying to get at the soul of the dandelion, its inner meaning, and finding existing books useless for that purpose, he concludes that 'there are no books; the books are yet to be written'.[105] Books, with their painstaking accumulation of facts, were burying the superstitions of the past.

> Thus men's minds all over the printing-press world are unlearning the falsehoods that have bound them down so long; they are unlearning, the first step to learn. They are going down to nature and taking up the clods with their own hands, and so coming to have touch of that which is real. As yet we are in the first stage; by-and-by we shall come to the alchemy, and get the honey for the inner mind and soul. I found, therefore, from the dandelion that there were no books, and it came upon me, believe me, as a great surprise, for I had lived quite certain that I was surrounded with them. It is nothing but unlearning, I find now; five thousand books to unlearn.[106]

A late notebook entry reads: 'Those thoughts I got from nature alone

---

[103] An education like that of the keeper's son in *The Gamekeeper at Home* ('that local intelligence, technical ability, and unwritten education which is the result of early practice and is quite distinct from book learning', (*GH*, p.26)) and Dickon in *The Amateur Poacher* ('absorbed rather than learnt in boyhood', (*AP*, pp.123-4)).
[104] *SH*, p.84.
[105] *FH*, p.31.
[106] *ibid.*, p.32.

of any value. Books, etc. in vain. Nothing to tell me.'[107]

In sum, Jefferies had a low opinion of conventional education. He was as repelled by it as by orthodox Christianity, by the organised religion of the Church of England. This may help explain why this most autobiographical of writers says virtually nothing about his schooldays. A prospective biographer scouring his works for evidence will come away disappointed. All we are told is that he 'learned Latin and Greek in the usual manner'[108] (and whether he did in fact ever learn Greek is moot) and disliked the French accent as a schoolboy.[109]

The reason for the silence is that Jefferies' schooling left no very profound mark. Conventional education gave him little. Indifference perhaps best sums up his attitude to the schooling he had received in Sydenham and Swindon. Like Hardy he was largely self-taught, a provincial autodidact.[110]

Ben Tubbs Adventures is the exception to the general silence, and the portrait of the school depicted in its pages is hardly flattering. It is, as said, a Dotheboys Hall: the headmaster makes Ben's mother pay an extortionate amount in fees, half as much again as the other parents; he is free in his use of the cane; and the school is divided into two factions, or gangs, with much bullying.

In 'A Natural System of National Defence' Jefferies says that 'in many schools there are regular factions who fight pitched battles',[111] an echo of the wars of the Logians and Chagians in *Ben Tubbs*.

In her reminiscences Audrey Horsell says Jefferies attended Daddy Hanks's school in Swindon where:

---

[107] *NB*, p.229. The undated entry appears in the notebook covering January-February 1887.
[108] Letter to George Bentley from The Downs, Crowborough, Sussex, dated 12 June [1886].
[109] In 'A Natural System of National Defence' he refers to the sweetness of 'those [French] accents, that we hated at school' on the lips of the children he watched playing in a park in Brussels. The article first appeared in three parts in the *Swindon Advertiser* in the summer of 1871. In August 2014 the Richard Jefferies Society published it as a booklet, where the above quote appears on p.4.
[110] Hardy was described as 'ce Saxon autodidacte' in F.A. Hedgcock, *Thomas Hardy, penseur et artiste* (Paris, 1911, p.458, n.1), a phrase to which he took strong exception, pencilling in the margin of his copy, 'This is not literary criticism, but impertinent personality & untrue'.
[111] *op.cit., ibid.*

It was a practice... to make a new boy run the gauntlet of two lines of boys armed with small stones tied in handkerchiefs, to initiate him into the life there with good hard blows about his back and head.[112]

This finds a faint echo in *Ben Tubbs* where on his first day Ben is tied to a post in the school playground and beaten on his bare bottom with the knotted end of a handkerchief by the other boys for sneaking.

Horsell also says Daddy Hanks was 'a terrible wielder of the cane', a phrase recalling the description of Dr Smales in *Ben Tubbs* as 'the wielder of canes'.[113]

It is possible, if not yet proven, that in his attempted march to Moscow Jefferies was running away from school as much as from home.

---

[112] Audrey Horsell, 'Reminiscences of Richard Jefferies', *The Countryman*, vol. 13, April 1936 [pp.40-44], p.41. However, apropos Horsell's memoir Fanny Hall commented, in pencilled notes written for her nieces in 1937 when she was 87: 'I never heard of Daddy Hanks.'
[113] *BT*, p.21.

Ben Tubbs Adventures

by

Richard Jefferies

Chapter 1

Benjamin Tubbs was born in an obscure village in the S.W. of England. He came of respectable parents. There is no doubt of that. Everybody said they were respectable and what everybody said must be true. Besides his father was a retired grocer and had an income rather above that called a comfortable competency. At any rate he lived in good style, rented a large house and larger garden, drank port wine and died at the age of sixty-five.

His mother was much the same sort of person, only stouter, she had a great idea of her own importance and said she loved her husband. She died four years after him, left the money to her son and probably went to heaven—should not like to insist upon the latter point because certain individuals said she was uncharitable. No uncharitable person, said they, could go to heaven, therefore, logically concluded and expressed a different opinion. However it makes but slight difference so we will proceed.

When his father died Ben was about fifteen but had not made even the most distant acquaintance with school, save what he could glean from certain young individuals who periodically came home for what was called a three weeks holiday. Three weeks, indeed. Of course they were too late for the coach and, as it went but once a week, the young scoundrels always made a month at least of it. According to these worthies it was a most dismal place save on Saturdays—he therefore determined to keep away as long as possible. This was no difficult matter as his father loved him to distraction and his mother could not "abear" the thoughts of a separation from her darling boy.

The cook had a different opinion of him. According to her, he was the most rascalliest, scoundrellest young, young —, she did not know what, and that was a fact. The truth was she could keep nothing, that is, tit-bits from him. Suppose the pantry door was left unlocked; that nice bit of chicken for master's supper, where was it? The cat had it. Of course she had. Was there ever a cat averse to meat, especially a tabby? Had it been a genteel black, it would have been different. Not the slightest shade of suspicion could possibly be attached to a sleek, well-fed, green-eyed, long-tailed, lazy, sharp-clawed black denizen of the parlour. But a tabby, a hungry, mewling, ravenous, tabby, there is no knowing what amount of mischief it may perform. This was "missus's" notion, but cook would have it that it was Ben's fault and loudly proclaimed her opinion upon every suitable occasion.

After the demise of Mr Tubbs, however, Ben grew so impudent and behaved in such an insolent manner to his only remaining parent, and indeed to everyone else, that it became apparent he must be broke-in—must make personal acquaintance with school. Mrs Tubbs, having been seized by this idea, was not long in acting upon it and called in a few worthy individuals to assist her in making a proper choice. There was old Mr Rubrick, Parson Snobbs, Widow Mull and Mrs Wulty. All these were sensible, practical and experienced persons.

It was true Parson Snobbs was a young man, that is young in proportion, but still from his position in society, clerical title and great piety, he was a fit person to be consulted.

Mrs Wulty was of the opinion that the very best "educational edifice," as she was pleased to call it, was situated at the outskirts of a town some twenty miles north.

Widow Mull agreed with her, but Parson Snobbs recommended one ten miles further on.

Mr Rubrick having uttered several preliminary hums, haws, coughs and so forth commenced a very learned and lengthy discourse in which he did not recommend any particular seminary, but showed in a very lucid manner in what consisted the excellency of a school, and ended by proposing that the merits of the two spoken of by Mrs Wulty and Parson Snobbs should be discussed in a candid manner. To this the assembled company acceded without a dissenting voice, and forthwith the parties commenced to arrange.

Mrs Wulty objected to the one proposed by the Parson chiefly on the score of the greater distance and consequent greater difficulty in transporting—yes, that was the word, transporting the youth thither. For some time this weighty argument was allowed to be convincing and Mrs Wulty actually grew so elated at the certainty of carrying her point, that she went so far as to declare that this was the only point on which she could oppose their respected pastor. Hardly were the words spoken than the Parson commenced speaking, and this time he bore down Mrs Wulty and convinced his audience of the superior merits of his school by showing, to their astounded understandings, that if it was further, yet in that consisted its great advantage. For should the youth at any time prove refractory, and disposed to quit the seminary, it would be impossible for him to do so because of being unacquainted with the direction and confounded with the distance of home. Mrs Wulty was silenced, so was everybody else and remained so until Mrs Tubbs arose and said that she fully agreed with the Parson and had decided upon sending her son to the school he patronised, and now concluded she, "This business being dispatched we will enjoy the evening and you must all stop to supper." They all assented cheerfully to this invitation and, drawing round the fire, commenced a little confidential chat of scandal.

Mrs Wulty commenced, she hoped, she wished, she did not think it probable that such a shameful thing could again occur as that which she had heard the other night. Hereupon she paused, winked at the Parson and looked mysterious, which was a certain method she knew of raising curiosity. Accordingly Mrs Tubbs smiled, said she thought she understood but would like to hear more particulars and concluded by going to a cupboard and producing a bottle of juniper juice, a sugar basin and some tumblers. The company evidently regarded this movement in a convivial light as Mr Rubrick chuckled, Mrs Wulty was all eyes, Widow Mull followed her example and the Parson tried to look shocked but could not. Of course not! Was there ever a bachelor, a young man past forty, not partial to gin and water? Mrs Tubbs went through the ceremony of asking what they preferred though she well knew that she had not mistaken the bottle. Accordingly everyone followed the example of Mr Rubrick who when asked, smiled, wriggled and requested her not to make it too strong. Mrs Tubbs was a woman of experience and she well knew what that meant, viz, a double dose. Having served them all and lastly herself, she drew up to the fire and, with a wink at Mrs Wulty, asked whether she referred to the elopement of Molly Tow the butcher's wife with Samuel Snaggs the baker. Mrs Wulty replied that it was a much worse case and seeing that all hung upon her lips she commenced her tale.

"You remember what a row, I can express the agitation caused by it, by no other word, that there was when Mrs Toll saw the ghost at the corner of Hum Wood?"

"Yes, yes," was the general exclamation.

"Well the mystery is solved and what do you think it was?" Of course nobody knew, nobody could imagine, nobody had the slightest idea and nobody could paint the throwing up of hands and rolling of eyes which attended the explanation. Who would have thought that the sanctified Molly Turner could have done such a thing; she that never missed a Sunday in her attendance at church, she who never had been seen with anything approaching a spread, she who always had a text of scripture at hand, she that never walked with the men—actually that she had met Bill Cumble and was married. It was astounding and with one accord each and everyone sipped their terrestrial nectar and expressed in various keys their astonishment.

And where was Master Ben all this time? He had been dismissed to the lower regions immediately on the arrival of the conferring parties. But with innate sharpness he suspected to use his own expression that something was "up" and presently determined to know what. He therefore slipped out of the kitchen and carefully ascended the stairs to an upper landing and, opening the door of a certain room as carefully, crawled to the fireplace and poked his head up the chimney. As he was directly above the company every word above a whisper could be plainly heard and judge of his astonishment and rage at hearing himself thus nicely disposed of.

"Oh, oh," quoth he, "school indeed Mister Parson, I'll school you, I'll tan your ugly skin just wait a crack—all right." And Master Ben formed a plan for serving out poor Parson Snobbs. The outline of this plan, as it first occurred to him, was to dress in white as he knew the Parson was very timid, and cross his path that very night on the way home. As the path to the vicarage, which stood somewhat out of the hamlet, was enclosed between high hedges rendering it perfectly dark the young rascal determined to meet him there. There was but one obstacle to the performance of this trick which was that Mrs Tubbs would most assuredly shortly order him to bed. Not to be defeated by this he began his preparations immediately and as they consisted in the secreting of a sheet beneath his coat they were quickly finished and he was soon out of the house and shivering with the cold. But having begun, nothing could prevent him from carrying out his diabolical purpose. So buttoning up his coat he started for the lane, where he purposed walking up and down until the Parson's footfalls announced his approach, when he would draw the sheet around him and stand in the way. But the night was cold and the Parson did not come. "He can't have gone round the road," thought Ben, "But I'll wait a little longer," and he drew the sheet around him.

About this time the party broke up and each set out upon his or her separate route. The Parson, with melancholy reflections upon the degeneracy of the times and the dirtiness of the roads, entered the dismal lane. Slowly, steadily and majestically he paced along, at times with scrutinising glances, surveying the darkness in front, at others trying in vain to find a dry road through a gigantic puddle. Suddenly he halted and put his hand to his eyes as if to shade them. A thrill ran through him, "No, it can't be," he muttered between his teeth. But it was. There, right in the way, stood motionless a white figure resembling in every respect the most approved descriptions of a ghost he had ever read. He was naturally a timid man and had been since infancy a firm believer in ghosts, goblins and spiritual apparitions of all descriptions, sulphurous or otherwise. He endeavoured to mutter a conjuration but now when it was wanted he could not remember a single word, and even if he had would not have been enabled to utter it. He was completely spellbound, mentally and bodily paralyzed for the time being. All his senses were culminated in one—that of sight, he watched it with agonising dread, his eyeballs almost starting from their sockets, and it is probable that had this continued much longer that the poor man would have lost his senses. But no, Ben thinking he had continued in one posture long enough resolved to alter it, and advanced two steps at the same time raising one arm. This motion was not lost upon the Parson—it awoke within him the instinct of self preservation, and as Ben again advanced, with a shout he turned and fled. Down the dark, dirty, briary lane he ran at his utmost speed, yet to him it seemed crawling, and he made still greater efforts. In his hurry he forgot that there was a gate at the end of the lane where it joined the road and he came up against it with tremendous force; his head, being inclined forward, received the brunt of the blow and he fell to the ground insensible. As for Ben, immediately the Parson had disappeared, he deemed his vengeance completed and divesting himself of the sheet he got through a gap in the hedge and made for home as fast as his legs could carry him.

He arrived exactly in the nick of time as Mrs Tubbs had just enquired of the servants, who were engaged in clearing the remnants of the supper, where he had betaken himself. They replied that they were at that time unacquainted with his whereabouts but thought he had gone out.

"Don't know? Gone out?" shouted Mrs Tubbs, her maternal feelings aroused for the safety of her darling. "Go and find him this instant Sarah, do you hear?" cried she in a louder tone. Poor Sarah, with both hands full, started off immediately and in her hurry knocking down half a dozen wine glasses.

"Dear, dear," said the cook in a sorrowful tone.

"Dear, ay you may well say dear, that girl has cost me, let's see—for two decanters, eleven mugs, fifteen tumblers, three teacups, ten ——."

Here Sarah entered and gently informed her "Missis" that Master Ben had returned and was now in the kitchen extracting his feet from his boots. This good news somewhat conciliated the old lady and she only admonished her to take more care and to tell Ben to come and kiss her before he retired for the night. Both of which Sarah faithfully promised to perform and saying "Goodnight ma'am" vanished.

Chapter 2

It will be seen from the foregoing chapter that Ben possessed a revengeful disposition. The fact was that he had been badly taught, if taught at all, and but slight restraint had been imposed upon him. The consequence was that neither of his parents could ever control him. He had naturally a fierce unforgiving temper and it had been greatly aggravated by having had his own way for such a length of time. Hence his love for his mother can only be described as ferocious and his hate for the Parson as reasonable. Having thus premised and given a slight insight into our hero's character we will proceed with the history of his adventures.

Mrs Tubbs was by no means an early riser and the consequence was that her servants followed her example. But their conduct was "unbeknown to missus," as the cook would have said, and judge for yourself as to what were her sensations on rising an hour earlier than usual to find the house quiet, the shutters up, the fires unlit and everything deep in dust. She was astonished, confounded, angry, savage and muttering vengeance rushed upstairs past her own door and made a dash for the attic. But it was no use, she was not so young as formerly.

The violent exertion, the unutterable rage which pervaded her proved too much for her lungs and she sunk upon the first step in a fainting state. How long she remained in this position Mrs Tubbs could never tell. All she knew was that there was a dreadful noise, an awful scream and, on opening her eyes, she saw extended before her something groaning and evidently clad in white. Mrs Tubbs was not naturally timid but just awakening as she was from a sort of swoon the apparition did not materially conduce to her happiness and she certainly started when, with an heart-rending groan, the figure rose upon its knees. Whatever were Mrs Tubbs feelings at this change of posture she had not had time to analyse them when two mighty bangs were heard apparently proceeding from below.

"Dear, dear," answered a treble voice above, "I'm coming, coming." There was a pattering of feet. Mrs Tubbs received a bump upon the back, another dreadful scream was heard, another awful groan and Mrs Tubbs, cook and housemaid rolled about on the landing in indescribable fear, indignation and confusion. Meanwhile the bangs continued below, at every succeeding stroke increasing in fury, evidently the knocker was getting savage, nay a voice could at times be heard shouting and bawling some unintelligible gibberish of "Shan't wait much longer!"

Mrs Tubbs now arose and commanded Sarah to attend and open the door. For a long time nothing could be obtained from the poor housemaid save that she was dying and wished to be left alone. "Let alone indeed," shouted irate Mrs Tubbs "you lazy, lay-a-bed, let alone indeed. Get up, I say, and open the door instantly." Here the cook put in her oar and with a mournful voice conveyed to Mrs Tubbs the melancholy fact that she was *hors de combat* and could not move. She was bumped, thumped and bothered, she said. Her head was broken, shaken and turning round; she could hear nothing, see nothing, do nothing. "Then I suppose I must attend the door myself?" demanded Mrs Tubbs in a voice of thunder. No one answered and she was about to descend the stairs when a thought struck her. She returned, disappeared and presently reappeared with Ben behind. "Go and open the door, sir," said she not very tenderly. Ben demurred. "This instant, sir," cried she raising her arm. Ben took the hint and jumping to the stairs slid down the banisters. He was just in time as the fellow was turning away when he opened the door and politely requested to know "what the deuce he wanted".

The fellow looked precious surly and presently replied that he had a note for "Missus."

"Let's have it," said Ben.

"No, no, don't 'xactly see that; shou'd loike half a pint first," said the man.

Ben said he should not and the man was about to depart when Mrs Tubbs, who had heard all from the landing, shouted "Go and get him some."

Ben replied that he had no slippers on and should catch cold on the damp cellar floor. This was plausible, so again Mrs Tubbs commanded Sarah to rise. But it was no use and boiling with rage she descended and drew a pint from the first barrel she came to. Upon receiving the cup the man handed the note to Ben. He then emptied the cup at a single draught and, returning it, walked off whistling.

Mrs Tubbs now took down a shutter and was soon engaged in wading through the note's contents. It was from Mrs Ung, the housekeeper at the Vicarage, and ran thus:

My dear Mrs Tubbs,

I sincerely beg your pardon for troubling you but I should be much obliged and so would Mr Snobbs if you would just walk down and see him. He is in a dreadful state covered from head to foot with bruises and suffering from a severe cold caught yesternight. He did not arrive at home until early this morning and you may imagine what a fright I was in. He says he was set upon and knocked but as he still has his watch it does not seem likely. I well know that you are a capital nurse and I wish to obtain some advice, so do pray come quickly.

I am,
   Your humble friend,
      Sarah Ung.

"And what is it to me, I should like to know," said Mrs Tubbs, "whether the parson's well or ill?"

"Ill?" said Ben inquiringly.

"Yes," replied his mother handing him the note. Ben could not resist laughing as he read the epistle. "Well what are you grinning at now?" asked the irritated Mrs Tubbs.

"Oh, nothing, nothing," answered Ben.

"Hum," said his mother, "nothing, oh," and she sailed upstairs in a dignified manner in the hope of finding the two servants groaning upon the landing and having a round at good hearty scolding. But they had both vanished, probably from fear of that young "himp," Ben. Mrs Tubbs shouted for "Sarah" and a voice above answered, "Yes ma'am, I'm coming ma'am," and presently the disconsolate housemaid appeared with her head bound up in a white something. Ben began laughing immediately but was silenced by Mrs Tubbs who next enquired where the cook was.

"Gettin' the breakfast ma'am."

"You'd better go and help her," was the forthcoming command and Sarah disappeared.

Although Mrs Tubbs pretended she did not care a fig about the Parson yet in reality she was burning with curiosity to see him and hear the particulars of his misfortune. So after making a slight breakfast she acquainted Ben with the fact that as he was to start tomorrow for school by the coach this would be his last day at home, and then departed.

Ben received this startling intelligence with surprise only equalled by his detestation of the measure, and forthwith determined upon enjoying his last day, i.e. doing as much mischief as possible in the time. Accordingly, shortly after breakfast, he commenced operations and, having by dint of threatening to empty the sugar-basin, compelled Sarah to put on his boots, and took a turn round the garden for the purpose of forming a plan. While leisurely perambulating his reflections were suddenly disturbed by the whistling and chattering of numerous important-looking starlings on the chimney. Ben winked and, picking up a stone, discharged it with might and main at the vociferous creatures. Of course it did not take effect as, before the stone had hardly left his hand, they were off with a tantalizing scream but, touching the brickwork, it rolled in and fell down the chimney. Great was Ben's delight at beholding this unexpected good luck and he directly ran in to see what damage had been done. To his mortification he found that, saving the smashing of a saucepan and frightening the cook into fits, but little had been accomplished in the way of greatly disturbing the economy of the place. This outdoor experiment having all but failed Ben determined to ascertain what could be done within and for this purpose commenced ascending the stairs, whistling as he went. But before he could gain the first landing Sarah shouted for him to wipe his boots upon the mat, but Ben continued to ascend and whistle.

"Oh! dear, dear, dear," cried the housemaid deprecatingly. Out came the cook, ladle in hand, from the kitchen with many kind enquiries as to what was the matter. Sarah replied that there was that "nasty himp a-trampin' up stairs with his dirty boots on," and she "couldn't stop him, no, not no way." Thereupon Sarah looked so pitifully woebegone that she excited the cook's deepest sympathy and with a "He shan't do it," she rushed upstairs. Ben was about to enter his mother's room when the panting cook caught him by the shoulder and violently pulled him back. He shouted, lowed, fought and would probably have succeeded in his object had not a reinforcement arrived in the shape of Sarah, and by their united efforts he was at last expelled from the house. This sort of treatment was not what Ben had been used to and he determined to be revenged for it. Having thought the matter over, he came to the conclusion that the best method would be to meet his mother on her return with a most doleful tale of the injuries he had received. With this idea he strolled towards the Parsonage until arriving at the entrance to the lane which had been the scene of last night's adventure. Here he made a pause and debated within himself whether she would be likely to return around the road or by the shorter passage of the lane. Many good reasons seemed to give the preference to the road and he therefore slowly strolled down it, meditating what he should say.

While all this was passing Mrs Tubbs was hearing the true account of his adventure from the Parson himself and her belief in ghostly visitations was confirmed by the dreadful narrative. Having heard him to the end without a single interruption she then overwhelmed him with questions directly or indirectly bearing upon the subject and received the most incoherent and incongruous replies. She then left the poor man's bedside and repaired below to have a chat on the affair with Mrs Ung. This concluded, she started for home promising to return bringing with her a certain preparation which was a sovereign remedy for all bumps, thumps, bangs or knocks of all descriptions, possible or impossible. Instead of taking the cleaner road she came down the dirty lane in the hope of perceiving the marks of the cloven foot. But although she surveyed the ground with the greatest attention yet not the slightest indication could she perceive until, just as she was about to give up the search, something close by the hedge caught her attention. It looked in the distance much like a pool of blood and she rushed, regardless of puddles, towards it. To her great disappointment it proved to be but a pocket handkerchief, dyed red, and imagine her immense surprise when upon opening it the letters which spell the resounding name of Benjamin Tubbs became apparent, worked with white. Mrs Tubbs was astounded. She could not move from the spot until she had ejaculated, "The young rascal—I see—oh lor," when like the Parson she turned and fled. On knocking at her door it was immediately opened by Sarah who began complaining of Ben in no very measured terms.

"Well what 'as he been doing now?" quoth Mrs Tubbs.

"Trampin' about the house with his dirty boots, ma'am."

Here Mrs Tubbs' wrath broke forth and had she not been somewhat restrained by the presence of Sarah it is impossible to say what Ben would have been called by his irate mother. She determined, that very moment, that neither pleas nor entreaties should gain him a single day of grace. To school he should go directly. Things were in this state when Ben returned with certain unpleasant forebodings of the welcome he would receive. However Mrs Tubbs' wrath had somewhat cooled down and she met him with a sort of grim expression on her countenance and in answer to his question of how the Parson was merely gathered herself up and walked upstairs to dress for dinner. Ben took his cue from her and spoke not a word during dinner. Immediately it was over he arose to depart but was stopped by an authoritative, "Come here, sir." "Sit there, sir," was Mrs Tubbs's next command and then, putting her feet on the fender, she dived into the recesses of a pocket and after various necessary contortions produced the handkerchief. "There, sir," said she, solemnly holding it up by the corners, "do you know that?" Ben's hand sought his pocket and not finding the accustomed occupant he answered reluctantly in the affirmative. "Where do you think I found that, sir?" asked Mrs Tubbs. No answer. "You don't know, oh don't you," said she ironically, "well I'll tell you. I found this, sir, in the lane, sir." Ben started, "and I insist, sir, on your telling me, sir, where you were last night, sir." No answer. "Sir," thundered Mrs Tubbs, "you were in the lane, sir, and you frightened that chosen vessel Parson Snobbs by playing the ghost, sir, now did you not, sir?"

Before the end of this speech Mrs Tubbs had risen to her feet and she now stood looking down upon Ben with such a grimly comical expression of face that in spite of himself, and dreadful apprehensions of what would follow, he burst into a loud laugh. Mrs Tubbs stooped and picked up the poker. "Sir," quoth she "leave off that giggle this instant, this instant, sir," and she waved the poker majestically over his head. He, poor fellow, startled for the safety of his sconce, immediately did as he was commanded and Mrs Tubbs, seeing she had produced the requisite effect, sat down and replaced the poker. "Now, sir," she again began, "listen to me. I had intended, though this morning I told you tomorrow was your last day, to have allowed you three weeks grace; but now, sir, since your disgraceful conduct last night and early this morning I cannot think of keeping such a young scoundrel about the premises, so tomorrow, sir, off you go."

Having uttered this dreadful speech she strode from the room leaving Ben to his own cogitations. These, to say the least, were anything but cheerful, however his was not a melancholy disposition and he soon recovered so far from the awful intelligence as to be able to wink continuously with one eye. This sign of returning consciousness was shortly followed by others and in half an hour he might have been seen, hands in pockets, strolling around the garden. The fresh air no doubt materially conduced to his complete recovery and after he had pulled up a flower or so, flung a stone into the next door neighbour's greenhouse and another at the cat, he felt none the worse for the cruel blow. He did not, however, feel quite so inclined for mischief as before dinner and therefore concluded upon retiring for the day. With this view he essayed to enter the house by the back door but it resisted his endeavours and he then walked round to the front. Here he was also repulsed and although he banged away with the knocker until tired, not the slightest effect was produced. Ben now concluded that it was no go and, seating himself upon one of the steps, tried to be miserable. But try how he would it was no use, not even the shadow of a tear could he drop and his utmost efforts to produce a good groan resulted in what Mrs Tubbs called a giggle. Disappointed even in this Ben began to foresee that he should spend a dismal afternoon when, involuntarily taking a look at the sun, he discovered to his great joy that it was rapidly declining, in short that there would be no afternoon to spend. Cheering, thought Ben, and whistling a tune he again took a turn round the garden. By the time he had completely encircled it the sun had entirely disappeared and darkness was rapidly settling upon the land. Seeing this Ben thought it high time for him to gain admittance and he again banged away with the knocker and again his efforts passed unnoticed. This began to look ugly as he had entirely reckoned upon being admitted to tea and the servants must have heard his knocking. He began to get savage. "S'pose they don't open next time by jingo but I'll see about it," he muttered half aloud and having formed this resolution he again assailed the front door apparently striving to beat it in by continued knocking. No footstep in the hall—not the slightest sound indoors. "Letherication!" bellowed Ben in a rage and he rushed to the back. Here he collected a heap of stones and discharged them one by one at the back door expecting to see it fall in with a mighty smash. But no, he could not make the slightest impression, beyond knocking out great splinters, and soon exhausted his stock of stones. He determined however to make another attempt and having collected another heap was about to fling one when a well-known voice cried "Well, I never," behind him and turning he beheld his mother standing in amaze and gazing upon the battered door. She had evidently been on a journey as her boots were muddy and her dress splashed. The fact was she had been to Parson Snobbs with the promised preparation and had given orders that until her return Master Ben should be kept out. Her orders had been literally carried out and she now saw the result of them. The back door was indented all over, great splinters were laying around and it was apparent that a few more volleys would have completely smashed it.

"You young rascal," said she turning to Ben who was surveying her from head to foot with great complacency. "Well, what are you staring at, sir, follow me, sir," and off she sailed round the house and gave a peculiar rap, rap, rappa, rap. The servants immediately knew who it was and the door was opened by Sarah. "Is tea ready?" enquired Mrs Tubbs. The answer was in the affirmative and, telling her to follow, Mrs Tubbs leisurely ascended to the upper regions. Ben, as leisurely, descended but instead of entering the breakfast parlour where he knew tea was awaiting passed on to the kitchen door and beheld through a chink the cook raising a teacup to her lips. He waited until it touched them and gave the door a tremendous thump with both fists. Up jumped the cook, down went the cup, over went the slop basin and Ben began to roar with cachinnation.

"That young himp agen," shouted the cook and rushed to the door intending to administer corporal punishment. But Ben was too quick for her and began ascending at a terrific rate. Unfortunately for him Mrs

Tubbs was descending at the same moment and, not being able to stop suddenly, an awful collision took place. Ben rolled backwards head over heels in no time making the bottom, while Mrs Tubbs quickly followed sliding very comfortably and, on her feet coming in contact with the floor, fell over and smothered him. Praise be to crinoline! Had it not been for its expanding folds Mrs Tubbs would have killed her son. As it was he was severely bumped and immediately after tea was dismissed to bed there to cogitate on the approaching morrow.

Chapter 3

The next morning, upon awaking, he was painfully conscious of the events of the preceding day by a tremendous stiffness of the joints. The crafty rascal immediately resolved to make virtue of his thumps and, by exaggerating their extent, number and severity to prove to Mrs Tubbs the necessity of his remaining at home for that day at least. But, although he manufactured a most pitiful tale and groaned as if woefully hurt, no one would listen to him, so he was obliged to rise from sheer hunger. Upon arriving at the lower regions he found everything in confusion, the cook running one way, the housemaid another, and Mrs Tubbs puffing and blowing from the immense exertion of locking a refractory box. She somewhat revived upon perceiving him and commanded extreme haste at the same time pointing to the breakfast parlour door. Ben was not long taking the hint and was soon agreeably employed in cramming. The command he did not exactly see and although each minute brought Sarah reiterating it yet, he cut away very leisurely without the slightest hurry. At last Mrs Tubbs appeared and Ben immediately put on an appearance of tremendous anxiety. But his mother was too sharp and, ordering him to put his boots on, she commenced to clear the eatables—the only effectual method of obtaining attention to her commands. Ben, seeing it was useless to demur, walked off and had just succeeded in lacing his shoes up when Sarah, who had been upon the watch, rushed down stairs with the alarming intelligence that she had stopped the coach. Mrs Tubbs directly began to scream for Ben and, he having appeared, she led the way to the vehicle. In a few minutes the luggage was placed in safely and they were driven away at a rapid pace. Ben curled himself up in a corner and looked sulky while

Mrs Tubbs sat bolt upright and looked as if immensely superior to the two other lady occupants who were lounging in easy positions. In this manner the journey was continued for two long tedious hours during which the only human voice heard was that of the driver as he swore at the horses.

They then stopped at the sign of the Saracen where a change of horses was effected. When this operation had been performed to his satisfaction the driver dived into the recesses of the bar to get "summat" and Ben, arising, got out to survey the place. Firstly he walked around the vehicle and unfortunately spied the whip which he immediately determined to hide and looked to see if he was observed. But no one was in sight as the three outside male passengers had followed the driver and were in turn followed by the ostler. The coast being clear, the next thing was what should he do with it? The stable door being open appeared exactly what was wanted, so snatching up the article Ben secreted it in the hayloft. He then returned to the coach looking perfectly innocent and in joyful anticipation of the row there would presently be. He had not long to wait before the driver and passengers appeared and the whip was immediately missed. The driver with a puzzled expression upon his countenance walked around the vehicle looking beneath it, below it and at it, while the outsiders watched his motions with great curiosity thinking the liquor had taken effect. But they were shortly undeceived as the man, convinced it had disappeared, shouted for the ostler who soon showed himself. "Where's the whip?" asked he, but the ostler disclaimed having any notion of its present position but added that he had seen it lying on the shafts. "Well it ben't thur now an' what be I to do wi'out 'un?" He could get no satisfactory answer and although they searched in every impossible and unlikely place yet not the slightest remnant could be found. The driver now began to wax savage and presently in the height of his indignation charged the ostler with the theft. This was more than the tender of horses could stand and in a moment he had rolled up his shirt sleeves and, placing himself in the most approved boxing attitude with fists rotating, called on his accuser to "Cum on." The driver, nothing loath, immediately divested himself of his coat and went to work in earnest. Soon their shouts and blows brought a horde of vagabonds to the spot and, some taking one side and some the other, a pitched battle commenced.

Meanwhile the horses had got restive and pawed the ground in impatience. Soon the various sounds arising from the scene of combat alarmed them and they commenced to plunge and rear. This made the ladies scream, and the men at that moment giving a tremendous cheer at a successful hit, they gave a startling neigh and dashed ahead at full speed. No sooner was this observed than the fighting ceased and numbers of men rushed down the road in the vain hope of arresting the horses' headlong flight and shouting, "the Canal, the Canal." The inside passengers knew not half their danger but those upon the roof immediately perceived that inevitable destruction awaited them should they continue in their present course. Right ahead, hardly one hundred yards in distance, they beheld the canal crossed by a narrow wooden bridge and it was apparent that, should they swerve a foot to the other side, the coach must roll into it. Two of them set up a most lamentable howl but the third, a cool-headed and sensible individual, contrived to gain possession of the reins and tugged at them with all the strength at his command. But it was useless, nothing could check their headlong speed and, giving up the attempt, he descended as low as possible upon the steps and sprang off. He, immediately upon touching the ground arose and, shouted to the others to do the same. But no, they were weak-minded and irresolute mortals and only howled the more. As to the inside passengers they were in dreadful alarm and their screaming conjoined with the outsiders' howl materially conduced to the horses continuing their mad flight. Ben, hearing the shouts of "Canal", immediately guessed what was meant and by dint of bellowing managed to make his mother understand. Up rose Mrs Tubbs and rushed to the door, which by a convulsive effort she opened. Then throwing up her arms to aid her progress she sprung from the coach closely followed by Ben. Oh! thou spouter forth of intense hatred to spreads, had'st thou witnessed its beneficial employment only this once, thy mouth would have been closed for evermore. Both Mrs Tubbs and her son arose but slightly bumped owing to the first's superabundance of dress. The other female passengers, seeing the successful issue of the experiment, rushed to the door but the foremost one could not bring herself to the act and hesitated upon the brink while the other had in sisterly affection clasped her round the waist. But at that moment the coach gave a frightful lurch as the off wheel passed over a stone and they both, losing their balance, fell forward and came roughly to the ground. Hardly had Ben, with great politeness, assisted them to their feet when a fearful scream arose and, looking forward to their horror, they beheld the coach totter for a moment upon the brink and then roll bodily into the canal. The two outsiders were of course thrown off and performed various gyrations in the air before coming splash into the water and were seen upon the arrival of the men to struggle valorously for their bare life. Suddenly however one stood bolt upright and with head and shoulder high above the surface and the other quickly followed his example. But his being considerably shorter than his companion in misfortune, his head alone protruded from the pure element and the slightest wave passed into his open mouth causing him to sputter most ludicrously. After many ineffectual attempts he was rescued from his unpleasant position by the grinning mob, his companion having with great consideration strided ashore and vanished. All of course now repaired to the Saracen, whose smiling, bowing, puffing owner wished in his heart that such a lucky mishap would happen every day. As the coach could not at present be extricated and one of the horses was lamed it was plain they must patiently await the morrow, in the meantime consuming heaps of the Saracens' provisions and of course paying for them. Since the owner had rented the house such a piece of good luck had not befallen him and might not again. Ergo, he determined to make the most of it.

One would have thought that such a narrow escape from a fatal termination of the affair would have completely cured Ben of his disposition for mischief. But no, he was perfectly incorrigible and grinned continuously at the successful issue of his experiment. Mrs Tubbs was dreadfully frightened and trembled exceedingly. She could not be made to eat a morsel but, greatly to the innkeeper's delight, swallowed large quantities of spirit. This of course, as her fear gradually subsided, as gradually arose in her head until nobody was more surprised than she was when in the evening everything appeared double. It must not be supposed for an instant that Mrs Tubbs was given to deriving the greater portion of her nourishment from suction. By no means. Mrs Tubbs was a very abstemious woman and never touched anything but the smallest of small beer except upon those extraordinary occasions when a friend or two dropped in, which was not more than three times a week, barring Saturdays. It was this very abstinence which caused them [the spirits] to now take such an effect upon her. She became on a sudden very talkative, poked the fire continuously (they had a private room) and had at intervals an almost irresistible desire to sleep. Seeing this, Ben presently insinuated that the wisest course to pursue would be to retire and sleep away the bad effects of the accident. For some time Mrs Tubbs was very indignant at his proposing such a thing, she talked grandiloquently about her superior knowledge in such matters, protested that her eyelids felt not the slightest inclination to close and then branched off to a number of more interesting subjects which caused her dutiful son to yawn. Presently however she really began to feel tired, and telling Ben to quickly follow, she called for a candle and commenced ascending the stairs, holding by the banister and rolling about in a very singular manner. Ben having seen her safely arrive upon the landing returned to the room and sat up to a late hour reading a musty old novel which he had found. It was a tragic tale full of ghosts and mysterious rhymes, trap-doors, dank dungeons, secret passages, awful tortures and Heaven knows what else. Ben was not naturally a coward, neither did he, like the Parson, believe in spiritual visitations. He was as valiant in the night as in the day and had the greatest contempt for those who were not. The reason of this trait was that he had not been terrified during his infancy, as most children are, with tales of bogies and other nursery fictions calculated to render darkness terrible. It is greatly to be desired that all children like him should be exempted from such superstitions as are often impressed upon them by the stupidity of nurses who, to save themselves a little trouble, invent all sorts of rubbish. But to proceed ...

Although Ben was, as said before, completely above any childish fear yet he certainly started when the first stroke of twelve from a large clock resounded through the room. The momentary impression soon passed away and upon hearing the time he flung the book on the table, unlaced his boots and called for a guide to the upper regions. In a few minutes the smirking chambermaid appeared and, by closely following her motherly injunctions, he was installed between two spotless sheets and snoring with great complacency. He was in a sound sleep but did ever a person in a strange bed on a soft mattress continue for long in that happy state? Certainly not. Accordingly, before half an hour had passed away dreams began to flit about him and presently settled down to a representation of the events of the preceding day and night. Firstly he fancied himself in the sheet confronting the Parson but instead of running away the expounder of texts began to "lay on load" as the romances have it. He began to find it no joke, when suddenly a singular lightness passed through him and, to his astonishment, found himself changed to a veritable ghost while the Parson's blows were no longer felt. With a spiritual sneer at the Parson's futile efforts to pound him into mash he dissolved into air. After floating about in this state for some time, the scene changed and he fancied himself in the act of leaping from the coach. He leaped and, after an apparently interminable period during which he was continually falling, came with tremendous force upon the road. The shock awoke him and finding himself very cold he essayed to draw the clothes around him. But he could find none and presently the truth dawned upon him, he was laying upon the floor. Raising himself he tried to find the bed, but that was no easy matter. However, after upsetting the water-jug, falling over a chair and breaking a shin, he fell upon it and rolled in. After vainly endeavouring to cogitate upon the matter he gave it up and surrendering himself unconditionally to the arms of Morpheus experienced no further interruption to his slumbers until the chambermaid knocked and announced breakfast. Having obtained a satisfactory answer she departed and Ben, after expending superfluous drowsiness in several interesting yawns, arose. The first object that met his view was the capsized water-jug and his two socks swimming. "Hum," muttered Ben and without further ejaculation he dressed and descended to the breakfast room. Here he found Mrs Tubbs presiding at the head of the table and after the usual preliminary kind enquiries as to how he had slept and so forth, he sat down and commenced to do justice to the viands.

"He possesses an uncommon appetite," quoth the innkeeper to himself and forthwith his heart warmed towards the youth.

When the meal was ended Mrs Tubbs arose and, beckoning Ben to follow, retired to her private room. Here her quick motherly eye soon discovered his want of hose and she demanded what had become of them. Ben demurred a little but presently gave a clear lucid account of his night's rest and of the position the unfortunate socks at that moment occupied. Mrs Tubbs was puzzled whether to get savage or laugh; however she presently smiled and sailed upstairs to see what could be done in the matter. On her disappearance, Ben sat down to finish the novel and was soon ankle deep in atrocious murders and other dismalities. He was very fond of reading or rather devouring tales of adventure or anything of that description and from this trait Mrs Tubbs argued favourably as to his scholastic ability. She never was more mistaken in her life. Ben had the great reluctance to do anything that did not exactly jump with his humour and as to sticking to books, as he was pleased to term it, it was his detestation, and he had long ago made a resolution that nothing should cause him to. His ideas of school were necessarily very confused but, such as they were, greatly strengthened him in this laudable determination. He supposed indeed that he should get bumped, thumped, whacked, banged and otherwise knocked about did he not comply with the rules. But for blows he entertained the most supreme contempt, as poor Mrs Tubbs well knew. It was this invulnerability to her hardest hits that first put the idea of submitting him to a more powerful arm into her head. She was now occupied with reflections upon the important subject of whether it would be more expedient to proceed or return but, after a little wavering, determined upon continuing the forward course and descended to the lower regions in search of the innkeeper.

Having at last found that smiling gentleman she requested to know whether he could accommodate her with a vehicle. With a bow she was informed that one would be ready in less than no time should she desire it. Mrs Tubbs however protested that half an hour's time would be plenty early enough and departed upstairs, pleased with the man who would obey her instanter, to undergo the operation of dressing. Before she went, however, she informed Ben of her intention, no doubt expecting to see the most violent exhibition of passion, but the news had no apparent effect upon him. The fact was, Ben had expected nothing less: consequently the dreadful blow did not descend so hard. It made him pretty sulky though, and when the vehicle was announced Mrs Tubbs had to take the book from his hand before she could obtain the slightest attention to her reiterated "come alongs." But now there was no excuse for further delaying the distressing moment Ben arose and with an injured air demanded what was the matter. "Matter, sir, there's nothing the matter, follow me, sir," Mrs Tubbs answered, in no very affectionate tone as her feelings had been somewhat ruffled by his disobedience of orders before the innkeeper, and thereupon she strode from the room. Ben followed with a mournful air, and they were soon comfortably seated in the carriage and rattling swiftly along. Silence prevailed for a length of time but Ben soon began to find it intolerable and therefore questioned his mother as to how far they had to go. Mrs Tubbs was puzzled by this question and being puzzled was also offended: consequently silence again resumed its sway. Ben began to get fidgety and arising from his seat surveyed the rapidly passing country through the window. It was a dull, dusty looking prospect and as far as he could see quite flat saving ahead where an apparently rather large molehill reared its gigantic proportions. Soon they neared this solitary elevation and he then perceived, built upon its side, a small town with nothing peculiarly inviting about it. It looked as if flung together and had not the slightest architectural beauty or novelty about it saving the church which lay in an exposed position and had a square tower at one end and a spire at the other. Ben soon perceived that their course lay towards this mushroom place and his heart beat a little faster when a turn in the road revealed, at a short distance, a large square heavy looking building. This he had not the slightest doubt was their destination and each minute confirmed the idea until it was rendered certain by the vehicle coming to a dead stop in front.

The door being opened by the driver Mrs Tubbs commanded him to wait and then, sweeping down the gravel path to the portal followed by Ben, rang the bell. It was almost immediately opened by a benevolent looking smiling damsel who enquired if they wished to see the Doctor. Being answered in the affirmative she ushered them into a small snug room and departed to inform the pedagogue of the fact that he had a lady visitor. While she was thus employed Mrs Tubbs had a chair and seating herself before the fire awaited the wielder of canes with great complacency. It was different with Ben. He could not take his eyes from the door and started at every sound. Presently a heavy footstep was heard in the hall, the door was flung open and Doctor Smales stood before them. Mrs Tubbs immediately rose and her example was followed by Ben. The Doctor advanced and with a courtly though rather stiff bow requested them to be seated. Then taking a seat himself he saved Mrs Tubbs a world of trouble by opening the conversation. He said that the object of her visit was without doubt to entrust to his care the youth beside her and assured her that he would do his best to render him fit for anything. Mrs Tubbs said that he had divined the object of her visit and requested him to give an outline of what he professed to teach and the sum he charged. Doctor Smales then looked serious and, laying the forefinger of his right upon the palm of his left hand, solemnly said that the principal were reading, writing, arithmetic, geography, history, grammar, drawing, astronomy and botany. All of these, he said, he taught in all their variations and branches and offered for a small extra to lead the pupil through the mazes of phrenology. With these Mrs Tubbs expressed her satisfaction and then again enquired what he charged for this comprehensive system of instruction. He named the sum, and Mrs Tubbs started. However she quickly recovered her self-possession and enquired if that was the price he always charged. "By no means," said the Doctor, "but you see your son is far past the usual age at which boys make acquaintance with school and I invariably find it more difficult to instruct them in such cases." While this conversation was going forward Ben had ample opportunity to study the personal appearance of his future master and he came to the conclusion that in an hand-to-hand encounter he could certainly thrash him. Ben's idea of a schoolmaster had been an immensely tall huge man with harsh resounding voice and corresponding features, but he found himself agreeably mistaken. Doctor Smales was the counterpart of his name, short, small, with a rounded countenance and was altogether of anything but a stern aspect. Ben felt himself considerably relieved upon discovering this marked difference to his preconceived idea and by the time tea was announced his boldness and self-possession had so far returned that he was enabled to wink at the servant, whereupon she smiled. This was observed by the Doctor and his sharp, bright eyes surveyed Ben from head to foot with a rather unpleasant gaze, which he returned with interest and even went so far as to elevate one eyebrow. But he immediately repented it and drank his tea and ate his toast in silence. This was such an uncommon occurrence for him that Mrs Tubbs could not refrain from occasionally casting a searching glance at him as if to confirm by her eyes the testimony of her ears. An elderly lady with mild features occupied the post of honour and was introduced to Mrs Tubbs as "My mother" (a bow), "Mrs Tubbs" (a smile). She expressed a wish that they might often have the company of Mrs Tubbs and then branched off into praises of the manly appearance of Ben. This excessively pleased Mrs Tubbs and accordingly she became very communicative and polite. As to the Doctor, thought she, why no one could be more agreeable. He sustained the conversation, handed the toast, filled the teapot and joked incessantly. Ben thought in his heart that all this looked suspicious, that extreme politeness certainly concealed something. He was not far from the truth as the Doctor, seeing Mrs Tubbs's inexperience, resolved to benefit thereby and he felt himself amply rewarded for his pains upon hearing her consent to pay a sum at least half as much again as the others. Shortly after tea Mrs Tubbs arose to depart and, of course, an affecting scene took place. Had the parting taken place privately it would have passed off much quieter, but Ben, seeing the Doctor watching him, acted admirably, even contriving to shed a few tears. It was presently ended. Mrs Tubbs stepped into the carriage with streaming eyes and a waving handkerchief while Ben, under pretence of sobbing, yawned terrifically and so well did he act his part that even the Doctor was taken in.

Ben certainly had a genius for two things, mischief and imitation, if he had for nothing else; and nobody could have guessed as he stood there with red eyes, waving handkerchief and deep-fetched sighs that he was laughing and yawning.

Shortly, however, the coach was lost to sight and with a last heartrending groan he was led unresistingly back to the tea room. Here he sat down and was immediately fastened upon by the Doctor who proceeded to question him as to what he knew, whether he liked tapioca pudding, and whether he was given to snoring. To the first of these queries Ben gave a very general answer and on further examination the Doctor found him woefully backward, to the second he gave a distinct negative, and indignantly repelled the base insinuation of ignoble habits contained in the third. Having satisfied himself the Doctor arose and, saying that he would introduce him to school on the morrow, placed a large volume of prints in Ben's hand and disappeared. Ben began to turn over the leaves and, finding them very interesting, was soon deeply absorbed. He was not however allowed to enjoy them for long undisturbed as, the tea things having been removed, Mrs Smales produced her work and, telling him to put the book away, commenced a tremendous cross-examination. Firstly she requested to be informed as to his exact age; to this Ben replied that he had always considered himself two years older than their old tabby. Mrs Smales stared with surprise and for a few moments was silent. She however shortly recovered herself and asked how many years the cat had numbered. "Seventy-eight," quoth Ben and, with the utmost coolness, resumed his book. If Mrs Smales was astonished before, she was angry now and screamed at the top of a very shrill voice, "Sir, tell me this instant—put that book down." Ben started but was in no hurry to obey until a threat of calling the Doctor struck him as sounding dangerous and he reluctantly submitted. "Now tell me, my dear, what is your age?" said Mrs Smales persuasively, at the same time smiling.

"Well ma'am I don't know, but fifteen, I think," answered Ben in as polite a tone as he could manage, for the fear of the Doctor was at that moment slightly predominant in his mind. Having at last obtained the required answer Mrs Smales turned her attention to another quarter and spent several minutes in stroking the soft fur of a tortoiseshell cat. "That's a pretty cat," said Ben, in imagination pulling its tail.

"Yes, it is a pretty pussy, ain't you Minnie, ah, ah, that you are," said Mrs Smales in a singsong voice stroking it with redoubled fondness. The vain animal purred and elevated its tail and altogether looked tantalizingly happy.

"Minnie, Minnie," cried Ben invitingly, but the cat seemed intuitively to understand that an enemy lay in that direction and refused to move an inch. This evident partiality for her pleased Mrs Smales and put her in a good humour for the rest of the evening. The consequence was that she did not ask another question and by the time the Doctor appeared and ordered him to bed Ben began to feel comfortable. However it was no use disputing the mandate so he quietly followed Mrs Smales to a small separate room where he was to pass the night. Here with many injunctions to be sure and put the candle out Mrs Smales left him and Ben was soon firm asleep.

Nothing disturbed his slumber until awakened in the morning by motherly Mrs Smales who informed him that breakfast was waiting. He immediately arose and having dressed descended to the breakfast room when suitable viands were placed before him. The meal over, the Doctor arose and, telling Ben to follow, strode into the hall, the atmosphere of which seemed filled with a buzzing sound. They soon arrived before a large door and, opening it, the Doctor ordered him in, which he did, and immediately found himself in the presence of his future schoolmates. They were seated at long desks which were placed at regular intervals. Upon perceiving the Doctor the whole lot arose and remained standing until he waved his hand when all sat down, as if by magic. When the Doctor conceived that Ben had observed the more prominent features of the place he consigned him to the care of an usher at the same time uttering the cabalistic term of "Four, R and W."

The usher bowed and placed Ben but a short distance from where he stood upon a form beside half a dozen wild looking young scoundrels. These, immediately their preceptor's back was turned as he went in search of a book, commenced under various pretences of admiring his clothing to administer certain snaps and pinches, one of which being particularly sudden and in a tender place caused him to bellow.

In a moment the Doctor appeared cane in hand and sternly enquired of Ben what was the matter. The youth immediately informed him that a certain long-nosed individual, to whom he pointed, had caused him to imitate the bull. Doctor Smales looked savagely delighted with this intelligence and, calling Nosey out, he, in Ben's phrase, "tanned" him unmercifully. Having finished the castigation the Doctor returned to his seat and as he placed the cane in its place smiled benevolently around as if satisfied that he had performed a meritorious action. And had he not, is not punishing persecutors of peacefully inclined individuals worthy of being held up for example? I leave thee to answer this question thyself, o reader, but relate its effects in the following chapter.

Chapter 4

When lessons were concluded the whole school rose and, with a joyous shout, poured bodily into the playground. Ben followed the throng and shortly found himself in a large square enclosure bounded on three sides by an high wall and on the other by the house.

Altogether he found himself very lonely although more than one hundred and fifty boys were hollering, bawling, and running about. Ben's nature however would not long suffer him to be miserable. He therefore commenced to whistle and walked towards a bevy of youths who were watching his motions with great attention. As he passed near them he recognised two or three as members of the class to which he belonged and noticed that they looked particularly savage. They were in fact waiting for him to enter a large shed which had been erected for the boys to practice gymnastics in and afforded a capital place for the performance of any nefarious proceedings, as it was impossible to see into it from the house. To this shed, which had attracted his attention, Ben now directed his steps and upon entering was agreeably surprised to find that it contained a number of upright poles, horizontal ladders, ropes and other accessories to learning the noble art of climbing. A few boys were amusing themselves by hanging head downwards from a cross pole which was reached by a rope ladder. Ben determined not to be looked down upon and immediately commenced ascending the rope ladder which swayed very uncomfortably.

He had hardly ascended one half of the distance when a chorus of "Sneak, tell-tale," caused him to look below when he beheld about a score of youths who were menacingly shaking fists and bawling the opprobrious epithets above mentioned. Ben immediately began to descend that he might wreak vengeance on the group below, but they did not exactly see the use of this, and catching hold of the rope ladder which trailed upon the ground so added to the pendulum motion of it that Ben grew dizzy and requested them in a loud voice to desist or he should make a disagreeable and rapid descent. But the more he shouted, the more they grinned and rocked the ladder. So, seeing it was useless expending his breath in that method, he again began to slowly descend. As he came within their reach they abandoned the ladder and raised blows upon him thick and fast. But Ben, first assuring himself that he stood upon terra firma, grimly smiled and then doubling his huge fists speedily made such havoc among the foremost of the combatants that those in the rear seeing and hearing the mighty thumps and whacks which he dealt so liberally rushed in search of reinforcements. These soon arrived in the shape of half a dozen eager wretches who charged with irresistible fury and bearing down Ben by superior gravity fell over, rolled, groaned, shouted and nearly killed those poor creatures whom Ben had extended upon mother earth. The shouts of those who, having recovered, were again rushing upon Ben mingled with the groans of the wounded reached the ears of four stately wights who arm-in-arm were perambulating the other side of the playground and enjoying the sweets of companionship and royalty. These were Mr Reginald Reeves, otherwise known, respected and obeyed as the Redoubtable King Log the Second. He was of immense height, strongly built with curling hair, black eyes and was the first on the first form. The other three rejoiced in and answered to the respective denominations of Mr Sam Smith, Mr Bob Trunce and Mr Harry Dump. They composed the privy council and proclaimed the orders of their monarch and friend through the length and breadth of his dominions. These were, as said before, gently perambulating and communing when the noise of the battle reached them. King Log immediately ordered Mr Sam Smith to hasten and ascertain the cause of the tremendous row. Although he went fast yet he came back faster and upon the receipt of the startling intelligence King Log immediately commanded a rescue and, putting himself at the head of a few youths, with a shout rushed towards the shed. Here confusion reigned supreme and many, seemingly having forgotten what they came for, fought against their comrades. But the greater number had adhered to their original purpose and had so far succeeded in it as to have squeezed Ben up in a corner where he as yet maintained the unequal contest though obviously nearly exhausted. However the arrival of King Log, with a dozen giants at his back, soon produced an effect for many fled when his dreadful name was shouted in their ears and the others although they still fought yet it was without the slightest hope of victory. Ben, finding himself released from his disagreeable position, as those who had been pounding him had turned to defend themselves, drew in a long breath and again engaged in the dreadful combat. But by this time King Log and his followers were completely victorious and the others expelled the shed to weep and wail over their discomfiture. Ben now advanced to thank his deliverers but King Log cut him short by commanding him to relate the why and the wherefore of his being the cause of such an awful skirmish. With dismal forebodings of coming disasters Ben told his tale which was received with black looks and other ominous signs. Upon his conclusion King Log coughed and commanded Ben to listen attentively whereupon his majesty wiped the perspiration from his brow and commenced.

"You have grievously offended against the laws of the commonwealth by turning accuser but, as a new arrival, will not be punished severely."

Here the surrounding courtiers uttered a deep "hear, hear."

King Log waved his hand and concluded his speech by sentencing Ben to be tied to a post and receive fifteen lashes with the knotted end of a handkerchief upon that part of the body which Hudibras designates the seat of honour. Ben started and jumping backwards requested in no particularly polite terms to be informed on whose authority he was to be castigated.

"On mine," said King Log and, having commanded that after the walloping Ben should be acquainted with the principles of his government, strode majestically from the shed. Upon his disappearance the courtiers seized on Ben and in spite of his struggles were about to carry out the sentence when the dinner bell rang and for the present he escaped. Ben found dinner very acceptable after the hard work he had been engaged in and although the viands were not of the best yet he did not disdain to send up his plate three times for meat, as many for pudding, which to his great delight was not tapioca but a moderately beplumed one. After they had all eaten or rather crammed into their voracious mouths enough to have lasted an ordinary person a year the Doctor arose and jerked out grace and they were dismissed for half an hour's play.

Ben would have stayed where he was, being fearful of King Log's courtiers, but an usher, seeing him lingering, pushed him out and locked the door. Thus compelled to go out Ben did and walked about for some time in no very enviable state of mind. Most of the boys were engaged in marbles, tops or some other game and being absorbed in them did not notice him. After a while, as no King Log appeared, Ben began to breathe a little more freely and was about to again proceed to the gymnastic shed when horror of horrors a small wooden door opened in the wall and Log stepped in followed by two of his councillors. They immediately saw him and, locking the door, hastened forward, seized and conveyed him to the shed. He was then bound to a post and the castigation commenced, King Log counting the blows. Not the slightest sound escaped the sufferer but he considerably wriggled and was precious glad when King Log's resounding voice announced the fifteenth whack and he was soon after unbound. King Log now again commanded that the principal features of his government should be explained and the two councillors commenced a short consultation between themselves.

Upon its conclusion councillor Sam climbed up the identical rope ladder while Hal departed to assemble as many youths as possible. Soon the major number of the whole school had collected in the shed and Councillor Sam seeing that all eyed him with impatience began his oration in as polite a tone as he could manage. "Gentlemen, you are called together and convened by order of his most gracious Majesty the Redoubtable Unconquerable King Log the Second." Here cheers mingled with groans arose and for a time interrupted his discourse. The noise having subsided he continued, "I say again, the Redoubtable Unconquerable Log has convened you that I may explain to the youth Benjamin Tubbs the principles of his majesty's government and that you may refresh your ears with the harmony thereof. His majesty's government then may be divided into three heads, namely: for the purpose of enforcing the laws contained in this,"—hereupon he drew a leather-bound book from his pocket and displayed it; "for keeping the whole community in order; and for resisting the encroachment of the Wobbles upon our football paddock. Now gentlemen I advise you to revolve in your nuts the extreme expediency of supporting his majesty's administration and I shall descend from my elevation." Whereupon Sam slid down and a hubbub went up.

Ben, even after hearing this clear, lucid and comprehensive explanation, still remained in much doubt as to the legality of the government and seeing a knot of youths eagerly conversing he strode up to one and stated his scruples upon the subject. By some chance this happened to be a member of an extensive conspiracy which had been forming for some time for the purpose of dethroning King Log, annihilating his aristocracy and then establishing another youth who was by them considered to possess a better right. Seeing the dissatisfied state Ben was in, the youth commenced to expound his views and was in a fair way of convincing his hearer when the two o'clock bell rang which was the signal for recommencing school. All the boys immediately ran in but the youths walked. King Log, being a youth and not a boy, thus had an opportunity of conferring with his right-hand man—Mr Sam the orator—and it ended by his majesty saying in a loud voice: "It must be crushed," with which gentle resolution he entered the house.

The afternoon lessons were much quieter than the morning, there was no buzz and the most noisy operation was that of scraping slate pencils which was performed with great delicacy and despatch by the experienced ushers. When the afternoon school was over the boys were allowed half-an-hour's play until tea or rather milk-time, after which all were confined in the school room to learn the morning lessons until seven when they had an hour of confusion and then were marched up the wooden hill. To Ben the hours wore slowly away, and when the order for bed was issued, he was heartily glad as he was tired of poring over uninteresting books, working impossible sums and wielding that mighty little article the pen which gave him the cramp. So he tumbled upstairs among the other boys with great gusto until arriving at the bedroom when his rejoicings were considerably modified on beholding the narrow couch wherein he and another youth—by name Edward Snicks—were to pass the interval of repose.

Mr Edward Snicks otherwise Ned or Ted Nidle laughed as he saw the expression of surprise upon Ben's face. "Ha, ha!" said he, "Don't you know, can't you see, haven't you got powers of penetration or undercumstumblation enough to understand why the Doctor limits us as to space?"

Ben confessed that he had not and wished to know.

"Why, because he doesn't want knees to chins," replied Mr Nidle, and rolled into bed where he was quickly followed by Ben who immediately expressed his desire to sleep by shutting his mouth, opening his nostrils and drawing in air at a fearful rate.

But no, directly Ned heard these indications of a wish to slumber he began to kick, roll and twist to an awful degree. Ben enquired what was the matter. "My friend," said Ned solemnly, "you're killing me. You're an air pump and a vacuum is forming." Whereupon he commenced his former conduct to Ben's great disgust and indignation. At last the persecution became intolerable and, irritated beyond measure, he administered a hearty thump upon Ned who immediately retaliated and a battle began which lasted with great animation and little effect until the usher came to take the candle. At the moment he softly entered the room Ben had slightly the advantage being seated upon his companion and pounding him unmercifully with the pillow. Sundry groans, kicks, and sudden alterations of the bedclothes convinced the usher that the walloping was not agreeable to the receiver. Rushing forward, he put an end to the contest just as Ben, having tired his arms, was upon the point of yielding to the continued writhing and gigantic efforts of his victim. The usher's mode of proceeding, however, resulted in a rather different manner to what he expected, as laying a strong hand on Ben's shoulder he indeed stopped the descending blow but received the ascending one as by a tremendous twist of the buried combatant Ben's head was sent with fearful force just beneath his chin and the usher staggered backwards howling. Recovering himself he rushed forward to take signal vengeance and aimed a blow at Ben's head, which missing him from another of Nidle's twists, he lost his balance and fell over them burying both beneath his ample body; the bed not being able to resist this added weight gave way and they all came to ground with a terrible bump which shook the house.

It startled the Doctor as he sat at supper, and exclaiming, "Some more foolery, I suppose," he rushed to see what was the matter, leaving his mother in a trembling state of suspense. It took him some time to find the whereabouts of the disaster, but he presently arrived upon the scene and beheld, to his extreme amazement, an usher seated on the ground holding his head and moaning, a bed torn from its fastenings, and two boys surveying him with a curious gaze. For a moment he stood looking from one to the other, but indecision was not a component part in Doctor Smales's composition. He therefore walked straight to the usher and gently reminded him of his presence by the application of his foot, at the same time indicating his desire to be informed why he reposed in that position. But he could obtain no intelligible answer from the poor man, who was apparently bound up in the contemplation of his wrongs, and therefore turned to Ned and sternly enquired of him. Ned had an answer ready and with great volubility informed the Doctor that he and Ben were enjoying a comfortable chat when the usher entered. Seeing they had not given themselves to repose, he rushed forward to administer corporal punishment when his foot slipped and he came upon the bed, thus causing the desolation now so alarmingly apparent. The Doctor appeared satisfied and having, by some means, awakened the usher to a sense of his degraded position the poor man arose and followed his superior from the room with faltering steps and dismal groans. Immediately on the door being shut Ned began to giggle with such apparent enjoyment that Ben joined him and thus cemented a friendship which had commenced under such trying circumstances. After they had thus soothingly passed half-an-hour Ned suddenly brought up in the middle of an interesting yawn and enquired of Ben whether he was a Logian or a Chogian. Although Ben did not exactly understand what was meant yet he had a glimmering. But being a prudent youth he resolved not to get involved in politics without knowing anything about them and professed his entire ignorance of the meaning of the two cabalistic words.

"You've been breathing the enlightened atmosphere of this intelligent place for more than twenty-four hours and don't know the difference of a Log and a Chog?" said the astonished Mr Nidle. Ben said that he supposed by a Log was meant King Log but who or what Chog was, he had not the slightest shadow of an idea. Ned immediately began to explain and the substance of his discourse was as follows. He showed that the great difference between a Logian, that is a follower of Log, and a Chogian, or follower of Chog, was that the one was wrong and the other right. Having thoroughly proved this by showing that Chog was the rightful heir to the throne inasmuch that he was brother to the last king; he proceeded to use all his eloquence in the endeavour to enlist Ben among the Chogians, of which party he modestly confessed he was one of its greatest ornaments and would if the conspiracy succeeded be at least a privy councillor. He ended by offering to get Ben knighted if he would tender his allegiance to Chog, who according to him intended to confer that honour only on those who distinguished themselves by conspicuous bravery in upholding the cause of right in opposition to that of might; whereas Log had bestowed the title so liberally and with so little judgment that in his army it had become no title at all, as all rejoiced therein. Ben enquired in what consisted the beauty of being a knight.

"A knight," said Ned "is a very honoured individual."

"Hum," quoth Ben, "I'll be a Chogian."

Ned appeared transported with joy at hearing this resolution and, with excess thereof, punched Ben continuously who, to obtain a little relief from this friendly proceeding, enquired in what state their cause was.

"Oh," said Ned "it's jolly, old Chog can't hardly keep 'em under. Fifty-two whoppers—seventeen youngsters all in a buzz to begin. But Log's up to it or I'm a nidle."

"Yes, that he is," said Ben and he mentioned overhearing Log's resolve to crush something.

Ned answered that he thought this looked serious and soon after announced his intention of going to sleep that he might dream the matter over and come to a reasonable conclusion. With this he turned round and in five minutes was snoring. Ben followed his example and was soon in the impalpable land of dreams where he performed various important actions such as cutting Log's head off and other meritorious and similarly gentle operations which lasted until morning when the brazen tongue of the breakfast bell informed him that he must arise and commence the business of the day.

He awoke and awoke Ned who opened and shut his eyes ten different times each time muttering "Serene, serene," before he could be brought to understand the true nature of the interruption. Then he leaped from the couch and performed his toilet in a singularly negligent manner, namely, huddling on his clothes, cat-licking his face and forming a superficial parting of his hair with what he denominated a rake and a besom. Thus he saved his character for punctuality and had already half devoured his breakfast when Ben appeared and voraciously attacked the viands which mainly consisted of a huge bowl of milk sops and a teaspoonful of sugar. The lamentably small quantity of the latter article completely destroyed his equanimity of temper for that morning; at any rate, no one looked more sulky, nobody could have said lessons worse, and nobody could pardon the contempt of the usher's orders which he displayed. The consequence was that the Doctor called him up before the desk and lectured pretty severely upon the subject, warning him not to again appear for the same thing. This made Ben still more discontented and when school was over wandered about the playground in a fit state for rebellion of any description. He would have probably presently committed some desperate wickedness had not Ned seized upon him and introduced him to a tall youth looking apparently made of wire. This was Mr William Lincoln, otherwise Bill Linkum, otherwise and in prospect, King Chog. He expressed himself extremely gratified to find that Ben had joined his little army and asked Ben's advice upon the important matter—whether they had better begin offensive operations at once or not. Ben was, of course, nearly overwhelmed with the honour but presently replied that he thought it would be best to leather the Logians directly. The fact was he wanted to obtain some redress for his morning's whacking. Chog said that he perfectly agreed with him and added that he had had so many courses proposed to him that very morning that he must retire and consider them. Whereupon he nodded and withdrew to a distant part of the playground while the two friends engaged in a furious splitting of tops, in which game they continued until the bell rang for dinner.

For two or three days nothing occurred of importance whether in the process of dethroning King Log or in any other. Ben had as yet made no further acquaintance with the town of Chilton than what he had seen from the coach window but on Saturday the boys were allowed to go beyond the precincts of the playground and few there were that remained behind. He was getting precious tired of books, slates and holding his tongue and was therefore much rejoiced when informed of the Saturday privilege. Ned proposed that they should take a stroll through the mushroom collection of huts, hovels and sheds dignified by the name of a town and on the arrival of the auspicious morn they set forth each armed with his particular bludgeon. Having paraded down what was called the High Street, looked at the church and flung a stone over it, Ned proposed that they should regain the high road and have what he called a "Scotty hunt."

For the information of those who do not understand this cabalistic term I will attempt to show the meaning thereof. Imagine, fancy, or conjure up before you a hedge, a cock-robin in it, a youth with a pocketful of stones on either side and both valiantly pelting the fluttering animal. Frequently a stone will pass through the hedge and, alighting upon the opposite hunter's visage, cause much ill-feeling and the compliment is presently returned with compound interest. Then begin desperate pitched battles which continue until one poor animal's stones are exhausted when he is unmercifully pelted by the other until his ammunition also fails. Then the parties approach and exchange mighty fisticuffs, fearful kicks, tremendous thumps, numerous blows, fierce threats—like glances, and exhibit astonishing powers of memory in calling each other everything wicked, bad and unmentionable in the United Kingdom, Europe, Asia, America or the whole world. But Ned and Ben were too fast friends by this time to act so uncharitably to each other; they therefore continued the manly, exhilarating exercise of "Scotty hunting" until the sun arrived at the meridian and the genius of hunger presented himself in the shape of many internal reminders. Like all boys they had forgotten that to live, i.e. to enjoy life, all must eat and had consequently forgotten to provide themselves with provisions. In fact their whole accoutrement consisted in the two aforesaid bludgeons, two clasp knives, ten marbles, five buttons, seventeen biscuit crumbs, a piece of cobbler's wax, and a slate pencil. What was to be done? Ben did not know. Ned had no idea. They were in a fix, five miles from the nearest village, seven from Chilton and probably four from the clouds.

At last an idea, novel and showing great research, suddenly entered the mind of Mr Nidle and, jumping from the ground upon which he had been reclining, he expressed it to Ben in these words, "I say."

"Well?" said Ben.

"I say, old chap, what singular dummies we were not to have kept that cock robin and cooked him. S'pose we leather's another?"

This plan struck Ben as peculiarly eligible and without further words the youths immediately proceeded to put it into practice. But the birds had very singular and comical ideas as to their right to continue alive as long as they pleased and flew off upon the approach of the hunters with tantalising screams, chuckles or gibes, which method of escaping so irritated our worthies that they gave up the project and flung the remaining stones at haphazard. On perceiving this, the feathered tribe took heart and on every branch perched whistling, chattering starlings, impudent sparrows who will not be killed, innocent-looking robins who hate cats, and sharp tomtits whose life is a perpetual round of hanging. All these and many more peopled the hedges on either side of the road apparently conversing with great gusto and greater freedom of opinion upon the futile efforts of the travellers. They walked on in silence each debating within himself what was best to be done and listening to the ever-increasing demands of that fiend hunger who now began to make his presence very disagreeable. In this manner an half-mile was passed, another and another, with still no signs of house, inn or dwelling of any description, whether in front or to the right or left. The prospect was anything but agreeable and the sun was sinking in the west, gilding with his almost horizontal beams each hedge and tree. The birds with one accord sang loud but sadly; the sun sunk and they ceased, save the loud scream of a blackbird or two who, frightened from his roost by some wandering poacher, gave warning of his approach.

Darkness began to steal over the earth and a twinkling star occasionally appeared, to be hid the next moment by the light cirrus clouds closely following each other across the vault of heaven. The worthies now began to feel, not exactly frightened, but they experienced a certain qualmish sensation near the pit of the stomach. They had all the time been walking away from Chilton in the vain hope of coming across some house or other where refreshment could be procured but, as they possessed no money, it looked as if a matter for serious reflection of which quality boys usually have but little. Now when darkness began to throw its pall around they stopped and for a moment each looked at the other inquiringly. Ned was the first to use his tongue and he proposed that they should return—if they could. Ben said he agreed with him and taking one long glance in front as if unwilling to relinquish the first project he turned and commenced the journey with slow and heavy steps.

Suddenly he missed his companion and stopping shouted his name. The hail was presently answered behind and in a few minutes up came Ned panting and out of breath. "It's all right," said or rather gasped he, as soon as possible.

"What's all right?" enquired Ben thinking that the moon which had just arisen had shed a peculiar influence over his companion and as the idea struck him he stepped into the shade.

"Why," jerked out Ned "it's a light—an inn—I saw it—ahead—behind."

"Oh," quoth Ben,"it's a light how?"

Ned presently explained that on taking his last survey in the direction they had been walking he fancied that he saw a star twinkle extraordinarily near the earth. Running forward a few paces it became apparent that it was no star but a candle and he now proposed that they should again turn and investigate the phenomenon. Ben perfectly agreed with him and shaking off his notion of the pernicious effects of moonbeams they both set out as fast as tired limbs and empty stomachs would allow. Soon it became apparent that the light proceeded from an house by the roadside and a few hundred yards showed it was an inn. And now a new difficulty struck the youths and simultaneously coming to a dead stop each enquired of the other, "How about the tin?"

Ben said that he had not got even so much as the ninety-fifth part of a mite and Ned, after ransacking and doubly ransacking every pocket he possessed, was obliged to own himself in exactly the same predicament.

"Botheration," quoth Ben.

"It's worse than that," said Ned, whereupon he stepped forward, set his foot upon something and drew back horrified—no doubt at the mere probability of having hurt a living creature. "It's a toad or I'm not Nidle," shouted he.

"No, it isn't," replied Ben, "something tinkled," and he began to search about with his feet.

"Too rul loo rul loo," shouted Ned the next minute, he having employed the time in the same manner. "Here you are—a purse by the living jingo." Hereupon he began to dance about in a very singular manner but suddenly brought up in the midst of a twirl and applied one hand to his stomach.

"What's the matter?" asked Ben, as the moon having cleared a clump of trees the slightest action was observable.

But before Ned could answer, before the words had left his mouth, before the shadow on a moon-dial could have moved the fifteenth part of a hair-breadth his hand also sought the same place and he knew what was the matter then. It was short but it was sharp and had Ben's face been photographed that instant the wonderful contortions which succeeded each other in such quick succession would have formed on the plate such a surprising conglomeration of eyes, nose and chin that it would have remained a standing wonder, curiosity and study for the whole world. The fact was that their stomachs, not having been accustomed to lengthy abstinence from food, had collapsed. Which operation produced a sudden griping pain causing them to assume stooping postures and dolorous looks. However it shortly passed away and they proceeded forward rejoicing now that they were relieved from all anxiety as to food or shelter.

As they drew near, the silence of the night was broken by snatches of jovial songs, shouts and other indications of a numerous and consequently not very respectable company at the inn. Upon coming within the streak of light that issued from the tap-room window a thought struck Ned and, taking the purse from his pocket, he divided its contents by guess at the same time hinting that it would be well to only produce the smaller silver pieces. This little arrangement settled, they walked to the door and banged away until it was opened by a fat-cheeked damsel who, with a smile, requested them to step in. Which they did.

Chapter 5

Following this beauty of a barmaid they were presently ushered into a large room crammed full of people who were employed in smoking, drinking, grinning, quarrelling and snoring. The moment her portly figure appeared in the doorway orders were shouted from all parts of the room accompanied with so many endearing epithets that she actually, although as hot as noon in summer, managed to blush and beat an hasty retreat leaving the youths to their fate. Her flight was hailed with a tremendous shout of horse laughter, intermingled with ironical expressions of disgust. As soon as possible Ben and Ned also beat a retreat and by some means contrived to find the landlord and to engage his attention for half a second. In this short interval of time by the aid of enigmatical signs, nods, winks and certain other indescribable movements of the body they conveyed to his brain the fact that they wished for a private room and a supply of eatables and drinkables. When he seized upon their meaning he beckoned them to follow and without a word led the way through a labyrinth of passages, up a pair of rickety creaking stairs, opened the door of a room with a fire in it, saw them in and departed. In a few minutes he returned with a huge mug of ale, a couple of plates heaped with cold beef, knives, forks and bread. These he displayed to their greatest advantage upon a small round table and then enquired if there was anything else wanted. The youths asked if he possessed a bed and were immediately answered that nowhere could be found better accommodation and, striding across the room, he opened a door and displayed the required article furnished with all necessary appendages. "That'll do," said Ben, who had followed him and the landlord nodded and withdrew. As for Ned, he had already made dreadful havoc of the contents of his plate and Ben quickly commenced to do the same. Neither of them ever ate, they always bolted, this however is a very common process amongst schoolboys although they are continually warned of its injurious effects. But as no effect is ever visible they will not believe it but continue the old round of opening the mouth to its widest stretch, shoving in a cartload and after many ineffectual attempts to reduce the size thereof, swallowing it. By the rapid repetition of this process they manage to convey to the stomach an immense amount of food, and it cannot be considered wonderful in the case now before us that the plates were three times emptied, likewise the mug, before the youths were satiated. Then the supper was cleared away and drawing to the fire each stared at it in a malignant manner and for a minute or two in silence. But the large quantity of malt liquor which had vanished down their voracious throats soon began to operate and first gave notice of its effects by both simultaneously shouting, "Ain't it jolly?" Hereupon both began to giggle and continued that interesting amusement for no less than twenty seven minutes when Ned solemnly laid the forefinger of his right hand upon his left paw and ejaculated, "Shan't we catch it?" Then his head fell backwards with a beautiful flourish, his jaw dropped and a nasal sound filled the apartment. This unfeeling proceeding greatly irritated Ben and, gently rising, he bestowed a bang so effectually full upon the offending organ that Ned came to the ground. At the same time the donor lost his balance and fell over him with irresistible force. Ned immediately awoke and, finding a tremendous weight upon him, fancied he had the nightmare. So laying hold of Ben he shouted to the landlord to help and catch it. That gentleman heard the thump and the shouting and, rushing upstairs, found Ben very comfortably sleeping and Ned bawling, "Th' nitmer catch me landlor'," at the top of his voice.

"Oh, oh," said Mr Trumel the landlord, "oh, oh," and, grimly smiling, he advanced, picked up Ben and placed him in a chair.

Ned finding himself relieved immediately began to sleep again, at intervals muttering unintelligible rubbish of "Th'—Th' nitmer."

Mr Trumel, seeing with his experienced eye the real state of the ease, stooped, picked him up and shook him severely. This mode of proceeding completely banished sleep and, rubbing his eyes, Ned stared sheepishly at the landlord who with another grim smile proceeded to awaken Ben in the same manner. Having at last succeeded, Mr Trumel advised instant retirement to bed and Ben, having sufficient sense left him to see the wisdom of this, staggered to the bedroom. Ned however had either imbibed a larger quantity of the intoxicating liquor or else was constitutionally obstinate as no amount of persuasion could induce him to move one foot. Mr Trumel, seeing it was no use talking, enveloped him in his gigantic arms and presently deposited him in bed. Once in Ned offered no further opposition but, muttering something about nobody-knew-what, immediately commenced to sleep. Mr Trumel waited until Ben did the same, he then took the candle and departed.

Neither of them dreamed in the slightest, both being much too tired for that, and consequently upon the chambermaid awakening them in the morning felt no inclination to rise. Ben notified this fact to her and she thereupon departed. Although neither arose yet they did not fall to sleeping again but lay in a dreamy half-unconscious state. Everything was perfectly still; not even the crowing of a cock was to be heard; and both, although it was opposite to their nature, enjoyed it. Both felt incapable of motion or of speech, even the faculty of thought lay dormant. They were in fact in a state of perfect rest and how long they might have so continued is a thing to guess at. Ben was watching the motions of a spider who was diligently spinning a web in one corner of the apartment almost above his head; Ned was occupied in observing a fly who pertinaciously flew in a circle near the middle of the room, when the ding, dong, doggerel sound of the village bells struck discordantly on their ears. Ned started up and shook his fist menacing, so did Ben.

"What a hang-nation bother!" said Ned as he sank back to his original posture and searched for the fly. But the little creature, startled by the vibration of the air, flew haphazardly about the room until unluckily it came in contact with the spider's web and was caught. It soon exhausted its little strength in vain endeavours to escape, seeing which the spider advanced and commenced to suck the blood of its victim. Ned started up and again shook his fist, "Hang the bells," said he, "my fly."

"Bless the bells," said Ben, complacently regarding the spider.

"Oh, oh, you say that—do you?" said Ned, brandishing his fists in a very bellicose manner.

Ben lazily drawled out a "Ye-ees," which filled the measure of Ned's indignation and, snatching up the pillow, he bestowed a heavy smothering blow upon Ben's mouth. A groan or rather half-suffocated growl was the result, and in a moment Ben was sitting up and returning the compliment with interest and bonus. Ned of course could not submit tamely to such a proceeding and a scuffle commenced which lasted without interruption until the chambermaid again knocked, when like sensible youths they agreed that they had been "kicking up a row about a humbug" and requested what she wanted.

"Oh, only as how that it's dinner time and master says as how as that maybe you'd want sum grub," replied the chambermaid through the keyhole.

"All right," shouted Ben, and she departed.

Up jumped the youths and having dressed commenced to eat voraciously of dinner which they found in the next room. When the meal was over they began to think about returning to Chilton and calling the landlord enquired its distance.

"Eight miles," said he.

"Hum," said Ben, "what's to pay?"

Mr Trumel struck his hand against his forehead, muttered something to himself, and then drawled, "Supper for two, two and sixpence; lodging for two, two shillings; dinner for two, two shillings; totality six shillings, and sixpence and sixpence for the chambermaid." Mr Trumel was astonished to see the little effect this enormous amount had upon his guests and muttered to himself, "If I'd only a knowed." But it was too late and he had to be contented with twice his due. He was about to depart when Ben stopped him and asked to be shown the way out.

"All right," quoth Mr Trumel and away he went closely followed by the youths.

In something less than twenty minutes of sharp walking a little daylight began to struggle through the distant doors and shortly before the half hour was passed they found themselves in the bright sunlight.

"Which is the road to Chilton?" asked Ned.

"Up there," said Mr Trumel, pointing with his hand, and with mutual "Good mornings" they started.

The road for some distance was level but it soon began to rise and did so for half a mile when it again became level and the hill of Chilton stood out boldly against the sky. Now that the termination of their journey was apparent they insensibly slacked their pace as certain unpleasant reflections as to the treatment they would receive upon arriving began to crowd on their minds. It must not be supposed that Doctor Smales had taken no notice of their absence: on the contrary, he had used every means in his power to discover their whereabouts but had signally failed. No one could give him any idea of the direction they had taken and he at last began to get alarmed. He determined that if they did return that he would make an example of them—in short, wallop them well. In his own mind he suspected that they had run clean away, but although he taxed his memory to the utmost to see if he could remember anything calculated to cause such a proceeding, yet he could hit upon nothing. Knowing the influence and power King Log possessed he called him up and in the close questioning which ensued Ben's castigation came out. That might have been sufficient to drive Ben away but Ned—what possible reason could he have in absconding? No one could answer this question, consequently it remained unanswered until Sunday evening when there came a gentle knock at the door and upon its being opened, which it was by the anxious Doctor, who should stand there but the missing youths. He motioned them in, shut the door, led the way to the parlour and mockingly announced to his mother who was within—"the repentant sinners."

"Oh I am so glad," cried the old lady, "come in my dears and sit down and tell us where you've been to." In her own mind she had not the slightest doubt but that they had lost their way and had maintained her opinion with great spirit against her son.

She was nearer the truth than he was and listened attentively to the story as Ben told it while he at times uttered unbelieving ejaculations. Ben omitted finding the purse as he was afraid of it being taken from them.

"Where did you get the money from?" asked the Doctor upon its conclusion.

This was a puzzler but Ben with an unmoved countenance said that they had it.

"Had it—oh—go to the schoolroom," growled the Doctor and away cut the youths.

Immediately upon entering it the one hundred and fifty-seven boys simultaneously asked exactly the same number of questions as to where they had been, what they had been "up" to, and others of the like nature intermingled with such exclamations as "How they would catch it" and "ain't the guvner savage?" Being unable to reply to so many queries at once, they replied to none but drew near the stove. King Log and his courtiers occupied the nearest seats, way was made and command given by his majesty that they should relate the history of their adventure. Clearing his throat Ben did so with sundry embellishments and dropping the finding of the purse. It was listened to attentively but of course no one believed it and on its conclusion Councillor Sam sprang upon a desk and delivered his opinion of the matter in these words:

"Shentilmen, you villpleash attend to mediscourse." Upon looking around and seeing all eyes fixed upon him orator Sam continued, "Venyesterneven shades ob de night was gettin' mighty strong ve all valk in de roomsh and begun serction. Vell it was den diskivered that there vas some one missin' an've all lookprethy humbugs. Vell in cum the Docshur and he look ugly so ve didn't feel nice an'sposeve look so an' he grin and valk out agen. Vell it was all right so much but sposeve goes wid dese young scoundrelsh and den vat ve see, vhydem both a sippin an' a suckin' an' snoring and joyin'therselfsh as if as tho' vevashn't a lernin'leshons or noth' elsh. Shentilmen,yer see I spectsyerwon't like dis so yer'd better make allmightysmashan' I'll begin."

Thereupon Sam jumped from his perch and laid violent hands upon the offending parties. He had only expressed the sentiments of the surrounding multitude and nearly all rushed to assist him in beating them black and blue. Those who did not were Chogians, those who did Logians, and Sam had brought down precipitate vengeance on the youths' heads merely because he knew them to be partial to Chog, who sat in a distant corner absorbed in conversation with one of his prospective councillors.

Directly he saw the rush Chog arose and shouting, "To the rescue, to the rescue," advanced leaping over forms with twenty youths to his back to aid Ben and Ned, whom having mastered the Logians were literally pounding. Seeing Chog rush forward Log arose and entered the lists. A dreadful battle, of course, immediately commenced as leaving Ben and Ned alone, the Logians turned to wallop the Chogians. Both sides performed prodigies of valour as it being the first open declaration of enmity the partisans of each were anxious to show their zeal. The two principal combatants Log and Chog strove to get near each other but the heaps of struggling youths prevented them and they had to be contented with distant menaces. Meanwhile the noise of the battle reached the ears of the Doctor, who, guessing the cause, called the ushers and strode to the scene. Opening the door, what a sight met his view, what terms grated on his cultivated ear, what dreadful blows, what awful crashes did he not see as he stood upon the threshold and contemplated the moving mass. The Logians were gaining the victory and those poor Chogians who were not disabled had collected in a corner where behind three or four forms they as yet valiantly maintained the combat.

Doctor Smales calmly surveyed the battle and then drawing a whistle from his pocket blew loud and long. Each combatant immediately turned and to his dismay perceived the Doctor smiling in the doorway. "Oh, this is the way you spend your Sunday evenings, do you?" said he and then, raising his voice while his countenance lost its pleasant expression and turned sour, he shouted, "To bed with you every one," and left the room.

It was always the custom for the elder youths to sit up an hour later than the rest and as may be imagined King looked particularly disgusted as he led the way upstairs. "His Majesty's out of humour tonight," said an usher and he was immediately rewarded with a withering glance of extreme contempt from the Head of the Administration. As for Ben and Ned they were terribly bumped, "covered with bruises," as the usher said when he reported that night to the Doctor. "I'm glad of it," said the malicious Governor General and he swallowed a glass of wine. The usher beat a retreat and informed his mates that the "Guvner" and his majesty were devilish savage. "Hum," was the response from all parts of the room.

That night both Ben and his companion underwent an awful lashing in the impalpable land of dreams, which was administered by no less an individual than the gentleman who is popularly supposed to clothe himself in black assisted by the whole twelve ushers each armed with a dreadful instrument—a compound of the birch, the cane and the cat o' nine tails. They awoke in imaginary dreadful pain and arose to their duties with awful expectations. Breakfast was eaten in silence, a rare thing indeed, and they entered the schoolroom with trepidation. All passed well until the clock struck ten with great emphasis, when the Doctor suddenly started up, drew forth the awful instrument, and called general attention to his movements by whistling loud and shrill. Each boy's eyes followed the Doctor, who, clearing his throat, commenced an oration short but to the point in which he solemnly declared, and enforced by a thump upon his desk, that the conduct of the new boy Ben and his companion surpassed everything he had ever heard of, or experienced in the course of a long educational career, and finished by commanding the youths to appear before his desk. Slowly Ben arose and followed by Ned, who sat beside him, wriggled to where he was told and, in obedience to a second order, presented his back. Then did the Doctor turn up his cuffs, blow his nose, look with the air of a connoisseur along the dreadful instrument, pass his hand through his hair and placing himself in a convenient attitude commence operations on Ben's back. At first the blows descended to a tune which the Doctor hummed but as he warmed to the amusement they descended with fearful rapidity and his face assumed what is denominated a demoniacal aspect. Not the slightest sound escaped Ben, not even so much as a smothered groan reached the ears of Dr Smales who, to assure himself that such was the truth, bent his head to one side. But no, nothing could be heard beyond the whistling sound the awful instrument made as it was brought through the air by the exasperated Doctor, who now determined that should it take him all day Ben should bellow. Presumptuous resolution! Ben—holler, bellow, groan? He, do such a babyish thing? Had the little Doctor even done as he would have liked, that is whacked Ben with a poker, the result would have differed only in one particular, namely, he would have got whacked himself. But the Doctor was a man, a humane man, and he therefore desisted when he was exhausted and could whack no longer. Consequently Ned had to be walloped by an usher, who, seeing no use in tiring himself, discontinued the exercise after forty dozen bumps and handed the awful instrument to the Doctor with a graceful flourish. That gentlemen received it with a frown on his otherwise serene perspiring face and in a loud voice commanded that the youths who had been castigated should immediately be put to bed, there to cogitate and repent. Ben heard this command with joy as he was nearly exhausted but Ned who had only been fly-bitten was extremely disgusted and could not help showing it by turning up his nose at the Doctor as they left the schoolroom. Luckily for him this was not observed and, reaching the bedroom safely, both quickly tumbled in. Ben immediately went to sleep but Ned could not. He therefore employed the time in reading an old novel, sucking an orange and at regular intervals enjoying a fit of yawning. In which intellectual amusement we will leave him and, taking a step of some thirty miles, alight (invisible of course) in the sitting-room of Mrs Tubbs.

The dear old lady had intended to write a letter to Ben but finding the paper damp, the pen bad, likewise her head, was sitting before the fire, feet upon the fender and thinking of her darling whom she firmly believed possessed every virtue under the sun save that of a due respect to his truly indulgent mother. To enable her thoughts to have greater power and scope of memory she had manufactured a sherry cobbler and now rang the bell for Sarah. Presently in came that unfortunate damsel with the white something still around her head, her petticoats tucked up, a huge besom in one hand and a fire shovel in the other. Mrs Tubbs surveyed her from head to foot with an expression of intense disgust and appeared to be gathering words for a storm.

"Did you ring for me ma'am, if you please, ma'am," timidly enquired the housemaid in momentary expectations of being roasted alive.

At the first sound of her voice Mrs Tubbs's brow darkened and, having waited with exemplary patience to the end of her speech, she then broke forth in angry expostulation. "You nasty, lazy, dirty, slutty, wicked hussy—not done work yet? Oh! I say what will become of you?"

"If you please ma'am" said Sarah, deprecatingly, "the milkman came, and the postman—."

"Oh, the postman, I know! If you have him here out you go, you—you—you slubberdegullion and I don't know what," broke in Mrs Tubbs rocking with rage to and fro on her chair until, rolling of her centre of gravity, the floor received a lovely burden.

Sarah, with the best intentions, rushed forward to help "missis" but it was a day of misfortunes and the carpet being in a crinkle her foot was caught and besom, shovel and head flew about the floor.

Mrs Tubbs was the first to rise, which she did with indignation written in every line of her face. "You, oh dear," cried she and rung the bell. In a few moments the cook made her appearance but stopped short upon beholding Sarah upon the floor mumbling, grumbling, groaning and moaning with great emphasis.

"Dear, dear," said the cook.

"Send for a policeman, a constable," shouted Mrs Tubbs.

"What for ma'am?" enquired the cook.

"What for? To remove that nuisance," answered "missis", pointing to the disconsolate housemaid, and cookee vanished. On her return with the tantalising intelligence that the constable was not to be found, Mrs Tubbs drew a long breath and commanded that Sarah be conveyed from the room and the door shut. By dint of coaxing, the first was presently performed and, by gently exercising the muscles, the other was shortly obeyed. Then with many ejaculations of she couldn't write well Mrs Tubbs commenced to scribble and after two ineffectual attempts succeeded in producing the following epistle. It must be remembered that she had been born in comparatively low life and had risen to her present position by the indefatigable exertions of Mr Tubbs deceased, seconded by herself, and had not had much time for self-education.

My dear, dear Ben

I hopes you gets on famous as of course you do seeing as what a scholar you was at home a reading every mortal book as came in your eyesight. Now dont you be contrary like and not do as you betouldbekase if you do you will break the hart of yourn own mother which would be a serius matter. Tell Mr Smales who is a polite man and nice speaking as that I hopes he'll look to you sharp and see that you don't break winders nor nothinbekase it costesses so much—I well knows that. But your a good boy Ben onlie a little ruff but you must rub that ofsumhow and then youll be fit to be a lard sum day and of course youll be a Member of Parliment and make the laws of your countrie Ben and so I hopes you will. You mind you gives Mrs Smales my bestest love and plinty of kissesses if as how she'ill let you bekase I likes her and respects her. I ain't much of a scholar Ben but I hopes as that you will be and now I'm to konkludbekase its dinner time and I must put on the yellow marked dress that you didn't like and so no more from your luvingaffekshunate mother.

Letishia Maria GeorgenaKarrilina Tubbs.

Having with infinite pains sealed this specimen of a letter in three places and directed it to Mr Doctor SmalesSkoolMaaster it was despatched to the post and Mrs Tubbs ascended to the upper regions there to undergo numerous toilet operations while we will return whence we came.

oooOOOooo

Ben slept and Ned yawned over his back until the usher brought up the first course of dinner when Ned, by a thump and pinch, awoke his companion. After many groans, winks, stupid looks, and other indescribable rollings and twistings Ben sat up and attacked the viands with great voracity. They consisted of pea soup intermingled with pieces of beef and duly seasoned with superabundance of pepper and salt. Soon this disappeared as if by magic down the tremendous chasms called mouths which graced that portion of the friends' countenances between the nose and chin. Having finished, certain smackings of the lips, rollings of the eyes and other pantomimic expressions without the aid of speech clearly showed that another plateful or rather panful would be acceptable. But it was not to be, as in a few seconds, a step was heard outside, the door was opened and an usher entered bearing in his hands two plates covered with great daubs of, horror of horrors, tapioca pudding. Ben could have borne anything else, but this was too bad and probably this notion of his was apparent as after depositing the plates upon a chair the usher departed with a broad grin upon his broader face. No sooner had he shut the door than the wrath of the friends broke forth with terrific fury. They kicked, they twisted, they rolled, they groaned, they uttered various inelegant expressions, and finally falling in each other's arms vowed vengeance on the Doctor, at the same time declaring that no possible nor impossible inducement should cause them to long remain in this disagreeable place. Having made this laudable resolution they commenced to render in their intelligent minds the means of putting it into practice. Suddenly Ned leaped from the bed and dived into the recesses of his trouser pocket. From the depths of this repository he presently brought forth the money which had fallen to his share as the division of the contents of the purse. Ben seeing what he was about did the same and upon putting the money together they found to their astonishment that it amounted to the sum of twenty-two pounds seventeen shillings and ninepence three farthings. "Hurrah," shouted Ned beneath his breath and he proceeded to equally divide it. Some difficulty was felt about the appropriation of the odd farthing but this was presently removed by Ben's insisting that Ned should pocket it. This settled, they returned to bed and began debating as to the best mode of proceeding. First came the difficulty of escaping except upon Saturdays but as neither had patience to wait until then they determined to, if possible, scale the walls. How this was to be done however was a matter for serious reflection and it was at last given up as impracticable. But in what other method could they get out? As to going through the house that was impossible. What then? This question remained unanswered until Ben remembered the small wooden door in the playground wall and mentioned it to Ned. That young gentleman struck his forehead forcibly with his hand, simultaneously shouting, "What an unmentionable nincompoop!"

"Who's a nincompoop?" asked Ben, beginning to take offence.

"Why, I am, not to have thought of it."

"Oh!" said Ben, and paused. Presently he said, insinuatingly, "King Log's got a key, wouldn't that act?"

"Hum," quoth Ned. "Come on, we'll have him," whereupon he jumped out of bed, when the plates of tapioca met his sight. He very coolly caught hold of them and, approaching the fireplace, which was stuffed full of paper, removed some and wiped it in. He then replaced the plates and got into bed again. Hardly had he done so when the usher entered with another grin on his countenance. On seeing however that the tapioca had entirely disappeared he looked from the plates to the boys and back again, as if puzzled, and then left the room wearing a dissatisfied aspect. The youths waited until his footsteps had died away and then getting out of bed cautiously opened the door and peeped out. No one was in sight, the upper regions were perfectly deserted and everything was still. Beneath, however, there was noise enough, as it was the dinner hour and the musical clatter of knives and forks could be plainly heard, intermingled occasionally with the sonorous voice of the Doctor as he shouted some order from the head of the table. This noise favoured their purpose and the youths stole softly onwards keeping a vigilant watch upon all sides with throbbing hearts and stifled breathing. Door after door was passed until one rather larger than the others was reached, this they slowly opened and entered the room. It was a large apartment and rather tastefully decorated with a couple of almanacs hung upon the walls. Behind the door, on pegs, hung several suits of clothes and these were immediately subjected to a careful search. Nothing was found in them and the adventurers moved to the dressing-table on which stood a large looking-glass. Beneath it was a drawer locked but the key had been carelessly left upon the table and with great expectations Ned unlocked it. He could hardly stifle a cry of joy as there, almost the first thing he set eyes upon, lay the identical key. He well knew it was the right one as in former times he had been a great favourite of Log's and often allowed to use it. In a low voice he communicated its discovery to Ben, who was ransacking the contents of a portmanteau, and, having replaced everything they had moved in as nearly as possible its original position, they slowly returned to their own room and, hiding the key beneath the mattress, jumped into bed. Burying themselves beneath the clothes the friends congratulated each other on the successful issue of their experiment and resolved upon attempting their escape that very night. Many reasons concurred in pointing out this as the best course. Firstly, the key would be shortly missed, it might that very afternoon, and they almost shuddered at the thought. Secondly, it would be next to impossible to escape in the full blaze of daylight with more than one hundred boys within sight. Thirdly, it best suited their own impatient natures to commence the enterprise at once. They therefore passed the time in contemplation of the approaching attempt until the usher brought milk-sops as a substitute for tea. After devouring this, their impatience grew more and more. By the time the boys were dismissed to bed they were in a perfect fever. When the ushers followed, their pulses were at more than one hundred, and when the Doctor passed the door, with his firm steady tread, their excitement knew no bounds.

Having waited what to them seemed two hours—in reality, ten minutes—they slipped out of bed and noiselessly commenced dressing. This operation was soon performed and, then having extracted the key from the mattress, Ned began to slowly open the door. He presently effected this and, followed by Ben, cautiously descended the stairs. Here they had apparently the option of two distinct methods of egress, one by the front door, the other by the more roundabout way of the playground. In reality however they had no choice as the Doctor, each night with his own hands, locked every door and pocketed the keys, this Ned well knew. But he could not lock the windows and this also Ned knew and he resolved to take advantage of it. Closely followed by Ben, he led the way slowly and silently into the schoolroom and between the desks up to a small window which he was aware opened easily and was but a few feet from the ground. By mounting on a desk he undid the shutters and as he did so a flood of moonlight poured in, startling Ben, who also stood below, and rendering visible the anxious countenances of the youths. Ned now opened the window inch by inch—that it might not creak—and motioning Ben to follow he slowly wriggled out. The window was small but Ned was smaller, and by a sudden jerk he drew himself through and disappeared. Ben now tried to follow his example but being considerably stouter experienced proportionate difficulty and presently stuck fast—half out and half in. However by the help of Ned, who seized his collar and tugged away, he was presently released and banged upon the ground. Ned now requested to be allowed to sit on his shoulder for the small space of ten cracks that he might shut the window. Ben immediately consented and the shutters having been pulled together Ned descended and again led the way to the small door. Arriving before it he applied the key and turned the lock but still the obstinate article would not open. They began to push and continued to push but it was no use: the thing was carved in the stone wall and painted apparently. But presently an idea descended from the smiling moon above and entered the head of Ben. That idea was that there must be a bolt and upon searching a bolt was found, drawn back, and the youths found themselves outside the walls and free to go wherever they listed.

For a moment both halted and looked up into the starry sky as if to ask for guidance, but receiving none Ned again put himself in front and led the way into Chilton past the church and along the road they had travelled that memorable Saturday. On, on they trudged now side by side, absorbed in thought and both thinking the same thing—what should they do? For some time they walked on, but the natural vivacity of their tempers would not allow them to remain for long quiet and Ned presently began to talk. What he talked about must forever remain unknown but the ice, having been broken, continued to break and in breaking gave off certain sounds that resolved themselves into the following conversation.

"I've been thinking," quoth Ben, "about what's up."

"So've I," answered Ned, "and I say cut for Aunt Billicum's. She's an innocent and will take in. What sort's your mother?" continued he.

"A brick, soft at one end, hard at t'other," said Ben.

"So's Dad, I've got no mammy," quoth Ned informingly.

"Too-ra-loo-ra-loo-ral, we'll 'xactly fit then," said Ben. "I've got no daddy."

Shortly after this desultory talk they entered the small village and passed their ancient acquaintance, the inn. But they passed on and soon left it far behind. Now certain rosy streaks of light conjoined with the fact that the stars looked precious dim warned the travellers that day was approaching. Suddenly the sun cleared the summit of a hill and shot his beams in all directions, causing the dew to glitter with a lustrous light; the birds woke up and the stars went out. The travellers had been proceeding due west and, now turning, looked at the glorious jolly red-faced luminary.

"He's been drinking," said Ned and by alternately putting one foot before the other he moved on his way. Ben did the same and the travellers, having again got into that swing which is so conducive to quick walking, opened their mouths and began to talk, in that respect imitating the birds who peopled the hedges on either side of the road. "They'll have just found us out," quoth Ned.

"Ha, ha," laughed Ben, "no fear. By the living jingo! Hark!" and before the words were hardly out of his mouth he began to scramble through the hedge. The fact was the rolling wheels of an advancing carriage had struck upon his ear and, thinking that the better part of valour was discretion, he resolved to provide against meeting the Doctor at the risk of tearing his clothes. Ned perfectly agreed with him and they both stooped down behind the hedge so as to see and not be seen. It rapidly drew nearer and, to their astonishment, they beheld standing upright in it and urging the horses to greater speed no less a personage than Doctor Smales himself. When it had passed the friends arose from their concealment and stared at each other.

"Whew!" whistled Ben.

"Whew!" answered Ned sympathisingly, "It's all up with Aunt Billicum. He's sure to go there—I say let's go to California and turn gold-diggers."

"By the jingo!" quoth Ben, "But we will, it's the ticket—come on," and he scrambled into the road again.

Ned followed and shouting "America!" they rushed down the road at a rattling pace. Suddenly Ben stopped, so did Ned and asked what was the matter. "Why," answered Ben, "the Doctor's been there," and he pointed to a collection of houses ahead, "so we'll be catched."

"So we shall behind—what must we do?"

"Cut across the country s'pose," laconically suggested Ben.

Ned nodded and they immediately commenced to put their new project into execution, steering as near west as possible. Field after field was passed, still no signs of any road, nothing but a few but little used footpaths and occasionally a short lane. They now began to feel hungry and looked about for houses but none were in sight and, what was worse, they suddenly came upon a large wood which barred further onward course. They followed its edge for some distance but it appeared endless and they therefore determined upon boldly entering it. At first their progress was much impeded by a great quantity of blackthorn bushes that grew so thick and close together they were obliged sometimes to crawl. But they presently passed them and entered a large plantation of ash that, beyond compelling continuous turns, offered but slight resistance. They thus continued to walk for nearly two hours during which the pangs of hunger continually increased until, feeling utterly exhausted, they sat down at the foot of a large oak to rest. While thus recruiting their strength a piercing scream suddenly rent the air apparently but a few yards distant. Both youths immediately rose to their feet and surveyed with startled and curious gaze the depths of the forest. Again and again the cry of agony arose and each time went to the heart of the youths and the rattling of a chain was now heard. They were neither naturally timid but now in the depths of an unknown wood with that fearful scream still reverberating through their ears, far from the haunts of men, they certainly were startled and amazed. But as no repetition of the scream again arose they summoned up courage and advanced a few steps to halt the moment the rattling of the chain smote upon their ears. It did and now appeared to come from behind a huge ash stem where the leaves were violently agitated. Again they summoned up courage, rushed forward, ran round the stem and beheld extended before them, apparently in a dying state—a rabbit. The poor creature had unwarily popped both its forefeet in a gin and had uttered the piercing screams from the air. It had completely exhausted itself in vain efforts to escape and now, having given up all hope, lay still with its dark beseeching eyes turned upon the friends. Even had they been free from the continued disagreeable reminders of hunger it is to say the least extremely improbable that the poor animal would have been released. But now, when Ben bent over it with cannibal looks as if half resolved to devour it raw, the poor animal perceived that its earthly race was run, and therefore quietly gave up the ghost before the stick which Ned had cut could descend upon its insensible sconce. Ben immediately set about collecting dry wood of which a large quantity was lying around and had succeeded in piling up enough to roast an ox when it flashed across their minds that it would be impossible to light it as they possessed neither flint, steel or tinder. The first and second difficulty was quickly dissipated by Ben picking up a flint and Ned producing a clasp knife. But the tinder, where in the world was that to be obtained?

"Burn a piece of my shirt," suggested Ned.

"And where's the fire?" asked Ben.

Ned looked considerably foolish but, as if with the idea of doing some notable action which would pass away the memory of his speech, ransacked his pockets with great diligence. His face suddenly assumed an expression of extreme delight and, dragging forth a large piece of brown paper, he shouted "Here you are," to Ben, who was watching his motions. The addressed party, who held the knife and flint, immediately approached and by dint of knocking his knuckles succeeded in producing in his own mind such a superabundance of disgust that he flung the instruments upon the ground. Ned picked them up and, by superior patience and skill, after simply skinning two knuckles, at length managed to produce a spark. Which spark lighted the paper, and the paper by blowing lighted some leaves, which leaves smoked and lighted the wood, and a roaring fire was the result. Of course they had forgotten that to roast a rabbit you must first skin and therefore had been putting the cart before the horse. Now however there was no help for it and they commenced to skin the animal. Ben held it and Ned first stuck the knife in and then—. But I will not detail the horrible process by which what had once been a symmetrical creature was reduced to a hacked, haggled, and smeared lump. However it was done, a long sharp stick thrust into it, and Ned seating himself tailor-fashion commenced to act as a roasting machine while Ben heaped on firing by armfuls. By the continued repetition of this last process such a heat was engendered that Ned declared the thing was done. So producing his knife he severed a leg and commenced devouring it. Ben approached and quickly followed his example. Both having eaten one leg, cut off another, and declaring that it was excellent smacked their lips, flourished their knives and looked exactly like of couple of cannibals. At last from sheer inability to eat any more they desisted and, stretching themselves at full length on the ground with their feet towards the ashes of the fire, their heads in the shadow of the oak and the rest of their bodies exposed to the glare of the midday sun, commenced a desultory conversation.

"I say, Ben," quoth Ned, "ain't it jolly?"

"Jolly," answered the addressed party, uttering a complacent groan and endeavouring to turn. Being unable to do so he gave another piggish grunt and dropped asleep.

Ned, finding that all his questions remained unanswered, concluded that the hard breathing he heard showed great insensibility and murmuring, "Forty winks, just forty winks—tinks—inks," followed Ben's lazy example. Rabbits drew near, but the sounds proceeding from the friends' nasal organs soon sent them with a hop, skip and jump to the right-about. Not so an impudent jay who, seating himself on an overhanging branch of the oak, tried to imitate the hideous noises which arose beneath him. But not being able he flew off with a tremendous scream, making the woods ring and, saving the distant tap, tap of the woodpecker, all was silent as the deserts of Arabia.

Chapter 6

Doctor Smales had rather expected some such escapade as actually took place and had risen earlier and proceeded straight to the friends' room. He had consequently discovered their disappearance long before Ned or Ben expected he would. Knowing, that is, having strong reasons for suspecting that they would go to Aunt Billicum's he set out that way and, as we have seen, passed the fugitives on the way. On arriving before the desirable freehold residence of Mrs Billicum, Dr Smales alighted, put on a stern unyielding aspect, and gave a tremendous flourish with the knocker. No one answered nor was there the slightest sound within indicating the presence of any human being. Having again hammered away Doctor Smales stepped backwards a few yards and then saw what he had not noticed before—that all the shutters were down. It was apparent that the inhabitants of the house, supposing there were inhabitants, were not early risers and it was also apparent that they slept precious sound—a fact insinuating the keeping of late hours. So thought Doctor Smales as, hand upon the knocker, he again attempted to beat the door in. This time he produced some effect as a slight disturbance occurred within and a window was thrown open above his head. Doctor Smales looked up, but he could not distinguish anything to be certain save the tip of somebody's nose and an immense window curtain, which, strange to say, rose and fell with great regularity. He had hardly time to notice this singular appearance when a shrill voice addressed him in the following words, "You there, you below, what do you want, ai?"

"The human bagpipe," thought Dr Smales to himself as he enquired whether he could see Mrs Billicum.

The shrill voice said, "Yes, if you'll wait," and the immense window curtain and the tip of somebody's nose, which, by the bye, had a little pimple on it, simultaneously disappeared, proving their intimate connection. After something more than an hour the Doctor, unasked, stepped in and looked around to see the opener. But he, or she, had mysteriously vanished; true, the door was drawn tight back, but resolving not to perplex himself with such trifles, Dr Smales walked on to the end of the passage. Here he found some stairs which, evidently, led to the lower regions; he momentarily paused but gathering up courage slowly and safely descended. Upon arriving at the lower floor he looked carefully ahead and there in a small room, apparently used to breakfast in, he beheld the remarkable nose. This time, however, it was not in the midst of a huge curtain but stuck somewhere about the middle of a face, which again was stuck apparently without the intervention of a neck upon an immense conglomeration of dress. This peculiar person no sooner beheld the figure of Dr Smales standing in amaze at the foot of the stairs than it arose and with majestic steps, its moon-face wreathed in smiles, advanced towards him and announced itself in the identical voice as Mrs Billicum. "Come in, come in," cried she hospitably, after wrenching his arm out of place, and with a rueful aspect Dr Smales did so and sank into a chair. "Do you take coffee, or tea?" enquired Mrs Billicum with one hand upon the repository containing the refreshing beverage and the other upon that which is strengthening.

"I prefer coffee, if you please," replied the Doctor, wiping his forehead with a genteel flourish. When the cup was placed before him Mrs Billicum enquired if there was anything the matter with her nephew. "Yes," answered the Doctor, "he has absconded."

"Absconded—run away?" echoed Mrs Billicum "What possible reason could he have for such a proceeding?"

"None that I am aware of save this," said the Doctor, and he related what had passed upon Saturday and the judicial and moderate walloping he had administered. On its conclusion Mrs Billicum expressed her entire concurrence with the course he had pursued and advised him to prosecute the search with all possible diligence. Dr Smales replied that he certainly should and that now, finding the youths had not arrived, he would drive to Ned's father and from thence to Mrs Tubbs, stopping and enquiring at each roadside inn.

Hereupon he arose and with a genteel bow, thus obviating the necessity of his arm being quite dislocated, took his leave and left the house murmuring to himself, "Déshabillé—that remarkable nose." He ordered the coachman to drive to Ambourn, waved his hand to Mrs Billicum, who stood at her porch, and disappeared with his vehicle.

Acting according to his instructions the coachman drove off at his utmost speed, urging on his horses with voice and whip. Could Doctor Smales have been driven at the speed of the hurricane, had he been riding upon a steam-engine, going by the electric telegraph, moving with the celerity of Mercury, with that of a comet, the result would have been the same—null. Consequently his chagrin was extreme when he found that, enquire as often as or how he would, not the slightest reliable intelligence could be obtained. Some said that they never troubled themselves with other people's business, others that they had seen two youths answering to the description he gave. "When?" eagerly enquired the Doctor. "Au summat loike a month ago."

Such answers as these incensed and disgusted the Doctor to such a degree that he at last ordered the man to drive straight on. This the fellow did and presently drew up before the residence of Mr Snicks who followed the lucrative profession of an auctioneer. By some lucky chance that gentleman was at home and his astonishment mingled with rage upon hearing of his son's disgraceful conduct was unbounded. He stamped, he looked ferocious, he would have swore had not the dark suit which Doctor Smales wore reminded him of the gentleman in black and it all ended in a tremendous heart-rending groan. Sinking into a chair he motioned Dr Smales to depart and continue the search promising to aid him with all the means at his disposal. Thus unceremoniously dismissed Dr Smales departed, doubtless with a heart bursting with sorrow for the disconsolate parent. However that may be, certain it is that he entered his carriage and was driven direct to the house of Mrs Tubbs, where he arrived just in the nick of time, as she was going to dinner. When Doctor Smales was announced by Sarah and, the next moment entered the room, Mrs Tubbs's heart misgave her and, rising, she motioned the Doctor to a chair and Sarah out of the room—a piece of unprecedented cruelty. Then in a tremulous tone she enquired if there was anything the matter with her darling. When informed of his escapade she burst into motherly tears and looked so miserably woebegone that the Doctor could but just smother a laugh, which however he managed to do by yawning, looking hard at the fire, and stuffing his handkerchief in his mouth—the disgusting animal. In a few minutes Mrs Tubbs recovered sufficiently to hear the details of the disaster which Doctor Smales told in an harrowing tone as if he delighted in ploughing up the exquisite feelings of an "affekshunate

Mother." On its conclusion another flood of tears ensued, expecting which the Doctor had his handkerchief ready and thus escaped. Presently Mrs Tubbs managed by some indescribable means to overcome her maternal feelings and invited the Doctor to partake of dinner. Doctor Smales having no objection gracefully accepted her invitation and proved to her satisfaction that he did not disdain to devour cold beef and floury potatoes. Dinner over, the dessert was spread and whilst sipping his wine and picking his teeth Doctor Smales explained to Mrs Tubbs his views upon the melancholy subject. Finding that, taken collectively, they entirely concurred with hers, he presently rose and, having promised to use his utmost endeavours to find the missing youth, departed for Chilton. After a ride of about three hours and a half he arrived at that thriving place and poured into his mother's ear the unsuccessful issue of his expedition. In which occupation, conjoined with that of masticating a piece of bread-and-butter, we will leave him and betake ourselves to the forest wherein the friends were left quietly sleeping.

Not such a tremendous long interval of time had elapsed after the jay took his departure before a squirrel made its appearance and danced about upon the oak with great enjoyment. In the course of a rapid evolution the graceful animal incautiously trusted its entire weight upon a dead branch which of course immediately broke and precipitated it from a great height bang upon the most prominent part of Ben's features. The poor fellow was of course dreadfully startled and, awaking from a state of somnolence in great alarm, applied one hand to his countenance to find whether or no the nasal organ remained intact. For some time he found it impossible to ascertain with any degree of certainty as the blow had completely banished feeling from the sensitive organ, and having for a length of time lain upon his hand, it was benumbed. However by using the other hand and employing a vast amount of patience he at last succeeded in finding to his great delight that he was not a nose-less being. This being the case, Ben gave a tremendous yawn and stretched himself. He then rolled over and over until, coming in violent contact with Ned, that young gentleman awoke, which was exactly what Ben desired. Not that Ned came to full sensibility at once: on the contrary it required two or three bumps and pinches before he could be made to understand that, as the sun was beginning to decline, it was necessary that they should make a move.

After a while however he comprehended and arising expressed his entire willingness to start.

But which way should they go was the question which occurred simultaneously to the friends and at the same time an idea entered Ben's subtle brain. This was to climb the oak and from its topmost branches take a good survey of the surrounding country; but it was easier to talk than to do in this case. The tree rose many feet above their heads without a single bough and it was much too large to "shin" up. Neither by one mounting on the other's shoulders could it be done, but as they were about to abandon the project a thought struck Ned and pointing to an ash pole he soon made Ben understand. His plan was to "shin" up the pole which gradually decreased in size until it bent with his weight and let him against the oak's first huge branch. No sooner said than done and Ben, rushing forward, in about a couple of minutes sat upon the bough everything having occurred exactly as Ned had foretold. After a slight rest he commenced ascending the tree and found no further difficulty as the boughs grew thick and strong. Upon arriving at the greatest height he dared to go, he took a long searching glance around. On three sides, the wood appeared endless but to the west it gradually thinned until it ceased altogether and was succeeded by pasture lands which extended to a small village which lay at about two miles as near as he could guess. It was a beautiful view as the sun, now fast declining, right ahead threw his last refulgent beams almost horizontally upon the land and it awakened even in the heart of Ben some slight appreciation of its beauties. For some time he contemplated it and would have probably done so much longer had not the impatient voice of his friend below disturbed his reveries by enquiring what he could see. Thus recalled to a sense of their peculiar position Ben shouted, "All right!" and quickly descended to the last bough, when swinging himself below it he hung for a moment, and then dropped. Ned having been acquainted with the news, they started at a sharp pace and after something less than an hour's walk arrived at the village just as the sun's red disk disappeared. After a little trouble they succeeded in finding an inn and what is more a civil, obliging and uninquisitive landlord who supplied them with Christian fare at a Christian price. He also informed them that he possessed an eligible bed, at which hook the youths immediately snapped and commanded that it be kept for them. After supping they requested to be accommodated with a private room and by following the landlord were presently supplied with one. The youths then drew their chairs around the fire and commenced to talk a lot of bald disjointed unintelligible questions which ended by their calling the landlord to be informed where they were. The worthy man shortly made his appearance with cuffs turned up and informed them that they were just then situated in a certain village twenty-two miles from Bristol. Having told them this he arose to depart in great haste and had in fact appeared to sit upon upright pins all the time. The fact was he had left a barrel running. "Wait a bit," said Ben. But it was no use. With an indistinct "I'll be here—," the landlord bolted. As he did not make his appearance and they felt tired, the youths thought it would be a good idea to go to bed and shortly put it into practice. Soon hideous noises filled the apartment showing that Morpheus had received them in his arms and there they continued until the sun had more than risen and the landlord awoke them by thundering at the door with one hand while the other rang a bell. To get rid of these discordant sounds the youths arose and, opening the door, flung a pillow out which had the desired effect as a smothered growl arose and the noise was silenced. Having performed their toilet they descended to the private room and quickly made havoc of breakfast. Then calling the landlord they requested to be informed how much "tin" was due and on being told that three shillings would be sufficient grinned, whistled and flung the money upon the table. The landlord counted the pieces, sounded them and having convinced himself that it was all right was about to depart when the youths requested to be shown the road to Bristol.

"Certainly, certain-ly," answered the landlord and it having been pointed out to them the friends parted with a polite "Good morning."

On and on they walked, at times pointing out to each other any peculiarity that appeared, whether in the landscape around or in the clouds above. Towards midday a small village was entered where they refreshed themselves with a draught of ale, having paid for which they again moved forward with light hearts and brilliant expectations of delectable adventures on land and at sea. About two hours after leaving the village the signs of a large town became more and more apparent. Numbers of pedestrians were met, large waggons of goods piled rather higher than sky-high were overtaken and passed while houses thickened on either side of the road. In another hour the suburbs of Bristol were reached and the friends frequently halted to note the long rows of apparently never-ending houses and the busy people. Before long they found it impossible to gratify their curiosity in this manner as the mass of moving people soon became too dense to allow of any remaining stationary—all must move or be moved over. Finding this they walked on side by side without having the slightest idea whither they were proceeding, but partly borne on by the crowd, partly by their own excited feelings.

After thus walking for about half-an-hour, as luck would have it, they suddenly emerged from the close streets and stood upon the wharfs. Several ships before them were discharging their cargo and the friends stood for some time motionless gazing on the lofty masts and symmetrical hulls. After having gazed their fill at a distance the friends drew near and watched with great attention the motions of the crew of a large United States vessel who were unloading her of baulks.

"By jingo, they're heavy." said Ben.

"Ah—now then—looky," answered Ned, pointing to a gang who were heaving away.

For some time the huge log resisted their utmost endeavours but it suddenly yielded and with a lumbering sound fell over upon the wharf making the very ground shake with the violence of the concussion. The friends remained watching the sailors thus engaged until the mate dismissed them, when Ned advised retiring for the night. And now arose a novel difficulty: there was such a quantity of public houses in the neighbourhood that for some time they found it impossible to choose. However they at last decided and entering ordered some provisions, a private room and a bed to be ready immediately. The landlord with a curious stare obeyed and, having supped, the friends commenced to chat. After an hour of which, feeling lazy, they called for lights and were soon fast asleep. In which thrice happy state they continued until awakened by the resounding knock and hoarse voice of "boots." That important functionary informed them that breakfast was waiting and then departed. With many enormous yawns the friends arose, descended and devoured breakfast.

Then, having paid the obsequious landlord his due, they strolled out upon the wharfs, there to try their luck with the gruff-voiced captains and important-looking mates. For a considerable period of time they wandered to and fro beside the rows of ships, neither of them having the courage to approach and tender their petition to be allowed to work their passage out. Such was their rough scheme which would enable them to save the money they possessed until put upon the shores of America. At last Ben, summoning up all the courage he could, approached an old sailor who was lolling against a pile of baulks, and in a tremulous tone asked whether a certain ship, which he pointed out, was to cross the Atlantic.

"I kalkilate yes youngster—to-morrow mornin'," answered the old man in a kinder tone of voice than Ben expected could proceed from such a gruff, grimed, gnarled and battered piece of States' humanity. Somewhat emboldened by getting a civil answer in a civil tone Ben next enquired whether they could work their passage out in her. The old man grimly smiled or rather attempted to and surveyed the two youths from head to foot with a scrutinising glance. Apparently satisfied with their appearance he grunted and answered informingly, "Yer'll hev to work smart."

"All right," said Ben, which sentiment was echoed by Ned.

"Cum 'long then," laconically ordered the old chap and away he sailed, threading his way with great dexterity between boxes, bales and piles of every description of merchandise, closely followed by the youths. In a short time he reached the side of the vessel and, beckoning them to follow, sprung up its sides like a cat. Ben and Ned also ascended and stepped upon deck. No one was in sight but a certain noise below, something between grumbling and growling, proclaimed that the vessel was not completely untenanted. The fact was, all the crew had gone on shore to dine saving a mate and two men, to whom the old sailor was extolling the outward appearance of the youths. This he succeeded in doing to such a degree that the mate, exclaiming "Just what I wanted," dropped his soup-spoon and rushed up the companion ladder. On arriving upon deck he approached the youths with hasty steps bawling out "Yer'll do," at the same time beckoning them furiously with one hand. Without being the slightest intimidated by this last proceeding Ben advanced to meet him and commenced his application. The mate heard him to the end, all the time surveying both attentively, and then shouting "My eye—yer'll do—cum 'long and grub," commenced returning whence he came.

With joyous looks the friends followed him and managed to descend the upright ladder without falling, though in continual dread thereof. When they again placed their feet upon an horizontal floor the mate had disappeared but by proceeding towards the sounds of "grubbin" which came from the forward part of the vessel they suddenly found themselves in his company again. He was seated at the head of a long deal table and engaged in the delicious operation of conveying a shovelful of pea-soup to his mouth. Two men were seated on one side of the same table and on the other they recognised their old friend, whose visage was now completely buried together with a large portion of his whiskers in a pewter cup. The mate, now having succeeded in his object, perceived the youths standing at the door and shouted out "Cum in, cum in, yer." He then filled a couple of plates with the same description of viand as that he had been devouring and shoved them down the table. At first sight the aspect of this food was not inviting, however a certain savoury smell was wafted to the olfactory nerves of the youths who sniffed it, advanced, tasted and devoured. The plates were then again ladled full from a huge tin bowl by the mate and again emptied. Meanwhile the pewter cup circulated freely and soon approached the friends who, having been agreeably surprised by the soup, were not dismayed but rather rejoiced thereat. Therefore Ben presently seized the article and, applying it to his lips, drank deep and long. Nor did he repent this audacious proceeding as it was filled with excellent beer and quenched his thirst. He set it down with a deep-drawn sigh of intense satisfaction which, being marked by Ned, he also seized the article and drank the remaining liquor. This concluded dinner and with a groan the mate arose, stretched his windmill arms and issued the necessary orders to the men who had now arrived. They were all strong wiry looking men and it would have been impossible to find a single fat one among them. Most were set to hauling in the remaining portion of the cargo and here the friends found plenty of employment. About the middle of the afternoon the captain and first mate arrived and the presence of new hands was immediately perceived. The second mate who had engaged the youths came forward and tendered his report with which the captain appeared satisfied and, first taking a good survey of them, descended below. He was a short but wonderfully strong man and had an eye which seemed to look through one. It was greatly by the means of this eye that his men were so completely under subjugation and never offered the slightest opposition to his smallest command. He had in fact the ship thoroughly under his command and he knew it. He was a capital sailor and was now about to pass the Atlantic from Bristol to

New York for the one hundredth time. This was the captain under whom Ben and Ned were about to court the dangers of the treacherous smiling ocean and they could not have wished for a better. When the day's work was finished the men were dismissed early to rest that they might be the fresher for the hard work which awaited them on the morrow. The second mate pointed out to Ben the cribs they were to occupy and his broad face was covered with a grim smile at the look of amazement with which they regarded them. Doctor Smales' bed had been in Ben's mind the very essence and model of smallness, consequently he was astounded upon beholding the cramped little box in which he was told to lay his weary limbs and sleep. Sleep indeed with his knees up to his chin how could that be managed? And in attempting to convince himself that it was possible he insensibly undressed and tumbled in. As for Ned he had already entered the regions of repose and gave evidence of the fact by snoring most awfully, thereby bringing down the vengeance of a sailor who slept beside him, in the shape of a pillow or rather bag of rags upon his denoted sconce. Seeing and hearing the dreadful punishment which had befallen his companion, Ben determined if possible to put in practice the maxim that "forewarned is forearmed" but was unsuccessful. However as the sailor had himself commenced to frighten all spiders in the vicinity he escaped for that night at least and awoke the next morning feeling refreshed though somewhat cramped. Breakfast over, the work of hauling the vessel out and turning her round commenced and lasted until dinnertime when the tide arrived at its greatest height. After a slight meal the tide-gates were opened and the work of towing the vessel down the river commenced. This was effected by horses and they were cast loose from them in rather more than an hour.

Now they were upon the great broad waters of the Severn, the men were sent above, the white canvas sails were unfurled and the ship with a joyous bound sprung on her way to the shores of the New World. 'Ere long the sun began to sink in the western horizon and the men crowded on deck to take a long last fond glance at the shores of Wales, which was all that could be seen of Merry England. As the sun sunk the wind freshened from the south-east, the waves sensibly increased in size, and the youths retired below with certain unpleasant reminders in the stomach and head informing them that the hated, dreaded rocking seasickness had laid violent hands upon them. They rose the next morning with white faces and shaking limbs and the mate, seeing that at present they were worse than useless upon deck, sent them to bed again. This command they gladly obeyed and would have slept had the creaking of blocks, rattling of chains, stamping of feet and other noises rife on board a sailing vessel in a heavy gale, permitted. But they did not, and as the day advanced and the gale continuously increased, so the melancholy feelings of the friends increased in proportionate ratio, until nobody but such a hard-hearted, grinning, grimed, weather-beaten old block as the mate could have laughed at their chalky faces and miserably woebegone groans. For two days this continued during which period neither ate the twelfth part of a morsel but remained cooped up in their narrow couches grunting, groaning, grumbling continually. However the third day the gale gradually decreased in violence until by dinner-time it had almost ceased to blow. The sea still ran high but the vessel did not rock to such a degree, the sun came out of the clouds, and the youths rolled out of bed. By slow and tedious degrees they contrived to dress and to tumble along to the mess-room where their appearance was hailed with a burst of derisive laughter. "Cum in," shouted the mate. "Shut up yer," continued he to the men and presently found both orders obeyed.

For a fortnight after this nothing particular occurred: they had favourable winds and the routine business on board was conducted in the ordinary manner. But who could expect to escape the vengeance of Neptune for ploughing the surface of his briny dominions without leave? No one. Consequently neither officers nor men were the slightest surprised when the wind suddenly ceased and a calm ensued early one fine morning. All day it continued, whistle as loud, as long, as shrill as they would, still the ship did nothing but rise and fall to the gentle swell of the waves. But as the red disk of the sun touched the surface of the water a few cat's-paws[1] appeared in the distance and shortly reached the ship coming from the north-west. The moment after, the sun sank and nothing but a red glow on the rapidly accumulating clouds remained to show where it had disappeared. Soon even this slight indication vanished and darkness reigned supreme. The wind had been gradually freshening and a slight show of canvas was now made to enable the ship

---

[1] A cat's-paw here means a light breeze that ruffles small areas of a water surface.

to have steerage way. Slowly she payed off upon the tack and thus became subject to a disagreeable sea which had like to have again made havoc in the friends' stomachs. As however they could be of no use on board they were dismissed below and turned in all standing,[2] to be ready for any emergency. During the night the gale rapidly increased until in the morning it blew a regular hurricane. Consequently when the friends arose they found it extremely difficult to move in any direction without some support. They had been kindly treated both by mates and men up to now and were of course slightly astonished when upon arriving on deck they were knocked about and swore at by everybody there. This being the case they made a rapid descent and, as may be imagined, were in no hurry to go on deck again. They had seen enough whilst there to startle stouter hearts than could be supposed to beat within the breasts of such youngsters. The waves were running as high as the main-yard, and occasionally a foam-crested monster towering above its comrades would approach with fearful speed, and striking the poop cause the mighty vessel, insignificant in comparison, to quiver from end to end, while the blinding spray flew high in the air to descend in the form of rain. As the day wore on such occurrences grew more frequent, and as night set in they followed each other with such rapidity as to cause great doubts in the minds of every experienced sailor whether the ship could long withstand them.

None slept that night, each and every one kept fearful watch and as every succeeding monstrous wave struck the ill-fated ship they listened with great attention to hear if it had taken effect. The bell was frequently sounded and as yet all was well, but none knew how soon the line might tell the awful intelligence of a leak. The friends sat side by side in silence each wishing in his utmost heart that they had not left the terra firma of Old England to trust the treacherous sea. Thus morning dawned and revealed to their sickened sight the same view as yesterday. Nothing could be seen but monstrous waves rising and falling in all directions. For the purpose of keeping the vessel head to wind the captain had kept up a small foresail of a few square feet. Even this slight resistance to the roaring wind was sufficient not only to keep the vessel in her proper position but to drive her forward with fearful velocity, and to occasionally bury her stern and forecastle deep beneath the waves. The

---

[2] A phrase used of a ship brought suddenly to a stop while all sail is set.

captain now reckoned that during the forty hours the gale had continued they had made no less than four hundred miles, so that they must be near upon the Canary Isles and would, supposing it continued, either go ashore upon one of them or, worse still, upon the inhospitable coast of Africa. These apprehensions he presently communicated to the crew, who received them, some with quiet despair, others with oaths. Ben and Ned thought of home, the one of his mother, the other of his father, and both felt some slight twinges of conscience for having left them in such an abrupt manner. But it was useless thinking of that now, they had taken the step and must abide the consequences.

During that wretched day the crew sat motionless. It was evident that they must trust in fate; no effort of theirs could ward off the dreaded result. Each man recognising this sat absorbed in melancholy thoughts. The captain alone appeared to have any hope as he, every hour, ascended the companion ladder and surveyed the surrounding horrors as far as possible with scrutinising glance. He also occasionally sounded the bell and as he did so each man watched his impassive countenance as if the only chance of life lay there. Towards evening he again lowered the line and on drawing it up even his iron self-command could not repress the groan that burst from his tight-drawn lips. The men with one assent arose and rushed to the place, the captain stood with his arms folded and, in answer to their questions, said "Five feet water in the hold." The cry of "five feet water in the hold" rang through the ship, and all gave up hope. True they had the pumps, two in number, but what were they to stem the torrent of water that was rushing in, whose bubbling sound could be heard despite the roaring tempest? Nothing truly. However, unwilling to abandon even the slightest hope they rushed to the pumps and worked until they were choked and would move no longer. Then did the feelings of the men break forth in varied manner. Some on their knees implored that God whom they had so long despised to deliver them from their present strait, others blasphemed, and others, among whom were the captain and the two youths, looked at each other in complete dismay. For half-an-hour they continued in this state when the instinct of self-preservation aroused itself within them instigating them to escape from the foundering vessel. There had been originally three boats on board, one each side and one at the stern. But the one to starboard had been stove in the first night of the gale and the following day that at the stern, which was the most capacious, had been washed away and lost. The remaining boat was a small jolly[3] capable of containing a dozen men and a week's provision, more it would not hold. As the crew surveyed this wretched little tub on which their safety apparently rested — for who could make a raft in such a sea? — their grief again burst forth and a shout of despair rose above the howling of the gale. As it died away, fifty strong-willed, strong-bodied men sprang forward, and regardless of the rolling of the vessel, the tremendous waves which each moment threatened to sweep the deck of its living freight, endeavoured in a fearful race to become possessor of a seat in the frail bark. Then commenced a dreadful struggle in which knives were drawn and had the rolling state of the vessel permitted, blood would certainly have been shed. The captain shouted, waved his arms at the mad fools who would launch such an eggshell, but all to no purpose. They were bent on their own destruction and, at last in a rage, he left them to their fate and returning below joined the two friends who, pale and trembling, listened to the sounds on deck. Up to the present moment not a man had perished, but now a tremendous wave advanced and striking the vessel's poop swept from stem to stern carrying with it twenty-eight men and the boat. The others had escaped by holding with the grasp of a dying man on portions of the rigging. But the instant the wave passed, and they were delivered from their perilous position, the boat, which had not been sunk, caught their sight and with one mad yell they each and everyone leapt the bulwarks and plunged in the remorseless sea. One after another they disappeared beneath the surface saving three, who by Herculean efforts reached the frail bark and scrambled in. But their safety only endured for a moment, the next the boat was overturned and with a wild despairing cry they sunk. Thus the captain and the youths were all that remained alive upon the unfortunate vessel. Soon it grew dark and as it did the horrors of their situation increased tenfold. In the daylight they would have had the consolation of taking a long, last glance at each other, at the ship, at the wild swelling waste of waters. But in the night how terrible it would be with the water rising higher and higher around them until some wave carried them off and plunged them in eternity. They shuddered as they thought of it and the two youths drew closer together, as for the captain he remained perfectly impassive with closed eyes and tight-drawn lips.

---

[3] A ship's boat.

Suddenly he started up and disappeared in the darkness, he had gone to procure a light but the candles were wet and would not burn, so he shortly returned. Slowly the night drew on, the gale continued, the wind still whistled through the cordage, the vessel still rocked frantically from side to side, and through the roar of the storm the sound of the gurgling water as it entered at the leak was plainly heard. It was as a death knell in the ears of the friends, and the captain, as it grew louder and louder, uttered a hollow groan. If such a man as he gave up hope there must be none, thought the friends, and there could be nothing to do save patiently await their coming dissolution. In this fearful thought they passed the night, and the morning broke upon a water-logged vessel and three despairing hearts.

Chapter 7

The captain upon the first appearance of daylight sounded the well and found as he expected that the water had considerably increased. From a slight calculation, which he made upon the spot, he reckoned that two hours was the extreme period of time upon which they could calculate before the vessel sank. During the last two days neither had eaten or drank anything beyond a biscuit and a sip of water. The captain now proposed to make a good meal and, finding that neither paid but slight attention to him, commanded them to eat and led the way to the storeroom. He here stuffed an immense quantity of ham and ale down their throats and they actually felt the better for it. They also fancied that the gale had somewhat decreased and in fact it had. Its great force was past and they were now being left behind by the roaring impetuous storm. At first this condition of things appeared much the better, but the captain hoped in his heart that it would have continued and thrown them ashore, instead of leaving them to founder at sea with scarcely a chance of escape. However he put a good face upon the matter and cheered up the drooping spirits of the youths when they perceived their mistake. But it was hard keeping up the spirits of others when he had none himself and he proposed going on deck in the hope of seeing a vessel that would deliver them from their dreadful situation. To enable himself to have a longer view, as the waves had not subsided, the captain sprung to the shrouds and was soon high in the air. For a long time he carefully scanned the horizon but no shout of joy reached the ears of the attentive listeners upon deck, and he presently descended looking, if possible, more grave than before. On arriving upon deck he imparted the bad news that there was nothing in sight and then descended the companion ladder. But the cabin floor was under water and he shortly reappeared. Now the vessel appeared to be fast settling down and almost every wave swept the deck, obliging the friends to hold tightly to the rigging. This position of suspense now became unbearable and, in a fit of desperation, they commenced ascending the shrouds with tremendous rapidity in the hope of seeing some distant sail. Carefully they swept the horizon with their eyes, so did the captain, and their united efforts resulted in disappointment. Once again did Ben bend a searching glance in the direction the captain had informed them that land lay, but no, not the slightest sign of land or ships could he perceive. Slowly he turned and looked out to sea—nothing but rising waves and screaming gulls.

"Stop a minute," he presently exclaimed, shading his eyes with one hand. "Yes," he now shouted, "It is, 'tis a sail."

"Where?" asked the captain and Ned at the same time.

"Yonder," shouted Ben, and he pointed out to sea. A moment employed in searching the spot pointed out by Ben convinced them and a shout of joy arose. It certainly was a sail and it certainly was rapidly nearing them, perhaps had seen them. But the captain was not as yet sanguine of escaping and he looked below. His worst fears were then realised, the vessel had but a few feet to sink and then—. Every moment might be their last and this the captain well knew though he said nothing. The vessel now rolled but slightly although the waves still ran high and the wind had not gone down. They prayed it might continue to blow if but ten minutes longer. For now the approaching vessel was but a quarter of a mile distant and had certainly observed them. Yet their deliverance was as yet but a matter of forlorn hope as the green waves now rolled almost uninterruptedly over the deck. The captain was astonished it had not foundered before but he knew that as it had held up so long it would go at last all the more rapidly. Now the fast approaching ship was hardly two hundred yards distant, a boat was lowered and they could see the men bend and strain at the oars.

"Can you swim?" shouted the captain.

"Yes," answered Ben.

At that moment, almost before the word had left his lips, the vessel gave a tremendous lurch forward, and they were thrown from the rigging. Ben's head struck the yard-arm beneath him and he remembered nothing more. The crew of the boat, when they saw the vessel disappear beneath the rolling waves, pulled and pulled with desperation and in less time than it takes to read it, certainly than write it, they arrived upon the spot. The first thing they saw was a dark body on the point of sinking, but by thrusting the hook back underwater and nearly half his body, the bowman managed to hook on and Ben was presently drawn on board. He was insensible and bleeding from a wound on the back of his head. The crew now shouted and listened. No answer. They shouted again and this time a faint hail was heard. By rowing towards the place whence the sound appeared to come they presently discovered Ned clinging to a spar and looking dismally woebegone. He was soon drawn in and questioned as to his companions and on being informed that there was still another the crew shouted and rowed, and rowed and shouted, but could obtain no answer. They therefore turned and made for the ship which lay to at about one hundred yards. By continued exertion they presently reached her and Ben, who was still insensible, was handed up the side while Ned followed with a sort of suppressed hop, skip and jump. Ben was immediately conveyed below and placed under the care of a surgeon, whilst Ned was examined by the commander as to the destination &c. of the sunken bark. Having given as much information on the subject as he could Ned looked hard at his questioner as much as to say, 'and who are you?' He noticed the look or rather stare, smiled and announced himself as Captain Tinglum of the United States from Guinea to New Orleans doing a little "nigger" business. After having volunteered this startling intelligence Captain Tinglum eyed Ned steadfastly for a few moments and then, turning on his heel, descended to his cabin, whistling with tremendous effect Yankee Doodle with brilliant variations. To which interesting and edifying tune Ned listened attentively until a heavy hand laid upon his shoulder caused him to turn somewhat precipitantly and survey the intruder. He was a short thick man, with a tremendous shock of hair, a flat nose much like a frying pan, and a huge mouth now extended to its utmost stretch displaying to view several cannibal teeth. "Ha, ha, ha," giggled the Yankee. Which mode of introducing himself astonished Ned who stared in silence.

"Ha, ha, ha," continued he of the frying-pan nose, "Yer kinder scared, air yer?"

Ned now was nearly scared but seeing no use in owning it merely enquired in dignified and polite language, "Who be you?"

Suddenly the Yankee ceased from giggling, popped his hands in his pockets, made a horrible grimace and bellowed, "Who be I? —I'll tell yer—Guess I'm fust mate Martin Finnikin an' as good a man as ar'n livin'."

After making this furious declaration, for the space of ten moments he uninterruptedly winked with one eye, then executing a splendid flourish with his right hand applied the tip of thumb to tip of nose and laterally extending the fingers of said hand whispered, "Humbug." Ned, thinking that this objectionable epithet was undeservedly given to him, was beginning to feel singularly bellicose, when the thought struck him that the Yankee's hand pointed slightly to starboard and, looking in that direction, he discovered the respectable Captain Tinglum standing upon the poop. All doubt as to whom Mr Finnikin intended his salute was removed when, with a sudden movement, Captain Tinglum turned and, with one still suddener, his first mate removed his paw and applied it to drawing forth a handkerchief. Which operation seemed endless and perfectly unprofitable as after five minutes thus spent he had only succeeded in getting his paw inextricably fixed. So calling Ned to follow, he jumped down the hatchway muttering several unintelligible Yankee curses. By the exercise of exemplary patience and equal agility Ned managed to keep him in sight and presently emerged into a long low room evidently used to mess in. The cook's apartment was at the other end of it, and that sable functionary was discovered luxuriantly lying at full length on a bench fanning himself. To this occupation he added that of superintending the operations of several little black wretches who, with great diligence, stirred a huge cauldron and occasionally received, as a reward for their virtuous conduct, a resounding whack. Blackee had just applied his broad hand rather forcibly on a little imp's ear when the mate entered followed by Ned.

"Holloa here, you lazy bag o' sut, you cockroach, you ink bottle, you——," but here his exclamations were interrupted by startled Blackee who had jumped up in great alarm and shouted, turning his white eyeballs in all directions, "Massa Fiking." As for the imps they retreated like so many black beetles and, when at a safe distance, turned and enjoyed the fun.

"Fiking! you fiddling black scoundrel, cut my pocket open," cried the exasperated mate shoving Blackee off his perch and occupying it. "Do you hear?" asked he of the trembling black, "cut my pocket open—this minnit."

Blackee in the excess of his trepidation hastened to obey and caught up a skewer. "You black d—l, air yer gwain to stick a lobster?—yer fool," groaned the mate.

Ned, seeing the dilemma Blackee was in, advanced and, pulling out his clasp knife, offered to perform the necessary operation. Mr Finnikin observed the act with a scowl but he rolled over and allowed Ned to cut his paw out. When it was done, he stretched himself, punched the "nigger" and slapping Ned on the shoulder in a patronising familiar manner left the room, first advising Ned to dry himself and Blackee to obtain some provisions. By turning round and round before the bubbling cauldron, from which a savoury smell arose, Ned contrived to make himself comfortable and, when he sat down to devour some corned beef, the little imps slowly and cautiously peeped from their hiding-places. Blackee at first contented himself with beckoning to them but as he found this dumb proceeding of no avail, he conquered his aversion to displaying his powers of bawling before Ned, lost all control of his serene temper and shouted shaking his fists, "Cum here you dam Sambo, you Jake you hear—ai?" But shout, bawl and curse as much as he would, none would obey him. He, therefore, with many groans commenced the task of driving them in and, armed with the poker in one hand and the soup ladle in the other, departed.

By dint of banging, poking, kicking and thumping he at last contrived to get the little wretches back to their place and locking all the doors produced a cane. Comical indeed were the looks of the young Sambos as with one accord they crushed up in a corner beneath the dresser and regarded the dreadful instrument with rolling eyeballs. They had evidently felt its weight before and knew pretty well what was coming. Blackee seemed in no hurry and he first passed his hand affectionately along the cane, all the while regarding the black lump of humanity beneath the dresser with the looks of a hungry cannibal. Presently he advanced and, stooping so that his body was in a horizontal line with the dresser, commenced to ply the instrument indiscriminately. Then did yells, and groans, and demoniacal expressions fill the apartment, splitting the ears of poor Ned and yet for the soul of him he could not help laughing. "Neow then Sambo—ther yer'll catch it," shouted the delighted "nigger" as he affectionately poked the unfortunate creature in the ribs. A yell from the attacked party arose and with a furious movement he dived beneath half a dozen of struggling, rolling, shouting, bawling, wriggling cockroaches or black-beetles. Blackee enjoyed the fun immensely. He laughed and laughed or rather grinned with very excess of merriment and consequently did not hear a knock at the door. But Ned did and he softly opened it. In stepped Mr Finnikin and looked around with an expression of intense disgust. "Wal, I niver," whispered he to Ned, and then softly and upon tiptoe approached unsuspicious Blackee, whose face shone with perspiration and who could hardly wallop for excessive cachinnation. The young black wretches saw Finnikin's intention and, in spite of their pain, began to grin. "Jako yer will—will yer," ejaculated Blackee and he applied himself still harder to his task. Just at that moment Finnikin lifted his foot and sent it with the whole force of his powerful leg against a certain unmentionable portion of Blackee's body, and with a cry of amazement, mingled with pain, that sable tyrant disappeared beneath the dresser. Before he could arise and resent this injury Finnikin grasped the cane, which Blackee had let fall, and applied it to his body. Then did he imitate the black beetles and a tremendous heart-rending, dismally woebegone yell arose and mingled with some gibberish of "Massa" floated on the savoury smell of the bubbling cauldron into every chink and cranny of the ship. It startled the captain as he sat absorbed in the contemplation of a map and he arose and fled to the scene. It reached the ears of Ben as he lay in his cot dreaming of battling with the waves, and sounded to him as the last despairing cry of his companions as they sunk beneath the sad sea. To the ears of the second mate it sounded as the knell of his hopes—he fancied that the slaves had escaped and were murdering the crew. The men thought the same and all looked excessively foolish when they rushed against each other and learned the cause of the demoniacal row. On Captain Tinglum entering the cook's room and finding him roaring beneath the dresser his surprise may be imagined. So may the look with which he regarded Mr Finnikin when that gentleman turned and beheld his commander, but they cannot be adequately described. However Mr Finnikin was an important personage whose authority was but second in the ship and he therefore cared but little for looks. After many groans, grunts, and other equally strong demonstrations of his entire disgust at the unprovoked attack he had received, Blackee arose and confronted Finnikin, who also for the space of one minute confronted him. Then with an horrible grimace Finnikin ordered that dinner be directly administered and, followed by Ned, ascended to the deck.

The vessel was long, very long, low in the water and evidently built for great speed. She was cleaving her way rapidly through the water on the starboard tack. She had been forced to scud with the storm and had thus arrived in exactly the nick of time. Now the wind had chopped to the north-east and she was making for New Orleans, having on board between two and three hundred blacks. The crew were mostly a very brigand-looking set of men, but there were some fine specimens of humanity amongst them. Most were tall and wiry, Mr Finnikin being almost the only exception. There was another though, a certain sailor who went by the name of Mike, his other cognomen being wholly unknown even to himself. He was sort of half an Irishman and between him and Finnikin there often passed very sharp repartees that occasionally ripened to a short struggle, affording an immense amount of merriment for the rest of the crew. But in reality they were firm friends and had known each other from boyhood. Captain Tinglum was not particularly liked—he was much too overbearing to fall in with the tempers of the unruly "do as I dam please" Americans who mainly composed his crew. He was obeyed, however, generally speaking, with willingness and alacrity as every man on board knew and respected him as a good sailor.

After taking a good look at the vessel Ned enquired for his companion and presently found himself in a small cabin, in a berth of which lay Ben in a sort of dreamy half-unconscious state. The blow on his head was very serious and the surgeon ordered that he be kept perfectly quiet. So, after a good survey of him, Ned returned on board. Here he was set to perform several small operations that lasted until darkness set in and those who were not on duty were sent below.

After supper they all collected in the forecastle and jokes, sharp rejoinders, and occasional thumps—not exactly in fun—were the order of the time. Mr Finnikin sat right in front of the cook's fire nursing one of his short stumpy legs and sipping occasionally with great gusto from a glass of grog. On his left hand, lolling against the side of the room, stood the short sailor Mike and beside him Blackee. Mr Finnikin, having indulged in a long pull at the grog, suddenly lifted his shaggy head and enquired where Ned was. That young rascal having presented himself, he was ordered to sit down, take a sip and unfold the history of his adventures. Ned duly complied and, on finishing, the grog was again handed to him while Mr Finnikin euphoniously said "Wal." Here he paused, looked at Ned and ejaculated "Yer cut from schule—did yer?" Ned answered in the affirmative. "Then ef I was schule-bos and catched 'e—guess yer get walloped—slick."

"Ha, ha," grinned Mike and Blackee, the last individual always enjoyed wallopping, that is, administering it, whether in prospective or in imagination. Therefore he put in his oar, and observed "So'd I."

Round turned Finnikin and grinned from ear to ear. "Oh yer wou'd—kalkilate yer'd he slick at it," and with a sneer of extreme contempt he again turned and commenced cross-questioning Ned. But that discreet young gentleman saw no use in letting out that, which by some impossible chance might be turned against him, and soon contrived by feigning sleepiness to retire, and laid his head upon the rolled-up blanket which served as a pillow with a sigh of satisfaction. Without performing the tedious operation of reviewing every action he had engaged in that day, whether good, bad, or indifferent, nay without forming a plan for the morrow, thus showing his negligent nature, Ned shut his eyes, opened his mouth and was soon in the land of dreams. To that shadowy impalpable place we will not follow him but await with patience the rising of the sun, which in due time that rubicund luminary did and shone upon the waste of waters.

To the eye of an observer at a distance nothing could have been more beautiful and soul inspiring than the fine lines, raking masts and immense spread of snow-white canvas which bore the "Lopez" swiftly onwards. But if that same observer could have drawn nearer and nearer until he sat upon the beam, and so could have beheld the length and breadth of her deck, his opinion would doubtless have changed for the worse. Dozens and dozens of blacks with hands tied behind them, covered with filth and with but the slightest clothing stood in long rows awaiting their triennial ablutions by means of a bucket of water thrown over them. The poor creatures turned their white eyeballs in the greatest alarm whenever a heavier sea than usual struck the vessel, causing her to roll and they to lose their equilibrium. As for the crew they had not apparently the slightest compunction for thus treating their fellow creatures, but grinned at the futile efforts of the slaves to preserve themselves in an upright position. Not but that Captain Tinglum was a humane man, he was doubtless a very humane man as he firmly refused to take more than his ship would hold, thereby nearly creating a mutiny. For be it known that almost every man had a certain share in the profits. However when Ned had paid a visit to Ben, who was still sleeping, and ascended upon deck his opinion of the humaneness of Captain Tinglum was very small. Not particularly caring for the sight of so many poor devils he descended to the mess-room and commenced to make a hearty breakfast with some fifteen men served by Blackee. That sable gentleman took good care not to approach too near Mr Finnikin who in a glorious humour presided at the head of the table. He had been thrown into this glorious humour by finding upon arising that morning that his suit of everyday clothes had disappeared and who should take them but Blackee, who would take them but that unscrupulous "nigger", who else could have such a black conscience as to steal a gentleman's standing rigging? Certainly nobody, so wait until after breakfast, you ink bottle. Thus thought and reasoned Mr Finnikin and upon the meal being finished he arose, called Ned to follow him and solemnly strided to the cook's apartment. On entering that sanctum Blackee was discovered licking a plate while his myrmidons, the black beetles, polished a bone. He no sooner beheld Finnikin than, divining like a practiser of the black art, as he was, the purpose of the visit, he would have vanished—but Finnikin was a little too rapid and locked the doors. Then seating himself upon a bench Finnikin began, while Blackee cast fearful glances around in the hope of finding some impossible means of escape.

"I say," said Finnikin, "Yer the mostis abominable black bag of humbuggian bones as iver I set eyes on."

Here Blackee put in his oar and deprecatingly ejaculated, "Massa".

"Massa," answered Finnikin, "I'll massa you, mash yer, I'll smash yer ugly nut ef yer don't out with it at once—ai," continued he warming, "Yer stole my fixing didn't yer neow?" In vain did the trembling black protest that he had never even thought of such dishonest proceeding, in vain did he roll his eyes thus making awful grimaces, in vain did he fall on his knees and join hands in supplicating gesture. Mr Finnikin was not to be turned from his purpose by such "humbuggian nonsich," as he was pleased to term it. Not he, the pleasure of retaliation—that is, of walloping an enemy— was too strong in him to be suppressed. Therefore he commenced operations. By the help of Ned, who did not dare disobey and enjoyed the idea, he bound the black's hands and feet. Then, laying him in the best position, Finnikin seized the hot ladle from the pot and began to bang and bump away. The black-beetles, cockroaches, spiders, imps or what you like, had watched Finnikin's operations from numerous small hiding-places in the vicinity, and, on seeing the tyrant who had anciently knocked them about, they set up a yell of delight, and emerging from their concealment commenced a triumphal dance around their fallen master. While dancing they made certain sounds with the tips of their tongues meant no doubt to express intense satisfaction, but which sounded in the ears of Ned so ridiculous that in spite of his pity for Blackee, who now also began to yell, he burst into a roar of laughter. Finnikin did the same and a most peculiar noise was the result.

Click-it, a Click-it-a, click, click, click went the beetles; ha, ha, ha, sung Finnikin and Ned; whack, smack went the ladle; and as for the yell Blackee made, it was perfectly indescribable. After having basted Blackee in this manner for a considerable period Finnikin suddenly stopped and bawled, "Here yer bittles bang away," and he handed the ladle to the first little imp that applied for it. Then did fearful groans, awful yells, frenzied shouts of laughter, numerous whacks, quantities of wops, innumerable smacks make the air of that apartment in such a state of vibration, that Ned was fain to show the white feather, that is, to evacuate the room and betake himself to the cot of Ben leaving Finnikin and the beetles in their glory.

When he arrived at the cabin, Ben was dressing, as the surgeon had said he might arise and enjoy a little fresh air. His countenance was very pale and he had been evidently seriously hurt. After having embraced, enquired how the other was, and all the other meeting ceremonial rubbish, Ben asked to be informed as to where they were going and on what errand. Upon being told that it was a slave-ship bound for New Orleans, he did not look so mightily overjoyed.

"What shall us do on shore?" asked Ned. "Go to California or how?"

"S'pose it's a good way from Orleans, ain't it?" said Ben.

"Guess it be rather, don't 'xactly know," answered Ned.

"S'pose we turns niggers an' sells ourselves an' then cuts," suggested Ben after a pause.

"Hum, t'wouldn't act, s'pose we buys sum guns and turns hunters?" said Ned.

"Wal, that'll do, s'pose we goes on deck?"

Having thus settled what they were to do on landing, though, it must be admitted, in a very general manner, they ascended the companion ladder, and lolled about the deck in certain undignified, independent positions. Presently however Captain Tinglum observed them and immediately set Ned to work, at the same time casting a severe look on Ben whom he knew at present to be incapable.

The "Lopez" had now run a considerable distance, so far indeed as to be considered out of the way of the British cruisers, and the watch was consequently reduced in numbers. Favourable winds with occasional tough gales bore them swiftly onward for three weeks until Ben had recovered and they entered the Gulf of Mexico. Now the watch was doubled as they had also entered the ground where they might expect to have an exciting chase or two. No one on board expected, guessed or calculated on more than this as they had the greatest confidence in the superior sailing powers of the "Lopez" above those of any British cruiser afloat. This confidence caused the men, who composed the watch, to be much more lax in their work than Captain Tinglum would have allowed had he known of it. The consequence was that one morning a large frigate rapidly nearing on the starboard bow was not perceived until she had advanced within a mile, when the man stationed forward sung out "Ship ahoy." They were within one day's sail of land and the excitement caused by this announcement was tremendous. In the midst of the general hubbub Captain Tinglum remained perfectly cool and would not allow his men to cumber themselves with arms—which they were rapidly doing—as they would not be enabled to perform any necessary manoeuvre with so much speed. All the men saw directly the wisdom of this and stood at their stations in readiness to carry out his further commands. The wind was blowing from the north-eastward, the "Lopez" was cleaving through the water on the larboard tack, while the British frigate, slightly inclined to starboard, was rapidly coming down across the wind. Captain Tinglum immediately ordered his vessel, which was schooner rigged, to be laid upon her starboard tack, so as to run slanting out to sea away from the frigate. As this was being performed, of course the frigate made a considerable way upon them but directly the "Lopez" felt the wind away she went, while the frigate, seeing she was being left behind, hoisted more canvas and fired a shot. The friends, who with nearly every man stood upon deck, were considerably startled upon seeing the white puffs of smoke arise, while at the same moment the water was ploughed up at the stem. "Ha, ha," grinned Finnikin, "blaze away my hearties." To the youths this seemed an insane speech but it is well known that firing slackens speed. The British seemed to know this as they fired no more shots but crowded on as much canvas as their yards would bear. Nor was Captain Tinglum sparing of his sails and the whole vessel seemed one mass of canvas while she appeared to fly through the water. It being a stern chase, the way they were gaining was not so apparent, but in reality they were leaving the frigate far behind. Ben and Ned, standing by the wheel, watched the now distant vessel with intense interest and saw firstly her hull, then her lower sails, disappear beneath the rolling waves.

Now the sun began to rapidly sink until his fiery disk touched the heaving waters; here he for a moment remained apparently stationary, as if taking one long last lingering look ere he retired to rest, then slowly descended until half his disk was hid, when a large wave suddenly washed him out, and darkness began to steal over the sea, for they were in a clime where twilight is of such short duration as not to be noticed. One by one the twinkling stars shone out until the whole heavens were one vast black vault set with sparkling gems of all magnitudes, while in the west the Zodiacal light stretched in the form of a cone of rosy-coloured light high in the heavens.[4] Ben and Ned remained on deck a long time, now gazing at the sky above, now at the scarcely less brilliant sea beneath, and saying but few words. Even Ben's turbulent, restless

---

[4] Jefferies describes the Zodiacal light in the essay 'Sport and Science' (collected in *The Life of the Fields*, 1884) where he writes: 'This very spring (1883), as I walked about a town in the evening, I used to listen to find if I could hear any one mention the zodiacal light, which, just after sunset, was distinctly visible for a fortnight at a time. It was more than usually distinct, a perfect cone, reaching far up into the sky among the western stars. No one seemed to observe it, though it faced them evening after evening.'
 The 'town' to which Jefferies refers was Brighton, where he was living at the time. A notebook entry for 16 March 1883 reads: 'Zodiacal light up to Aries.' (*NB*, p128)

spirit was somewhat subdued by the sight of so many beauties. Truly it was a beautiful night, such a night as one rarely, if ever, sees in misty humid England where half the time the heavens are obscured by clouds. It seemed to them almost sacrilege to break the deep silence, as the crew did by bawling out some bacchannalian song from the recesses of the forecastle. However the spell being broken they felt it could not be renewed, so taking one more glance at the star-spangled sky they descended the companion ladder and, after many impromptu bumps against the sides, managed to reach the forecastle, that sailors' sanctum sanctorum, and, opening the door surveyed the scene of joyous carousal. But they were quickly observed and a shout of "Cum in," immediately arose.

Chapter 8

They immediately did so and were soon seated listening to the tough yarns some of the old sailors told—those who had been round Cape Horn. Occasionally something more substantial was handed them by Finnikin, who again occupied his old place in front of the stove, in the shape of a sip of grog. Not that Finnikin was a sot. On the contrary he "couldn't abear" such goings-on but he did like a glass or two and a pipe to warm his mouth.

Of course he must have a pipe and he had one. A very peculiar pipe it was too with a stone bowl and a stem something between two and three feet long which came into lengths and could be carried in the pocket. Where he procured this pipe, nobody seemed to know although everybody pretended and everybody made a great fuss about it. Everybody else's pipe had a yarn a hundred yards long attached to it, but Finnikin's pipe was unfathomable. "Yer med smoke it, look at it, wink at it, but by Jasus," as Mike used to say, "Yer couldn't dhraw nothin' from it." Some a little wiser than the rest conjectured, nay openly expressed their opinion, that the thing had no yarn at all, but the others were not to be stuffed with such rubbish, they knew there was a yarn and there was a yarn if Finnikin had chosen to have told it. This evening in particular, this particular pipe excited particular attention and Finnikin was particularly pestered on all sides by persons who wished to know the article's history. But it was no use—it only made him savage, got him into a glorious humour, made him drink like an horse to cool his excited feelings and finally made him drunk. That is to say it drove him into a state in which persons are very ready at falling about, grinning and altogether rammed, jammed and primed for all descriptions of mischief. There he sat, leaning as far back as possible without falling, humming Yankee Doodle and telling the most tremendous bouncers[5] to any who chose to question him on his past life.

"Wur was yer barn?" asked a lanthorn-jawed, lathical[6] man leaning at full length upon a bench.

"Oh—yer—wants tu kneow upsters," jerked Finnikin.

"Well yer fool —."

"Who ses yer fool?" shouted Finnikin raising himself, "Cos I'd wallop 'un."

"Oh yer woud—woud yer," said the lathical man sitting upright.

Round turned Finnikin and surveyed the fellow from top to toe. Apparently satisfied he arose and began the twirling of fists by most supposed to be essential to good boxing. "Cum on," he shouted. Up jumped the lathical man, off with his coat displaying to view the smallest proportions ever beheld, even in America. A yell of laughter arose as he swayed his windmill arms about and approached diminutive Finnikin with lengthened strides, and bellicose intentions gleaming from his deep-set gray eyes.

Up jumped the crew and rushed forward that they might get a good view of the display of skill about to take place. As for poor Finnikin he could barely keep upright. However he managed to preserve his equilibrium until Lathy, as he was there and then christened by the crew, punched his nose a little flatter than ever—if that was possible. Then up went his arms and backward fell poor Finnikin to be caught before his head came in forcible contact with the floor by Mike who had rushed forward to help his friend. Being placed on his legs again Finnikin attempted a blow but again overbalanced himself, this time however upsetting his antagonist whose sconce came bang against a seat, and there he lay rubbing the afflicted part and blinking ludicrously. As for Finnikin, he with his head pillowed on Lathy's bosom was

---

[5] Jefferies here seems to be using the word in the sense of 'tall stories', which we were unable to find in any dictionary.
[6] Another word not in the dictionary but presumably meaning 'thin as a lath'.

indulging in several preliminary snores before permanently entering the land of Morpheus—which he presently did in spite of the crew's efforts to keep him awake. Lathy, however, by no means desired to continue the contest; he was settled for the next three days at least.

Matters were in this state when there was a tremendous clattering and pattering of feet above, a rush, the door was thrown open and in ran a sailor shouting, "The Britishiers by gosh, the Britishiers, shiers, shiers," cried he almost choking with excess of hurry to communicate the melancholy fact.

This announcement created a fearful commotion, each man struggling to be the first on deck that they might corroborate the assertion with the testimony of their eyes. The more haste, the less speed is a very true saying and it was now exemplified. At last they all did contrive to bundle on deck and the first thing they saw was a dazzling flash of light followed by a tremendous explosion and a shot flew whistling overhead. In a few moments the facts of the case were plain to everyone on board and they were these. The wind had dwindled to a calm shortly after night had set in. So the British Commander ordered out his boats, and after a two hours pull they had arrived within fifty yards of the "Lopez" before their presence was discovered by the sleepy watch.

Captain Tinglum was on deck and he gave his orders with coolness and precision. He caused the two four-pounders they possessed, and which were loaded almost to the muzzle with musket bullets, to be run one to starboard and the other on the stern, so as to sweep the deck should the British gain possession of it. The men were immediately armed—which operation seemed done by magic, such is the power of willingness—and stationed along the sides. Hardly were these orders obeyed when the first boat ran alongside and its crew, with a loud hurrah, commenced to scramble on board. This would have been comparatively easy as the "Lopez" was low in the water, had the bright rows of muskets, now pouring forth their deadly contents, been empty. But now it was not such an easy achievement for the slavers had tremendous advantages, if not in numbers, yet in position, and many a man was flung back by the deadly shower to rise to more. Ben and Ned, not knowing what else to do got behind the main mast, but the position was soon rendered untenable by another boat attacking from the opposite side and bullets flew about very uncomfortably. The continued flashing of the muskets, pistols and at intervals a great gun banished darkness, so that the friends, who now wandered like melancholy sprites about the deck, thus making themselves capital targets, could see the combat with great ease. But they actually began to think about retiring below when Captain Tinglum brushed past and saved them from that infamous proceeding by handing Ben a musket, Ned a pistol with some cartridges, and pointing aloft. They immediately understood and scudded up like lamplighters inside the shrouds thereby in a great measure escaping observation, although Ben had a pike thrust through the lower portion of his coat uncomfortably near the seat of honour. Seating themselves comfortably on the cross trees they began to choose a proper person to pay a heavy compliment to, but for some time this was impossible as no one kept still for a longer period than one crack, and neither of the youths professed to be a good shot. Ben however quickly got tired of aiming and so, taking the article down again, as a man, evidently an officer, was about to roll upon deck—he fired. When the smoke had cleared away Ben found that the man was nowhere to be seen; he had probably fallen overboard. Somewhat encouraged by this success they blazed away at a rattling rate, so fast indeed that as Ned fired the last of the cartridges into a marine they began to attract attention, and a few bullets whistling by hastened their otherwise rapid descent—of course for more ammunition. But somehow Captain Tinglum could not be found, search and search as they would, so laying down, each began to reflect upon the best thing to be done. While they were thus intellectually engaged, the combat grew faster and faster. Two more boats came up, each containing twenty men and a large pivot gun. This reinforcement gave the British awful odds and the slavers' men began to yield. As this was observed, a tremendous cheer arose from the attacking party and thirty men, closely followed by others, leapt upon the deck of the "Lopez." Then began a fearful hand-to-hand fight in which the combatants only beheld each other when the flashes from the boat's guns for a moment banished darkness. The friends were now obliged to arise as the surging mass of struggling men would have quickly crushed any poor person so unlucky as to be beneath. Occasionally, as a shot struck the vessel crashing through the woodwork, a fearful yell arose from below—from the blacks who, chained to the under-deck, were in continued expectation of death. The British by superior numbers—for the slavers fought with desperation now—drove them back towards the stern where stood Captain Tinglum, match in hand, watching for an opportunity to sweep the deck. Several times his hand approached the touch-hole but he quickly drew it back as his own men stood in the way. He seemed to bear almost a charmed life as bullet after bullet was sent flying towards him, but still Captain Tinglum rejoiced in the possession of a whole skin. As he was a tall man and in a prominent position this was the more remarkable, but Brown Bess[7] was never particularly true in her shooting capacity. The two friends with considerable good sense, if not a great portion of valour, had long ago disappeared down the hatchway, ostensibly for the purpose of bringing up Mr Finnikin. They found him still sleeping but Lathy had vanished, probably gone to the dogs long ago. By dint of forcibly applying his knuckles to the appendage from which apparently proceeded peculiar sounds, Ben managed to bang into him a little appreciation of his disgraceful position. In short, he awoke, sat up, winked and looked like an owl in daylight.

"Wal", he presently ejaculated, "what's the row?"

At that moment Captain Tinglum, seeing the way pretty clear of his men, applied the match and off went the article, killing some half dozens and wounding others innumerable. Up jumped Finnikin, now wide-awake and perfectly sober, "Gosh," he shouted "what's up—Britishiers?"

"Yes," answered Ben.

No sooner was he sure of the fact than drawing a pistol from his pocket Finnikin rushed to the companion ladder and had ascended about halfway, when two dozen valiant Britons simultaneously jumped into the orifice, making a rapid descent and crushing unfortunately burly Finnikin. The ship was in fact taken. The gun Captain Tinglum fired was the slavers' last resource; it had produced a momentary effect but nothing more. The British quickly pinioned the slavers' men and placed them in the boats while the blacks, in the exhilaration of victory, were set loose by the sailors and danced about on deck, uttering the most absurd noises and, as Lathy observed, as he, not being killed, was handed into a boat, "raisin de Hal considerable."

The black race never have much control of their feelings and it cannot therefore be much wondered that the poor wretches should hail their liberation with the most extravagant demonstrations of joy.

---

[7] Nickname (origin uncertain) of the British Army's musket.

Ben and Ned with Finnikin, who groaned ludicrously, were treated as prisoners and bundled into a boat. Blackee the cook was left on board the "Lopez" to serve those who had charge of her and at first the poor man knew not whether it would be proper for him to bellow with grinning or to blubber. But when he saw Finnikin disappear over the side into a boat Blackee understood and, mingling with his sable brethren who danced around the mast to a rat-a-tat-tat performed with a thwart[8] upon the deck by a fat "ol' nigger", shuffled it with the best.

On arriving upon the frigate the prisoners were all sent down below and confined wherever there was room for them. Ben and Ned stuck to Finnikin and were locked in a small cabin there to spend the night—the two youths in sleeping, he in groaning and lamenting the loss of his reputation and part of the cutaneous covering of his nose. However the longest night will have an end, so Finnikin remembered, but not until looking through the cabin window he discovered certain rosy streaks of light which, to his experienced eye, denoted the approach of morning. And he was not mistaken: in a few minutes the sun arose above a bank of red-tinged clouds and displayed to view his rubicund claret visage. Finnikin, on observing him (why the sun should be 'him' is a question), uttered a peculiar sound usually represented in black and white as 'Tchek', three times in rapid succession. Then turning on his heel he awoke Ben, doubtless by punching.

"Hulloa," shouted that hero rolling about under the influence of the punch Finnikin had bestowed exactly upon the place where Aldermen are popularly supposed to deposit their turtle.[9] "Hulloa," he said again, looking as if mystified at the cabin, Finnikin and the sleeping Ned. Having satisfied his curiosity he arose and enquired of Finnikin what was the matter. Whereupon that burly flat-nosed personage approached him in such close proximity that had he come of cannibal stock Ben's ear would have been in chancery.[10]

"I say youngster," whispered Finnikin in the before-mentioned organ, thereby breaking his word, "I say," he continued.

"Wal," said Ben, who had begun to get Americanized.

---

[8] A rower's bench across a boat.
[9] Ben's stomach presumably, 'turtle' being turtle-soup.
[10] In an awkward predicament (*slang*).

"We ain't gwain to quod[11]—mind that neow," communicated Finnikin under his breath and contradicting facts, for were they not in a British frigate bound for Sierra Leone and then for England?

This fact was at the moment uppermost in Ben's mind and in spite of his entire reliance on Finnikin he only said "Ain't we?"

"Neow," quoth Finnikin "we ain't, anyhow we won't—cos we'll get stretched—twon't fit yer see."

"Whew!" whistled Ben—that idea had never struck him before, but now it appeared almost certain that they would some fine morning appease the vulgar appetite for the horrible. It did not seem particularly desirable and he now perfectly agreed with Finnikin that they must not go to "quod." But how to obvert the necessity of making acquaintance with that place where you are fed and clothed and strangled without the slightest trouble or expense to your relations, your wife, your family? That was a difficult question to answer. For the present, in fact, it was unanswerable, but Finnikin said that doubtless something would turn up and in the meantime they had better conduct themselves decorously—like turtle doves—and appear perfectly destitute of any hope of escape. Ben promised he would and they then awoke the sleeping Ned. When he had recovered the perfect use of his faculties, which was greatly expedited by sundry bumps judiciously expended, he was made aware of their purpose and duly cautioned. He also promised to keep his own counsel except to his two more intimate friends. Hardly had he made this laudable resolution and expressed it sufficiently loud to catch Finnikin's ear without awakening suspicion to any possible eavesdroppers, when the door was unlocked and breakfast shoved in. All three were beginning to feel a little hungry: consequently the food thus unceremoniously given was not despised and they made a hearty meal. Afterwards they all and each relapsed into silence, probably contemplating (at least Ben was) the desirable position they now possessed, and the still more desirable, because more elevated, position which would be theirs upon arriving at the land of his birth.

Presently Mr Finnikin started to his feet and struck his forehead as if trying to knock something in. Apparently successful he approached Ben in his ancient position and whispered, "I kneows." Then without waiting to answer Ben's euphonious "Wal?" he withdrew and made the

---

[11] Prison (*slang*).

same communication to Ned. He then sat down, knocked his two fists together, popped his head between his knees and remained in that position—deaf to questions—until the cabin door was again opened and they were ordered on deck. Here they were permitted to disport themselves in any posture for nearly two hours, always under the eyes of armed marines, and were then sent below and locked up for the remaining portion of the day.

The frigate went by the name of the "Oporto". It was armed with thirty-five guns and manned by two hundred and sixty British tars—not nearly sufficient to properly work the guns. They were enough however to work the frigate and to keep the slavers' men, now reduced to thirty-eight, well under.

The captured vessel sailed alongside with just sufficient men to keep her in tolerable trim with the greater number of the slaves on board. For a whole week they sailed quietly forward without anything of importance occurring; the slavers' men of course looked particularly black but the voyage seemed likely to be a prosperous one. Although Ben and Ned were continually hammering away at Mr Finnikin yet not the slightest information as to his plan escaped him, he only repeated the mysterious action of rubbing his knuckles. When it came out that he had been an officer he was allowed much more freedom of movements and was allowed to stay on deck twice as long as the others—saving Captain Tinglum—and several other small privileges. Doubtless he made good use of them, so on we go.

It was Monday night; the watch was nodding in a corner when he suddenly coughed awake and looked around—nothing but the silent deck and equally silent sky. The sea could scarcely be called silent as it occasionally dashed against the stern but the noise it made was little, very little. The stars shone and although he looked attentively at them yet he could see nothing peculiar, no comet, no meteor, nothing but a quantity of sparkling winking points looking calmly down upon him. The wind was but little, barely enough to give the vessel steerage way. Seeing all this and hearing nothing suspicious the man thought all was right and leaning his head against the bulwark looked up into the sky and fixed his gaze on a ruddy-hued gem. As he looked at it a strange kind of dreamy stupor came over him and he did not notice that the deck was getting covered with moving figures. He thought of home, of his Highland lassie and his "twa bonnie bairns", now probably fast asleep, and wished himself with them. Completely absorbed thus he saw not three men, tall, thin but wiry men take the man at the wheel and gag him, heard not the stifled shout which arose. Suddenly he felt a hand at his throat, the knuckles were pressed firmly in so that he could utter no sound save a slight gurgle, and at the same time his arms and legs were firmly pinioned. Where were his bright visions now? Gone, utterly gone, and in their place arose the certainty that he was a gagged, bound, helpless, ill-used mortal, and as such lay quiet. But if he was still others were not, the whole thirty-eight slavers' men were moving slowly about upon the deck and obeying the commands of their ancient captain. Softly and slowly the long boat was lowered into the sea and man by man she was filled, almost to overflowing, but the waves were small, although fortunately the wind was rising. Ben, Ned, Finnikin and the captain occupied the stern while the others gently pulled, as the oars were not muffled, in the direction of the "Lopez", whose black hull was plainly visible about one hundred yards distant. In a few moments they arrived within ten or fifteen yards of her and then commenced the most difficult part of the undertaking—how to secure the man at the wheel without being discovered. But ordering under his breath the men to lay on their oars a few yards from the "Lopez", which was slowly passing through the water, Captain Tinglum divested himself of his coat and gently slipped overboard. Finnikin quickly did the same and the two quickly disappeared in the darkness. They soon made the broadside, which as before stated was low in the water, and scrambling in commenced to crawl towards the wheel. But they had no need to have been so cautious as the man had lashed it and surrendered himself to the arms of Morpheus. He consequently proved an easy prey and, having secured him, the two commenced a laborious and diligent search for the watch on hands and knees, but to their surprise found none. This considerably simplified the business, so having fastened down the hatches Finnikin approached the stern and uttered a low, a very low, whistle. In a few moments the boat bumped alongside, the men filed on board and could, with difficulty, be restrained from giving a tremendous cheer. But half a crack employed in reflection, and that is a long time for sailors, convinced them that it would be an extraordinary foolish proceeding and without a murmur they relinquished the idea. They then stood to their stations and soon made all sail in accordance to Captain Tinglum's directions in an almost contrary direction to that the vessel had been proceeding. The wind had considerably heightened and to their delight continued to do so to such a degree that in three hours the crew of the "Lopez" could not even doubt the successful issue of their enterprise. But it was not terminated yet, they were still five or six days good swift sailing from New Orleans and there were eighteen men below, all well-armed. Still, they were asleep, which circumstance would give the attackers great advantages, and Captain Tinglum resolved not to let the opportunity pass. He therefore ordered all the men that could be spared and himself led the way. As Finnikin had predicted all were easily "fixed", that is, pinioned, excepting one or two who awoke and offered some resistance. But on seeing the enormous odds against them they also yielded and the victory was complete. As for the slaves—some two hundred were on board—nobody expected the slightest trouble from them. Nor was there.

When morning broke upon a rough sea, a south-easterly gale, the "Lopez" bounding merrily along under its influence, the poor wretches found themselves in the hands of those whom they had hoped never more to behold. A loud yell arose and flinging themselves on the lower deck they indulged in the bitterest despair. Thus it is ever with the uneducated natives of Africa, one moment they are transported with joy, the next plunged in the abyss of grief. Let not this be understood to also apply to the civilised "nigger."

By no means. I grant that he has a few grains of self-control and concentrated action but even he has but little. Almost at the same moment that the yell of despair arose from the "Lopez", one of surprise mingled with rage came from the decks of the "Oporto". The commander of that diddled vessel conceived upon awaking in the morning that she was rocking and rolling in a very singular and unaccountable manner. To find out the cause he arose and, on arriving upon deck, what was his surprise to see two pinioned men, the ship perfectly at the mercy of the waves, and seas from time to time dashing over her? It was unbounded. He was astonished but in a moment the truth burst upon him and he rushed forward to unbind the man at the wheel. On finding himself released the man sat up but for some time could not speak owing to the gags having been so long in his mouth, although the captain was stamping, almost raving, before him. Presently he managed to gasp out in answer to the rapid incoherent enquiries of the captain, "T'was 'em." This brief speech confirmed the captain's suspicions and he tumbled below to order immediate pursuit. He did not stop to examine the prisoners' apartments, he knew it would be useless and he could not waste time. Soon the whole two hundred and sixty diddled sailors were aware of the disaster, which at one blow shattered their hopes of prize money, and then arose the above-mentioned yell. Vengeance, vengeance was the cry, partly embodied in the eloquent shakings of fists, partly in the growls of "D—n 'em," which the presence of their commander hardly suppressed. But they were too much enraged to waste time in vain threats. Besides, the position of the ship, as the wind had considerably risen since the discovery, was getting imminently dangerous. They therefore huddled on a slight clothing and hastened to obey the impatient captain, who trumpet in hand was bawling and shouting unintelligible orders by the dozen. All of which were shortly obeyed, and the frigate, being rounded to, was sent speeding on her way to intercept, if possible, the fugitives before they arrived at New Orleans. As for the unfortunate watch and the man at the wheel, both were solemnly assured of their future walloping, and both, not being able to offer anything like a reasonable excuse for their behaviour, hung down their heads and believed the assurance.

Captain Tinglum having had a happy example set him of the risk attending an insufficient watch resolved to take warning by others' misfortunes. Which resolution he carried out to the full and the result was that early one fine morning he entered the mouth of the Mississippi without having seen even a sign of the dished "Oporto". Up the noble river they went with a favouring wind right into the city of New Orleans and were presently moored to a wharf, which partly belonged to the "Lopez" owners, who received Captain Tinglum with every mark of genteel joy or rather satisfaction. They lazily climbed up the side and critically examined the blacks while Captain Tinglum was relating the story of his adventures and escape from the British. Genteel astonishment appeared in their faces as they listened to the tale and, on its conclusion, they with great suavity shook him cordially by the hand and invited him to dine with them. This was the extreme length their generosity could go but was declined with thanks, Captain Tinglum urging as an excuse his wish to disembark the slaves. Directly he refused, their politeness doubled, they pressed him with anxious faces, nay would have used force had it accorded with genteel bearing. But Captain Tinglum would not retract his word and the "great guns" as

Finnikin termed them had to sheer off with every mark of regret. No sooner had they disappeared than Captain Tinglum ordered that disembarkation should commence. Accordingly long rows of blacks soon began to file down the plank which connected the "Lopez" to the wharf, each with his hands tied behind and casting curious glances around. Thus they marched through the crowded streets of New Orleans until their owner's yard and covered building prepared for their reception were reached, when they were singly released and shoved into a square place, enclosed on every side by high walls. In one corner was a small covered building used as a sleeping apartment and littered with straw. Here they had to pass the time, some groaning, grumbling, grunting, others dancing, others singing something in their own unintelligible gibberish, until it was convenient to the Messieurs Dible, Dible and Quits to hold an auction. Which they did in three days and at which Ben, Ned and Finnikin were strolling about as spectators.

Somehow, for it would have puzzled him to explain how, there had sprung up in the heart of the rough sailor Martin Finnikin a deep attachment to the youths. Whether it was having no child of his own, or what, he could never rightly understand. His had been a roving, lawless wild life. At one time he had been an hunter ranging over the boundless prairies and woods of Mexico and Texas, later a miner in California, and later still a sailor. His great strong common sense, fearlessness and daring had caused his rapid rise in the latter profession, but it was not the thing in which Finnikin rejoiced. He still remembered how free he had been when chasing the buffalo on his brave mustang, still wished to be flinging the circling lasso, still thought of his unerring rifle. In the hurry and bustle of the day these thoughts were never uppermost but in the still, dark hours of the night they came over him with irresistible force, and at such times Finnikin would arise and walk the deck. Finnikin's was not a poetical or romantic disposition; he well knew that in the eyes of the world he now held a much higher position than as a half-clad wild hunter. He was now fast verging on fifty and, as each year flew swiftly on, he lamented the days gone by and resolved that each voyage should be his last. But the urgent entreaties of Captain Tinglum, joined with the tempting bait of gold he held out, had hitherto prevented him carrying out his resolution. Now however, when he saw two mere youths on the point of throwing into the desert, the example was too strong, too much accorded with his natural inclination, and resisting the offers Captain Tinglum made of still higher wages, Finnikin threw up his appointment and joined the youths, who joyfully hailed him as a companion and guide. Two days afterwards the "Lopez" hoisted her snow-white canvas and sailed away on her ancient errand of evil. After seeing her well out of sight the youths and Finnikin, who had stood upon the wharf turned and plunging into the crowded streets made for the auction mart. They arrived exactly in time to see the first trembling wretch put up for sale. Intending bidders were requested to examine the "article", which they did by making the black jump and open his mouth, and by punching him to try his soundness. When the auctioneer conceived that the "animal" had been sufficiently examined he began operations by giving the desk before him a smart rap to attract attention. Then clearing his throat in the most approved style he with various appropriate pauses started the following speech:

"Genel'men, here's a fust-rate article, warranted sound, good bellis, rale muscle an' twenty-five. Look at him neow, five feet ten, plenty of ballast an' awfully skeared. Genel'men, I say buy 'un. Neow auction begins."

Whereupon he flourished the hammer and brought it down bang upon the desk again, thereby almost drowning the first bid of two hundred dollars. But his ear had been too well schooled to pass over even the slightest indication of a bid and he shouted apparently savage, "Two hundred dollars, harky neow." He had not long to remain in a state of pretended rage as a little man with two bright eyes, hands in pockets, and a snuffling voice pushed forward, closely followed by one still shorter with one eye and a red necktie, and snuffled, "Three hundred." "Ah," sighed the affectionate auctioneer, "Not so mean, three hundred,"—"and fifty," shouted the one-eyed man, finishing the speech for him. "Eighty," sung out someone behind. "Four hundred," snuffled the little man, elevating one eyebrow. "An' fifty," bellowed the dwarf. "Seventy," shouted the snuffler, now getting into a fearful state of nervous anxiety while his burly antagonist remained perfectly cool. "Five hundred," shouted someone in the crowd. A pause ensued and the auctioneer took it up. "Five hundred, genel'men offered only five hunderd, a rate article." "Fifty," cried the snuffler, and bidding recommenced. "Seventy," calmly cried the dwarf, apparently enjoying his antagonist's anxiety. "Six hundred," gasped the snuffler, wiping his forehead of the perspiration. The crowd now desisted from bidding and all attention centred on the fidgety snuffler and the one-eyed resolute dwarf who now shouted "Eighty," thereby making a bold step and probably thinking to crush the other by it. "Goin' goin'," shouted the auctioneer with tremendous hammer flourishes. "Seven hundred," gasped the snuffler. The dwarf looked at him and grinned, he then bellowed "fifty," and the snuffler was now obliged to retire as he could not afford more for what he now designated "a bit of unedicated lumber." Having watched the sale for some time the friends began to feel what Finnikin called a little "peckish", and left the place to resort to a cook's shop, there to indulge in the "needcessities" of life and discuss future operations.

Chapter 9

In this cook's shop we will, for the present leave them and using the well-known and equally well-used privilege of writers, put on a pair of imaginative seven-leagued boots and after a few preliminary skips, hop with one gigantic bound from the New World to the Old, and alighting in the parlour of Mrs Smales remain there in the form of some persevering smoke which will not go up the chimney.

"Dear, dear," ejaculated the poor old lady, "What shall I do, suffocated by the smoke, freezing with the doors open? Oh dear, Oh, dear, Ooo de-ar."

Here a pantomimic throwing up of hands ensued, trying to drive back the detestable smoke. But it was no use and giving up the attempt she continued her work of darning stockings with exemplary patience. Suddenly there came a slight knock at the door. "Come in," cried the old lady. Whereupon a smiling, short-petiticoated damsel appeared and, opening her enchanting mouth, thus began.

"If you please ma'am, it's Master ma'am, he's come back ma'am, and—."

What other "ma'am" she was about to say, no one can tell but at that moment Doctor Smales himself in all his prim severity brushed past and shut the door in the poor girl's face. Seating himself by the fire the Doctor leaned back in his chair and groaned.

Mrs Smales, who was apparently seated on upright pins, now timidly and under her breath enquired what was the matter and whether he had found them. Without taking the slightest notice of her questions the Doctor indulged in a loud soliloquy, to which his mother listened with an awful expression of countenance.

"To think," quoth the Doctor, "To think that I—I—a man of my ability should have wasted a whole month in hunting those vermin, those ungrateful wretches, who now peacefully—aye peacefully repose beneath the sea."

Here Mrs Smales arose all trembling and echoed inquiringly, "Beneath the sea?"

"Aye," answered the Doctor, "I found their track at last—they went to sea from Bristol and the ship was lost, pieces have been washed ashore."

Mrs Smales gave a terrified, shocked scream, and sunk back upon her chair. But had she known only what Doctor Smales knew and not what he hoped she would have been considerably less frightened. The fact was he had ascertained that the fugitives had sailed for America but by continually repeating to himself the wish that they might be drowned he had began to regard it as the truth, and as such communicated it to his worthy mother. When he thought Mrs Smales had sufficiently digested the length and breadth of the matter, he arose and saying, "I'm going to Snicks and Tubbs, shan't be back till night," jumped into his carriage and departed.

After about an hour's drive he arrived before the residence of Ned's father and was presently admitted to the presence of that august personage. Gently as he could the Doctor broke the news to the disconsolate parent who stared at him like one possessed for the space of two minutes, then, uttering various endearing epithets, stamped around the room pulling his hair. Suddenly he stopped in his violent perambulations and rang a hand bell. A servant immediately appeared and was ordered to bring a greatcoat. Mr Snicks then turned to the Doctor and requested to be allowed to ride with him as far as Mrs Tubbs's, whither he made no doubt the pedagogue was going. Doctor Smales politely replied that he should be most happy to have the pleasure of his company, and Mr Snicks, having enveloped himself in his greatcoat, first offered some refreshment, which was refused, and then led the way to the carriage.

On entering they were rapidly driven to their destination, and on the way Mr Snicks communicated in faltering accents his intention of "shuttin' up shop" and taking his departure to search for Ned. Doctor

Smales gently tried to persuade him not to, that is, egged him on until they arrived before the residence of the ex-groceress, Mrs Tubbs.

She, dear old lady, was sitting disconsolate before a large fire thinking of "poor, poor Ben" as she now always designated that young scoundrel, when the rattle of wheels, which seemed to stop before her door, disturbed her meditations. Up she jumped and rushed to the window there to behold the equipage of Doctor Smales. Dismal thoughts now chased one another with fearful rapidity through her melancholy brain, and the moment Doctor Smales entered the room he was requested to tell her the truth at once. Which that pedagogue did and murmuring "gone to Ameriky" Mrs Tubbs sank to the ground, almost fainting. Of course, as there were two gentlemen in the room, she was not allowed to remain a moment in that position and Doctor Smales lifted her into a chair while Mr Snicks furiously rang for water. That paragon of housemaids Sarah appeared instantly—she had been listening outside—to disappear and reappear in the same time with a bucket of the pure element. Lifting this in his gigantic arms Mr Snicks was about to bestow a bath gratis when, luckily for her best dress, Mrs Tubbs awoke and waved her delicate hand as if disclaiming all idea of swooning. Then Mr Snicks relinquished his intention and the bucket to Sarah, who nevertheless remained watching the proceedings. From time to time, as Mrs Tubbs sighed, she ejaculated consolingly, "dear, dear." Presently, however, "Missis" recovered and Sarah was dismissed to communicate the joyful intelligence of "Master Ben's gone to Amerikay" to her partner the cook who was bedizening herself in the attic.

When Mr Snicks conceived that Mrs Tubbs had perfectly recovered the use of her faculties he communicated his project, insinuating that, at the same time, he could search for Ben if his travelling expenses were half borne. Mrs Tubbs eagerly caught at the idea, much quicker than he had expected, and in the excess of her appreciation of the notion offered a guinea a day. But Mr Snicks assured her that he could not think of taking such a heavy remuneration from a "sister in misfortune" but would be well satisfied with half that amount.

Mrs Tubbs was on the point of closing with this proposal when Doctor Smales, who had heard Mr Snicks with intense detestation, suggested that it would be the better plan to offer a certain sum, say eighty guineas, to any one who would bring Ben home alive and kicking. Mr Snicks here cast a savage glance at the Doctor who repaid the compliment with one of extreme contempt. Mrs Tubbs, not noticing this little interchange of civilities, now said that she should place the matter in the hands of Doctor Smales, in whom she expressed herself to have the greatest confidence. That gentleman said he was almost overwhelmed with the honour but promised that he would use his utmost endeavours to find her son.

Hereupon he rose to depart and Mr Snicks did the same as in duty bound but as a last resource said with a bow, "Then I am to consider myself engaged at half a guinea per day?" But Mrs Tubbs only referred him to the Doctor and, with another bow to conceal his mortification, Mr Snicks departed. Doctor Smales truly enjoyed walloping, it mattered not what, so long as it had feeling and could show it. He therefore accepted the honour Mrs Tubbs conferred on him with delight—it gave him the opportunity of mentally thrashing Mr Snicks, whom he knew would most assuredly depart in search of Ned, Ben and eighty guineas.

And so it turned out that in a week's time Mr Snicks, having concluded arrangements with Doctor Smales, sailed for New York in about as savage a mood as possible.

As for Doctor Smales, he returned to his old round of instructing miniature men while his mother darned stockings, and Mrs Tubbs gave tea parties and sometimes supper parties. Thus all carried on their ancient business and we, by a sort of imaginative electric telegraph, will transport ourselves to the other side of the "herring pond", that is, to America.

oooOOOooo

It was evening on one of the immense prairies of Texas, the sun was sinking fast, and a slight wind waved the tall grass around a small coppice which appeared as an island of wood in the midst of a sea of vegetation. Three hunters with their rifles lying near sat around a sparkling fire, at which the eldest of the three was cooking a large piece of deer's-meat. "By jingo," quoth one whom we recognise as Ben, "how long's that gwain to be?"

"Ha, ha," grinned the addressed party, "Yer peckish, air yer?" by which speech we know him as Mr Finnikin, who as neither Ben or Ned understood the mysteries of cooking was obliged to turn cook for the nonce. Presently the meat was pronounced "dun" and speedily commenced to disappear before the mighty bowie knives which from time to time attacked it.

"Good!" ejaculated Martin as he finished the last morsel.

"Jolly!" echoed the youths and, leaning back in an attitude generally supposed to be extremely unfavourable to digestion, they grunted forth sighs evidently of intense satisfaction.

Mr Finnikin also leant back, but it was against a tree, and commenced to sing or rather hum a favourite verse of his –

My Nancy was a lovely girl
I niver seed none sweeter
I allus loved to kiss her well
She war a splendid creature.

which lasted with some variations until the sun sunk and darkness fell like a pall over the earth. Then all three rolled themselves in blankets and drowsily saying "Good Night" were soon sleeping.

They were on their way for California but as yet had not made more than sixty miles because Finnikin judged it best to let the youths get a little used to the rifle 'ere entering the territory of the Indians. They had therefore been merely moving about for the last week but on the morrow proposed starting for the far-famed goldfields.

Early in the morning, then, Finnikin awoke the slumbering youths and, having made a slight repast, they mounted on their mustangs, who had been tethered near, and rode forward at a gentle pace. When in England both Ben and Ned had been much addicted to the exhilarating practice of riding refractory donkeys and were therefore in capital training. For he who can ride a gypsy's donkey — which they could — can ride anything. As for Finnikin, once on, his old skill returned and he now sat his horse with the ease of a Comanche. And that is saying something, for those Indians are a sort of modern centaur and from childhood may be said to live in the saddle, thus saving the squaws the trouble of rocking cradles.

All that day the three rode forward only stopping for an hour at midday when the almost overhead sun was unbearable. Once or twice they passed a settler's habitation but they were few and far between; and when they stopped for the night Finnikin calculated that they had passed the last hut for three and probably four hundred miles of alternate prairie and wood. They had entered the country of the Indians and the greatest caution must be observed. They must now shoot only when necessity compelled, while watch must be kept by one or the other all night supposing that they wished to preserve their scalps. As they sat around the fast dying embers that night Finnikin communicated this to the youths who promised in every respect to carry out his injunctions.

That night Finnikin said he should keep the first watch of two and a half hours, then Ben and lastly Ned. By this arrangement he gave the youths plenty of time to recruit their strength for the morrow. Having acquainted them with this intention he seized his rifle and leant against a tree and the youths seeing him thus employed rolled over and commenced to sleep. As for snoring Finnikin would allow of no such thing, it would betray their presence he said, and whenever any indications of such a proceeding appeared the offending party invariably received a punch. But by this time no punching was required as they were both pretty well schooled to sleeping quietly. When Finnikin considered that about three hours had gone by he awoke Ben and, pointing out a large star, told him to awaken Ned when it was over a prominent tree. Ben promised he would and Finnikin enjoining him not to sleep rolled himself up in a blanket and lay down.

Ben, who was half asleep, took his stand against the tree and stared at the particular star endeavouring by fixing his attention upon it to cast off drowsiness. But in spite of himself his eyes would close occasionally and each time for a longer period, so that upon opening them he presently found it impossible to distinguish that particular star from any other and giving up the attempt to find it, resolved to go by guess. He then thought of his present peculiar position, thought of this, thought of that, but could not fix his thoughts upon anything, and yet he could feel that if he did not think he must sleep. No earthly power could keep him from sleeping thought he, and murmured "no, no." But thinking of sleeping soon began to exercise tremendous power and, at last unable to control himself longer, his jaw fell down, his eyes shut of their own accord, and he began to snore most vociferously. How long he thus remained he knew not. All he could remember was that he suddenly fancied himself standing on the edge of a precipice, that the earth gave way and he felt himself sinking, sinking down an unfathomable place, then came the sensation of flying through the air followed by his coming in contact with some soft substance, which shrieked out but broke his fall and he found himself looking up into the star-spangled sky, while the soft substance beneath was heaving and groaning.

It was in fact Ned upon whom he had descended with tremendous force and crushed out the shriek. When he came to a sense of his position, which was materially aided by the numerous blows Ned bestowed upon him, he rolled off and sat up. In a short time, having satisfied Ned who had seized his rifle, that he was neither an Indian nor a bear, he announced it as his intention to keep watch another hour as a sort of punishment for his former conduct. Hearing this joyful news Ned laid down while Ben again leant against the tree and began to search for the particular star. At length he satisfied himself that he had found it and resolving never to lose sight again commenced to stare the poor creature out of countenance. Whilst thus engaged the most monstrous absurdities flitted across his mind in reference to the particular star. He fancied that he could see the inhabitants of the twinkling thing compounded of sixteen different animals all twisting and twirling about in a ball or celestial dance. Presently he himself alighted upon the star having been drawn thither by its magnetic twinkling, and was immediately employed in the dance by a beauteous creature made up of an old shoe, a few wafers, and a couple of tea-caddies. This engaging article took him by the arm and, directing a melting glance from its deep green eyes, enchanted him. Round and round they flew to the music of the spheres while the creature kept murmuring a humming accompaniment. He thought it never would end and had almost danced his legs off, when she, or rather it, dexterously steering through dozens of the like articles flung him into an armchair. Now this was a most desirable thing, but the confounded article began to run backwards from the shock, until reaching the edge of the star it toppled over just as a most tremendous shake of the double drums by Jupiter himself split his ears and he awoke. Awoke and found an overpowering smell of sulphur, the sun shining brightly on him, Mr Finnikin loading his rifle and Ned grinning.

"Yer a pretty felloer—ain't yer neow?" said Finnikin as he rammed the bullet home with great emphasis. "Yer wur snoring like ole Hal[12]—but I shou'dn't a fired onlie I kalkilate it 'ud skear yer more—Yer see."

---

[12] Presumably a euphemism for 'all hell'.

Ben presently said he did see and sat down to make a slight meal. It over, the three mounted upon horseback with rifles at saddle bow[13] and bowie knives stuck in belts, and away they went at a swinging pace — through the tall prairie grass sometimes reaching to the knee, occasionally over a large plot of short greensward, and then entering a forest: a solemn looking forest of gnarled oak trees placed at some distance apart and all apparently many centuries old. Such a forest in England would have suggested mysterious Druid rites and mistletoe; in America it gave rise to thoughts of remorseless scalping Indians. As yet they had not seen a single member of the latter named fraternity although diligent watch was kept on all sides. Huge herds of buffalo were occasionally sighted and fled at their approach, while deer would sometimes start almost from under their horses' feet. Flocks of wild turkeys — enormous birds — rose from time to time and, wheeling high in the air, flew towards the south.

As evening drew near they entered another forest of altogether a different description; here the trees grew thick and were matted with various creepers in one thick impenetrable wall of vegetation. There was no passing through this forest but by the winding buffalo paths trodden deep in the earth, which allowed but one horseman at a time and were frequently obstructed by creepers, under which the buffaloes had passed but which Finnikin — who rode foremost — was obliged to cut down with his hatchet. Few persons, once well in such a forest, would find their way out again, but Finnikin was a regular Indian in all but the colour of his skin, and even then, there was but slight difference. Just as the sun sunk they entered a sort of clearing some fifty yards in diameter which offered a capital place for a bivouac, especially as a large pool of water stood nearly in the centre. To this pool it was evident that the buffaloes came to drink as not only the path they had been following but five or six others coming from various directions led down to it.

"Rippin'," quoth Finnikin as he emerged from the path into the above-described clearing, "cou'dn't a been better."

"Why?" asked Ben who followed him; which question was echoed by Ned who also followed him.

"Why?" answered Finnikin dismounting, "Ere's sum grass, sum water, sum buffalo to be leathered and what not."

---

[13] The arched front part of a saddle, aka the pommel.

Ben chuckled, he delighted in shooting and was already tolerably expert with his rifle, which he involuntarily cocked.

"Cum off yer 'osses," said Finnikin and down they jumped. He then led the horses or rather mustangs a considerable distance back into the buffalo path and there tethered them. Then returning he began to cast about for a good place where it would be possible to have a fair shot at one of these enormous animals, which he knew would shortly make their appearance. Presently he selected a large tree, thickly covered with moss and creepers, into this he mounted and was soon followed by the youths.

"Yer kneows wur to fire—neow don't yer?" asked he.

"Yes," answered they.

"Wal then don't till I goes so," and he snapped his finger and thumb, "then yer med blaze away."

"Alright!" sung out the youths and they began to comfortably install themselves beneath the creepers so as to see and not be seen. This done they awaited with growing impatience the coming buffalo.

The moon was high in the heavens, casting her white light into the clearing, silvering the surface of the pool, and enabling the sportsmen to take good aim whenever it should be necessary. Ben began to get fidgety and impatient and was about to ask Finnikin whether he saw any, when taking a long survey of the clearing he fancied that something moved at the entrance to a buffalo path. He strained his eyes to pierce the darkness which then reigned supreme as the moon threw that spot in deep shade.

"It was something, I kneow," said he to himself, and it was something as the moment after he was made fully aware of its appearing full in the light of the silver moon.

There with a waving plume of dark feathers over his left ear, standing bolt upright, with a short firearm in the hollow of his arm, stood an Indian. Yes, an Indian. He could not be mistaken. Finnikin had described their appearance so often and so minutely that it had become engraven upon his memory. Ben's heart beat fast. Thump, thump, went that all-important organ. He almost fancied that the Indian could hear it but for the life of him could not have stilled it. During the time his eyes had been firmly fixed on the Red Man, who still stood bolt upright and perfectly motionless. A thought struck Ben. Should he shoot him? Ben had not the slightest twinge of conscience as this thought passed quicker than lightning through his mind. Finnikin had often talked of their cruelties—how they would torture any unhappy white who fell in their hands until death released him from his sufferings. Ben's rifle had been placed in such a position that, without being observed, he could cover any portion of the opening. He gently brought it to bear on the Indian, looked along the barrel, got the sights in a line with each other and the Red Man's breast and, with his finger, pressed the trigger. It momentarily resisted the pressure. That moment's resistance changed Ben's intention. He withdrew his finger from the trigger but still looked along the barrel. The moment after another Indian appeared on the scene. Ben's heart, which had somewhat desisted in its attempts to burst his breast, again began to beat with renewed violence. Another Indian appeared, another and another, until the place seemed full of Red Men. Ben's head also to him seemed to swim with them, and he took his hand altogether away from the trigger of his rifle lest he might unwarily pull it and reveal their position. A conversation now began between the Indian who had first appeared and another in a low tone of voice. Ben of course could not understand a word. But while they were thus engaged he, with great trouble as the opening now was almost enveloped in shade, counted them and they amounted to forty-eight. "Forty-eight," he mentally ejaculated. "Lucky I didn't shoot." Lucky indeed.

    As for Ned, he also had observed the Indians, his heart also beat considerably faster than it usually did, but he had not entertained the murderous intentions Ben had. Finnikin also observed the Red Men but he was not like the two youths surprised and alarmed. No. He was much too old a woodsman for that. He had been surprised that he had not seen any before but he knew that they would see them—probably hear them—another time. He had only been in a little suspense— whether the youths would fire or not, but they had not at one and certainly would not at so many. Therefore Finnikin, although he had certain misgivings as to the mustangs being presently discovered, was in no particular alarm. He well understood the language of most of the Indian tribes inhabiting the immense prairies around and those he did not yet he knew sufficient to generally get at the sense. The Indians before him he knew to be Comanche and of their language he was a sort of walking vocabulary. He therefore listened attentively to the before-mentioned conversation and although but a few words reached his ear yet he contrived to get at its substance, which was this. That the Indian who first appeared was a chief and that he had discovered a small band of whites. He then branched off and proved according to his reasons that it was a meritorious act to kill a white, and then proposed that they should ambush in the buffalo path, which each warrior there knew to be the direct road through the forest. To this all agreed and praised the wisdom of their chief, who returned the compliment, and proposed that as the whites could not as yet have left the Wood of Oaks they should have a feast. A loud grunt of satisfaction arose and preparations immediately commenced.

Finnikin felt considerably relieved when he saw what was going forward, as it gave them the chance of escaping by slipping, if possible, through the forest behind and regaining their horses. Ben still watched the Indians with a continuous stare, his whole soul peering from his eyes. He saw them make a pile of the driest wood and another strike a light and apply it. Then up blazed the crackling fire casting its deep warm glow on the dusky bronzed forms of the Red Men seated around it. Not all seated, two were employed in the cooking of a large piece of buffalo hump which had appeared as if by magic. Whilst thus employed the others all drew a large bowled pipe from their pouches and commenced smoking with the utmost gravity. Amongst the Indians, in fact, smoking is regarded not only in the light of a refreshment, with them it is a necessity.

Ben still watched them with untiring interest and so deeply absorbed was he, that he could barely repress a shout when a heavy hand was laid upon his shoulder. But he was the next moment reassured by a well-known voice whispering in his ear "Don't be skeared—neow." He turned and by the curiously mingled light of the moon and fire beheld Finnikin. That gentleman in a few words communicated to Ben what he had already to Ned—namely the Indians' intentions.

"Neow yer see," continued Finnikin under his breath, "we ain't 'xactly gwain to shove our noses in this blessed trap—kalkilate no."

"Ain't we?" said Ben. "How?"

"Why slip down this yer trunk and crawl through the wood to the 'osses."

"Alright," said Ben, and he slowly and carefully turned round and commenced descending behind the stem. Ned was already on the ground on hands and knees, and Finnikin in the same posture in front of him. In a few moments Ben reached terra firma and having notified the fact to Finnikin, that acute individual commenced the task of crawling fifty yards through an American forest within hearing of forty-eight Indians. It seemed almost impossible to Ben, who last of all slowly crawled along, carefully feeling his way for the fear of dead sticks and receiving from the hand of Ned those switches of the undergrowth which would otherwise come in forcible contact with his face. Slowly they wound along like a huge serpent, Finnikin its head, his rifle its fangs, and Ben's legs forming the tail. In spite of the most scrupulous care which all three observed, occasionally some slight sound was made, some small stick snapped, some small bough flew back against a tree. At any other time such insignificant noises would not have been noticed. But now, when all had the fear of tortures worse than death to which one moment's indecision might lead them, nothing was unobserved, nothing passed unheeded. Thus passed half-an-hour, five it seemed to Ben, and still Finnikin stealthily moved along. Ben had the greatest confidence in the ex-sailor but it seemed very singular why they had not as yet emerged into the buffalo path, and he was beginning to think that they had missed it, when Ned suddenly bounded forward and stood upright. A moment after Ben did the same and found himself right in the buffalo path but no mustangs in sight. To the left down the path could be seen a glow indicating the presence of the Indians and their cheerful fire. He had hardly time to notice this when Finnikin again commenced to move and, to his astonishment, he walked with slow and stealthy steps towards the distant light. In a few moments, however, the cunning of this proceeding became apparent. By emerging above the mustangs and walking down to them Finnikin guarded against the presence of sentinels as well as he could. Shortly they reached the mustangs, untethered them and mounted. Once on, Finnikin uttered a slight almost imperceptible Tchek'to urge his horse forward. They did the same and at that moment, just as their horses started forward, a flash of light illuminated the dark buffalo path, the crack of a rifle reverberated through the forest and a ball flew whistling past.

They were discovered. "On, on," shouted Finnikin, and all three kicked their mustangs and in momentary expectation of another bullet—more deadly in effect if not in intent—were carried swiftly forward.

Chapter 10

Down the buffalo path, with bodies bent forward as if to aid their headlong flight, fled the three. The shouts of the Comanche could be plainly heard but it was also plain that they were leaving them far behind. The fact was the Comanches' horses were not to hand and some time necessarily elapsed before they could mount and pursue the fugitives on equal terms. But once on, with a wild yell and their chief in front, they dashed with headlong speed down the narrow buffalo path. Ben, who was again the hindmost, fancied that at intervals he could hear the tramping of the Indians' mustangs and, as he did so, he felt a certain sensation which, if not, yet was much akin to fear. As yet he knew there was no fear of being overtaken as their horses were of the same breed as the pursuers and moreover they had a considerable start. But then in the usual course of things their horses would be presently tired out; true the Comanches' would do the same, but certainly not so soon, as they would most assuredly slacken speed when they found it impossible to overtake by a sudden burst, and consequently keep up for a much longer time.

It must not be supposed that these thoughts passed through Ben's brain in quick succession. By no means, he was occupied for the first half-hour in listening to hear above the tramp, tramp of their horses; the terrible war cry of the Comanche. But no sound, save the aforesaid tramp and that of the air as it went whistling by, struck upon his attentive ear.

Finnikin, who was still foremost, now slackened the speed of his horse, thereby causing the youths who rode behind to do the same, although they would much rather have put a longer distance between them and the Indians if possible. But Finnikin knew it was not possible, the mustangs already breathed hard and were, as they could feel, in a bath of perspiration. These signs indicated that it would be impossible to continue their present rate of speed much longer and he therefore pulled up his mustang from a headlong surging gallop to a rapid trot. Shortly afterwards they emerged from the dark, dreary forest out upon the moonlit boundless prairie, and Ben's hopes of escape, he knew not why, expanded as he beheld the open grassland. Whether it was the suddenly leaving the desolate forest, which seemed like a prison where even the winds could scarcely come, to find himself on the free prairie, or what, he knew not. The sensation struck him and, as it was very pleasant, he carefully nursed it. Finnikin, without a moment's hesitation, struck out into the prairie and was closely followed by the youths. Whither he was going they knew not but having the most implicit trust in his judgement followed him without a question. Away he went right out away from the forest which soon began to appear as a dark strip upon the horizon. He evidently knew what he was about and where he was going—not merely riding in a haphazard way from the Comanche.

The moon was now rapidly sinking and her fading light showed that morning was approaching. Indeed in the eastern horizon certain rosy streaks of light, with which the sun is wont to herald his approach, had already shot up into the sky and was rapidly increasing in brightness. The stars were going out, one by one, until only the most splendid remained to testify that there had been such things, and these also soon disappeared. Then up rose the glorious sun sending his refulgent beams right in the faces of the fugitives and gladding their hearts with his splendour. To the left they could see immense herds of buffalo who, upon perceiving them, immediately took to flight and went scouring over the undulating prairie, now rising up some slight eminence, now disappearing the opposite side of it. Finnikin shook his fists at them and growled. As for the youths they were too much occupied with their own thoughts to particularly notice any of his actions. The mustangs now greatly flagged in their exertions, it was evident that they would not keep the pace up much longer. This fact damped their spirits which had risen upon beholding the sun. But Finnikin, who up to now had not spoken a word since leaving the forest, save occasionally a cheering one to his horse, broke the silence which had so long reigned by saying, "Neow then yer needn't groan behind—cos we'll do di-rectly."

Which elegant speech opened the mouths of the youths and they both simultaneously ejaculated "How?"

"Why guess yer sees a wood yonder?" said Finnikin. Being answered in the affirmative, he continued "Wal, there's a creek ther as ain't to be jumped 'xactly." But the youths were now about as wise as before, whereupon Ben notified the fact to Finnikin who turned and grinned. "Yer'll see pre-sently," said he, and would vouchsafe no more. Hence the youths had to trust in time. That fleeting gentleman solves innumerable questions and as the youths expected he shortly solved this. In less than a quarter of an hour they entered the wood which was pierced by numerous buffalo paths, down one of which Finnikin led the way. Presently he stopped and then, through the trees, the youths beheld a river, an unjumpable river too as it was between fifty and sixty yards broad. Finnikin had halted upon its edge but from the thickness of the trees and the narrowness of the buffalo path they knew it not until he communicated the fact. From the flatness of the country the river rolled steadily onwards, there was no rapid, nor anything even approaching one. Finnikin took a good look at the opposite bank; he then turned and said, "Wer'er gwain across."

"Whew," whistled Ben. "How?"

"Why ossback how else, neow hold yer rifle an' yer powder 'bove the water an' cum on."

Hereupon Mr Finnikin kicked his horse's flanks and by continual repetition of that agreeable process caused the animal to enter the water with a loud neigh. It then walked without further hesitation until the water lifted it off its legs when it valiantly struck out for the opposite bank. Finnikin's weight at first sunk the animal to its head but it soon rose and, without particular exertion, presently landed safe and sound. Ben had ridden close to the water and watched his proceeding. Seeing him arrive right as ninepence, though dripping, he seized his rifle and powder horn and, holding them above his head, compelled the mustang to enter. Like its fellow the animal first neighed and then, walking in, struck out. Ben, being a much lighter weight than Finnikin, of course did not sink so deep and he escaped a wetting further than his lower garments. Ned now followed and being much lighter still crossed in a shorter time. Ben regarded his dripping garments with a doleful look and Ned felt particularly damp in his lower extremities as, obedient to Finnikin's commands, they dismounted and followed into a strip of wood, which reached a few yards from the river and then gave place to the prairie.

"I'm wet," quoth Ben sententiously.

"So'm I," said Ned.

Mr Finnikin grinned, it could not he called laughter, and said he, "Yer do look mighty like a drowned rat—but twon't hurt—t'will dry presently."

After finishing this complimentary speech he tethered his mustang and commenced to pick up dry wood. With this he made a fire and, producing a piece of deer meat, which, said he, was the last, proceeded to cook it. This operation was quickly performed and he then while shovelling in recommended the others to do likewise. But the youths still remembered the Indians and ate but little.

"Ha, ha," grinned Finnikin. "Yer thinkin' bout the Injuns—air yer, cheow away, no particular hurry," and seeing that they ate but little, he made up. However he presently finished and wiping his mouth with a sigh of satisfaction ejaculated "Th' Injuns—ai?"

"Where?" asked Ben, considerably alarmed.

"Hay ha, alright," said Finnikin, and he pointed across the river. Not being able to see anything there Ben looked puzzled. But Finnikin deigned no notice and suddenly starting up said "We mont cut neow." Thereupon he mounted his mustang and, holding his rifle and powder horn in hand, again commanded them to do exactly as he did. Having obtained a faithful promise, he led the way back to the river again, thereby causing the youths to look at each other. It seemed running into the very mouth of danger but as he went steadily forward they had nothing to do but follow him. Mr Finnikin having arrived upon the edge of the river stopped and again firmly impressed upon them the necessity of doing exactly the same as he did. He then compelled his mustang to enter the river in a direction corresponding to that in which it ran, and slantingly out into it. Soon the animal lost its footing and of course immediately commenced to swim. Finnikin allowed it to keep the old direction for about twenty strokes; he then pulled it short round and commenced ascending the stream and slowly crossing it. Thus he went up the stream for about sixty yards and then again pulling the animal sharp round was soon landed in safety. Ben now walked his mustang into the water and by dint of patience soon found himself standing by Finnikin. Ned closely followed him and, seeing that they had arrived in perfect safety, Finnikin turned and led the way into the strip of wood bordering the river. He had landed at the entrance to a buffalo path as it would have been impossible to have moved in any other place, and now began to follow its windings.

In a few minutes the wood began to thin and when daylight was visible between the trees Finnikin turned sharp to the right and led the way at a fast walk in a direction corresponding to ascending the river. This mode of proceeding was continued for two hours at the end of which time he calculated that they would be completely out of sight of the Comanche should they have not yet left the prairie. So leaving the shelter of the wood they entered it and went forward at a sharp trot. In about another hour, the sun having arrived at the meridian, and the mustangs getting short in their breathing, they halted and dismounting allowed the animals plenty of room to eat or roll to their heart's content. By this time too the sharp exercise had begun to tell upon the youths, and they were not in a fit condition to proceed further without rest. Finnikin, being much more used to fatigue, told them to sleep if they liked as he would watch and in five minutes the friends were agreeably employed in snoring, which to their great delight was not now broken by Finnikin's punches. That eccentric gentleman produced a bowie knife and, cutting a bough, began to whittle it with such untiring perseverance that, in the hour he allowed the youths to sleep, it entirely disappeared. He then judged it time to proceed and awoke Ben, who rolling over awoke Ned and both sat up looking ludicrously alarmed. In a short time they were reassured and, having complied with Finnikin's demand that they should mount their 'osses', were soon cantering over the prairie alongside the wood. Ben presently asked whether they were out of danger and received as answer the following speech to which he listened with the greatest attention.

"Wal—I shou'dn't 'xactly kalkilate on bein' skinned a...," here his mustang suddenly entered a gully and pitched him forward. Upon recovering he concluded thus, "skinned alive, becos yer see t'wou'dn't suit, but anyhow maybe them blessed Injins is a trampin, downstream— mighty likely." Here Mr Finnikin uttered a complacent grunt at the thoughts of his own skill in "doin' the Injins" as he termed it. Shortly after having thus euphoniously delivered himself, he, by taking a westerly look, found that the sun had almost gone down, and by another ahead discovered a large herd of deer some eight hundred yards distant who had not as yet perceived them. Mr Finnikin, seeing these two things, suddenly stopped his horse and ejaculated "Ripin'." The friends also stopped, probably by force of example and enquired what was so peculiarly gratifying to him. Mr Finnikin replied that it was the prospect of having a good supper and pointed forward.

"Oho!" quoth Ben and down he jumped. Mr Finnikin had already dismounted and entered the skirts of the wood. Here he tethered the horses and, looking to the priming of his rifle, began to stealthily walk through the wood in the direction of the unsuspecting herd. Neither of the youths was slow to follow him and the three, under shelter of the trees, stole slowly forward. The herd was grazing on the summit and side of a small hill and, being scattered, the effect was very striking. The three, having now arrived within two hundred yards, had to observe the greatest caution as deer in common with all wild animals possess particularly sharp ears and noses, not to mention eyes. The evening was perfectly still, not the slightest breath of air waved the tall prairie grass or moved the smallest bough. Slowly the three drew near until they arrived at a spot about one hundred yards distant from the nearest deer and nearly opposite. Here a slip of wood ran thirty or forty yards out into the prairie and the hunters immediately determined to take advantage of it. Now they were upon hands and knees crawling forward and making use of every small bush of undergrowth, as the deer being upon an eminence could survey the wood with great ease. Presently they arrived as near as they dared and Finnikin, gradually raising his rifle to his shoulder, covered a fine buck at about one hundred yards. Ben aimed at another rather nearer and Ned at another at about the same distance.

"Air yer ready?" whispered Finnikin.

"Yes," answered they, and the next moment three bullets sped upon their errand of death. The whole herd immediately took to flight save one, who was left by his comrades kicking upon the earth and vainly endeavouring to rise. It was the buck Finnikin covered and had been hit in a vital part—behind the shoulder. The poor animal took one piteous glance at the hunters with its liquid eyes and then ceased its struggles 'ere Finnikin could draw his bowie knife. To the youths' great mortification not the slightest trace could be found of the deer they had vainly endeavoured to kill, no blood to show that the animals were wounded, it was a clear case of miss and did not put either in the most agreeable humour. However, as the more they testified their displeasure, the more Finnikin grinned, they were obliged to put up with the misfortune and help him to cut the best pieces. This done, the rest of the animal was left for the wolves and, each carrying a proportionate quantity, the three returned to the mustangs as fast as possible for the sun's red disk now touched the horizon. They soon arrived and found them peacefully grazing and much in the same position as they had left them. A slight fire, for Finnikin would not allow of a large one, was now kindled and a few titbits soon roasted. These, with a few biscuits or two from their store and a draught of water from the river concluded the meal and, after a minute or two spent in conversation, the youths notified their desire of slumber and rolled over.

Certain sounds soon arose calling down upon the producers a few kind thumps from Finnikin who, seated with his back to a tree, kept the first watch. The fire had been suffered to die out, had in fact been assisted to depart, and but a few embers remained. These occasionally flared up and threw a flickering glare for a few moments upon the sleepers, but Finnikin soon stopped it by flinging a quantity of ashes over it. He was then almost in darkness for the moon had but just cleared the eastern horizon and but few of her beams penetrated the dark silent wood.

Finnikin gazed at the sky, it was covered with sparkling gems. He thought them beautiful and gazed again. Suddenly something obscured them, he almost started to his feet although he immediately perceived the snow-white plumage of an owl. Slowly the night wore on and he felt great difficulty in keeping awake. He had exercised himself more than usual during the last two days. When he judged it about midnight he awoke Ben and told him to take his place, which that promising youth reluctantly did. Then Finnikin curled himself in his blanket and was soon where he wished to be—in the land of dreams. Ben was barely awake when he took his rifle and, seating himself with his back against the tree, commenced to keep his watch. He presently remembered his beautiful adventure of the particular star and resolved upon this time resisting the "starry influences." To accomplish this object he from time to time pinched himself, punched himself, asked himself whether it was for Ben Tubbs to disgrace his name. "No" said he, and again pinched. Suddenly he desisted from the latter agreeable [14] operation, he thought he heard a sound as of boughs being forcibly parted and the passage of some body between. He listened attentively, now thoroughly awake, with his eyes bent in the direction it seemed to come from and rifle ready for any emergency. Yes, there was a sound and something more than a sound—it almost made him shout. There in the direction he had watched were two gleaming round balls of light apparently immovably fixed upon him. Ben was no coward, but he actually felt startled,

---

[14] The transcriber changed the perhaps ironic 'agreeable' of Jefferies' MS to 'disagreeable'.

especially when in another moment two more balls of light appeared. What could it be, he asked himself. Surely not an Indian on all fours. Finnikin had never mentioned that their eyes glared in the darkness and he certainly would not have passed over such a remarkable thing. Ben knew cats' eyes gleamed in the night but these were much too large for cats, if by any chance a cat could have been present in a Texan forest, which, to say the least, would be extremely improbable. While he was watching these mysterious lights one pair slowly moved as if surveying the sleepers. The other shortly did the same and a low growl reached his ears and his heart began to beat uncomfortably fast. A thought struck Ben. Could it be the gentleman in black? Not unlikely, thought he. Suppose I shoot him, said Ben to himself. But there was two and as he looked and looked, by Jove! there was three. Three devils. Nice company, thought Ben, very, very nice indeed. What was he to do? He could not awake Finnikin or Ned without moving and he felt that was impossible; he felt chained, stuck, glued, rivetted to the spot. Suddenly he fancied that one pair of shiners had moved nearer. By Jove! it was no fancy. It had, they all three had moved nearer, were moving nearer. Ben began to get really alarmed. Still the eyes moved nearer and nearer, yet he could hear no sound. No rustling, no breathing. It *must* be devils. What else could move without sound, without air. Nothing, the thing was plain as, as... He did not know what. Already he fancied he felt the first warm glow of a certain hot place—perhaps it might be from the red balls that had gradually approached within half-a-dozen yards. He had no means of knowing, nor did he particularly desire to. His eyes began to start from their sockets. Oh for one glimpse of daylight. Hardly had he mentally uttered this wish than a flood of light poured down upon him, so suddenly that in spite of himself he jumped up. It was the moon, she had been hid by a cloud but had emerged just in time to prevent Ben going mad and to reveal—What? Three prairie wolves.[15] Ben experienced a sudden agreeable revulsion of feeling: from being fearfully frightened, he determined to fearfully frighten. He gently raised his rifle to his shoulder, drew a head upon the largest wolf and fired. With a terrific howl two vanished, the other lay dead at his feet. The report awoke the sleepers who started up in dreadful alarm and seized their rifles.

---

[15] Now more commonly known as coyotes.

"What's the row?" asked Ned.

"A wolf," said Ben.

"Yer shouldn't a fired at 'im" said Finnikin "cos he woud a cut mighty skeared had yer bellered."

Ben explained that he had not been aware of this fact but added that he should know next time. With this sententious observation he commenced to load his rifle and having done so asked Finnikin if he had watched long enough. That gentleman, being just in the act of going to sleep, did not care to disturb himself in such a happy moment but merely grunted. Taking it for granted that he meant to have answered in the affirmative Ben shook Ned and acquainted him with his hard fate. Slowly and reluctantly that slim gentleman arose and ensconced himself in Ben's old position while his friend in return took his. By the exercise of great self-control Ned managed to keep his eyes open until the sun arose and having notified the fact to Finnikin rolled over for a short nap.

Finnikin yawned and arose. He then collected a quantity of dry wood and having alighted it commenced to cook a piece of deer's meat. It was soon done and first helping himself to the best half he awoke the youths. All of which actions show his disinterestedness. All three being tolerably hungry, the viands soon disappeared and Finnikin then gave it as his opinion that it was time to proceed. With looks of dolour the youths agreed with him and mounting the mustangs commenced to canter over the rolling, undulating prairie.

For three hours they rode forward through the long tall grass which, at the end of that time, began to sensibly thin and shortly changed to a perfect greensward. In another hour they passed this and then entered a new description of ground. Here instead of the furrow-like rolling prairie it was broken up by numerous small conical mounts, some covered with vegetation, the greater number of sand. The herbage here was very scanty and large boulders of a grey stone began to strew the ground. Still they rode alongside the river which had now decreased to about thirty yards in breadth while the wood on its banks had all but disappeared. Here Finnikin halted and dismounted. His example was soon followed by the youths who then ate a biscuit or two—but the heat was too great to allow of eating much.

Mr Finnikin then volunteered to keep watch and, getting somewhat under the shadow of a huge boulder, the two youths commenced a duet with variations by the great composer Morpheus. Meanwhile Mr

Finnikin took a piece of deer's meat and, spreading it upon the hot boulder to dry, commenced to hum his favourite verse which was elsewhere noticed. This he continued to do for about an hour and then thinking that enough time had been wasted awoke the youths. He then put the dried meat in the bag which hung at his saddle; and first taking a long draught of the clear though not cold river, they all three mounted and rode forward.

In less than an hour the scene again changed. It was now a succession of sharp eminences, bare of vegetation, but in the valleys between which grew a luxuriant grass. Each time they rode down these hills, that in front grew higher and higher and with more perpendicular sides. Mounting these hills was terrible work both for mustangs and riders and at last they found it impossible to do so. The only route which they could then pursue was that of keeping on the shore of the river as the hills all broke off into sharp cliffs and left a path some dozen yards broad between their bases and the water. After a moment's hesitation the travellers entered the path though not without some indefinable presentiments of evil. Why they could not say unless it was the sensation of being enclosed in impassable walls which, from the formation of the cliffs, seemed a very probable termination to their journey. Certainly they could turn back but there was something even in the contemplation of a retrograde movement very chilling. However as there seemed no help for it they entered the path and, under the shadow of the ever-heightening cliffs, cantered swiftly along upon the yielding sand. Finnikin, who rode between the two, observed the feeling of chillness which had come over the spirits of the youths and to a certain extent he felt it himself.

"Queer place, ain't it?" said he, and received an affirmative answer from both. "S'pose," continued he, "s'pose the creek war to ris—nice—ai?"

But neither of the youths saw exactly the nicety of the thing and by their silence demurred. Finnikin now also began to feel a little dull, especially as the cliffs rose upon either side of the river, forming an impenetrable wall up which it would be apparently impossible to climb. It certainly did begin to look a little ugly he acknowledged to himself. Suppose the Indians were on their track—nice place to be caught thought he. Very nice, especially if some obliging cliff projected out into the stream and continued for an hundred yards so as to be impassable.

The Comanches would then have them at their mercy and he well knew that they possessed but little of that article — if any. However they were in and certainly would not turn back unless compelled. Therefore it was useless thinking and supposing, it only made it worse.

No sunshine reached the surface of the river, and they could only tell that the sun was still up by the brightness of a cliff upon the opposite shore, whose extreme point was illuminated by what they felt sure must be his almost horizontal beams. Night was therefore fast approaching and still the cliffs continued, nay if anything seemed higher still. Shortly Finnikin stopped his mustang and dismounted, saying that he knew the sun was down and it would be perfectly dark in a few minutes. Slowly the friends dismounted, there was none of that joyful hurry which had characterised their halting for the night hitherto. A pall seemed to have fallen over their spirits and they tethered their mustangs in silence.

There was no herbage, nothing but a few plants growing on the face of the cliffs and they afforded but slight nourishment. There was no wood to be found and now the meat Finnikin had dried came in very useful — they wished there was more of it. After a hearty meal, for the coolness of the air had sharpened their appetites, the friends proposed immediate retirement to rest. Finnikin agreed and spreading their blankets as close under the cliffs as possible, for there the sand was driest, the youths were soon in a hearty slumber, he again keeping first watch. As there was no tree to lean against he walked gently to and fro, casting scrutinising glances in all directions. Once and once only he fancied that he saw something upon the summit of a cliff on the other side of the river but it quickly disappeared and he saw no more of it. It put him upon his guard however and rendered him doubly cautious.

As he walked slowly up and down he at intervals examined the face of the cliffs beside him in the hope of finding some scalable place that would enable them to survey the country. But search and search as he would, for a long time he could find none, and thus occupied did not notice black forms creeping slowly along on the opposite side of the river, which was in deep shadows cast by the silver moon high in the heavens.

Finnikin was full in the moonlight and consequently to an enemy on the opposite shore would have been a capital mark, but the black forms remained passive spectators of his doings. Finnikin continued to search for a scalable place and presently uttered a low exclamation of delight.

He had found one, difficult it was, true, but he thought quite practicable. Without a moment's lost time he hastened to awake the youths who grumbled excessively but, on being informed why he interrupted their peaceful slumbers, arose and seizing on their rifles expressed their entire willingness to follow him. For they also wished to see the country and the brilliant moon rendering the place almost as light as day seemed to expressly invite them to the attempt. On beholding the place however their enthusiasm considerably subsided.

"By jingo," quoth Ben, "It don't look easy!"

"Kalkilate it aint—but here goes," said Finnikin and he began to ascend looking much like a fly on a wall. Notwithstanding the difficulty of the ascent he soon arrived halfway when he halted apparently to rest but in reality to make a step with his bowie knife. This done he again started and did not stop until his dark form appeared at the top, full in the moonlight. He beckoned them to follow and Ben springing forward commenced the ascent. It was much easier than he expected, especially as Finnikin had enlarged natural cavities and made several in difficult places. He therefore arrived at the top in much less time and was quickly followed by Ned. Arriving safely by Finnikin, what a splendid view burst upon him. They were standing close to the edge of the cliff. Behind, about twenty yards from its edge, began a dark, impenetrable forest, while on the opposite side of the chasm stretched a boundless prairie. Beneath all was darkness save here and there, where a stream of silver light sparkled up on the water. As they looked down the youths shuddered. It was a fearful depth and they wondered whether it would be ever possible to gain the bottom in safety.

The placid murmur of the river, as it rolled steadily outwards, was the only sound that broke the stillness of the night save once when they fancied that a sound as of splashing arose. It was so slight however as to be deemed but fancy. Neither spoke, the scene was much too grand. It was awfully grand and the silence was oppressive. A sensation of powerlessness, as of being a mere atom, came over the three and anxious to escape from it Finnikin commenced the descent. He was closely followed by Ned, who was again followed by Ben. The last person deemed it prudent to hear from his companions before too closely following and therefore remained half down.

"Air yer safe?" cried he.

"Yes," was the answer, "we—." The rest of the sentence was drowned in a fearful yell that went through his heart and for a moment rendered him powerless, clinging to a root lest he should fall. The next, two shots struck upon his ear followed by a shout of "Cut, cut," and springing forward Ben commenced to scramble for the top.

Chapter 11

Up, up he went, scrambling as fast as legs would carry him and tearing the skin from his hands on the sharp projections of rock. But he felt not the pain, he only thought of the Comanche now probably having found but two below, fast following him up the narrow path. In a few minutes he arrived at the top panting with the exertion and, turning, listened. No sound reached his attentive ear and, thinking that he should have a good start, he made for the wood, which, dark and frowning, approached within twenty yards of the precipice. But he could not enter it, so thickly were the trees matted together with creepers and brushwood. Finding all his efforts vain, Ben stood still to think what he should do next. What even if he did escape the Indians? He had his rifle, ammunition and bowie knife but the powder would not last forever. Anything, however, was far better than remaining where he was. He therefore began striding at a sort of swing-trot by the edge of the gloomy forest in the direction the river ran far beneath. On he went as fast as he dared for the edge of the cliff was uncomfortably near and it might at any time slip with his weight. The moon, high in the heavens, cast her bright beams upon him, the barrel of his rifle glittered in it. He could see his way before him for some distance but any one on the opposite bank could also see him. He knew not what to think about, in fact he could not think, save one thing—that he heard the pattering of Indians' feet behind, and yet dared not look back to reassure himself.

Away he went, occasionally stumbling over stones and roots of trees, otherwise the path was pretty clear. For more than half-an-hour he kept up this swing-trot, from time to time quickening it as he fancied he heard the before-mentioned pattering, and then began to feel what is technically called "winded." He was getting exhausted. In the excess of his fear he had already covered nearly three miles, but he felt that he could not continue the pace much longer. And so he found it, in about ten minutes more, his legs refused their office, his lungs struck work at the same time, and he flung himself on the ground to recover. But it was much easier to think of recovering than to do so. Ben had a capital pair of lungs or, as Finnikin would have said, "considerable bellis", but he had put them to the utmost and they could do no more. He lay upon the ground almost insensible, his heart thumping at a tremendous rate, his breast heaving, his limbs quivering with his great exertions. Thoughts of Ned, of Finnikin, of his own probable fate chased themselves with lightning speed through his brain. The Indians, he'd not a doubt, knew there were three; consequently one had escaped and they would immediately set about tracking him. He had often heard from Finnikin of their wonderful powers of following a trail, and as the path he had pursued was of loose sand they would have no difficulty in his case. Very uncomfortable reflections certainly and not calculated to reassure him—thus he continued on the ground, gazing into the sky for a long period of time, until he felt himself pretty well. He then jumped up and continued his way alongside the wood in the old direction.

Whither he was going he knew not nor did he particularly care, but as he knew, which was about all he did know of geography, that most rivers empty themselves in the sea, he supposed that after many days of uninterrupted travel he should come upon the ocean. But he thought of the fearful sufferings his friends were probably now undergoing, or would undergo, and as he did so, he half resolved to deliver himself up and suffer with them. Another moment's reflection convinced him that such a proceeding would be very foolish and worse than useless. He could not relieve them by so doing, it would probably only add to their miseries. Besides it was no joke if the Indians did as Finnikin said. To have burning sticks thrust into one was in prospect very disagreeable, what must it then be in reality? Ben shuddered as he thought of it. He determined from that moment not to be killed by inches. It was much too slow a proceeding to suit his impatient nature. "Therefore," said Ben to himself as he cocked his rifle, "I'll shoot the first Indian that comes near enough." After making this laudable resolution he quickened his pace and continued to move at a rapid rate until, as he was beginning to feel fatigued, day burst upon the scene and almost alarmed him by its sudden appearance.

The fact was that, absorbed in thought and picking his way, he had not noticed the gradual dying out of the stars nor the fiery heralds of the morn in the eastern horizon. The sun consequently rather surprised him by suddenly casting his beams almost full in his face. But although surprised, he was not offended but exactly the opposite, and he felt his spirits rise as he looked for a moment at the glorious luminary. He now began to feel certain gentle reminders in the stomachian regions that gradually increased in strength, and he now looked ahead with some anxiety to see if the cliffs went down or the wood receded. But look and look as he would, rub his eyes and stare, nothing could he perceive but the same unending vista of the cliffs, wood, and path. He then glanced back and almost shouted as he beheld some quarter of a mile behind a body of Indians rapidly gaining on him. Ben ground his teeth, there seemed not the slightest chance of escape. He almost resolved to stand where he was and fight to the last extremity, but as he looked more attentively and could count some twenty men, the instinct of self-preservation was aroused within him and he turned and fled. Fled at his utmost speed, leaping over fallen trees, large stones and roots that now strewed the path, which to his extreme consternation seemed to get each moment narrower. Yes, it certainly did and probably had done so for a long time. There was hardly five yards now between the fearful precipice and the impenetrable wood. On he went as fast as legs could carry him, noticing this but indistinctly. In less than ten minutes the path so rapidly decreased in breadth as to leave barely two yards. He now saw distinctly enough the awful fate that awaited him, and groaned in despair. As yet he had not again looked behind but he fancied that he heard the shouts and yells of his demoniacal pursuers. Neither had he looked in front. With head hanging down, eyes bent upon the path beneath to keep him from stumbling over the roots which obstructed his way, and over which he could hardly scramble, he dashed along at his utmost speed.

  Now the path cleared a little, he raised his head and looked forward. Horror. Within thirty yards of where he brought up, suddenly the forest came right down to the cliffs. The trees grew thick and scrubby, they were perfectly impassable save in one way and he shuddered as he saw it. Beyond, the wood again receded, the cliff turned sharp out to the river, and then as sharply turned back. This he noted in a moment and then looked behind. As he did so, a yell rent the air, it apparently proceeded from all sides, beneath, around. It sounded as if a legion of devils had combined to make the most horrid noise that ever smote on the ears of man. Ben shook with agitation. He saw the Indians barely one hundred yards distant and rapidly advancing. He looked beneath and saw the blue river running placidly, noiselessly along. It seemed to mock him, so quiet, so undisturbed by events, did it appear. A fearful thought struck him. It would be far preferable to die thus easily than to fall into the hands of the remorseless Indians. One step, a sense of falling and all would be over. He involuntarily looked above. Was he in a fit state to meet the Almighty? Ben knew but little of Christianity beyond the name, he had but seldom bowed the knee, never had he trusted in God, never offered up a prayer in the real sense of the word. But now with death beneath, and worse than death behind, a sense of dependency came over him and he mentally prayed the Great Maker of the Universe to deliver him.

The next moment another fearful yell smote upon his affrighted ear and he sprung forward, resolved to pass the spur of wood or perish in the attempt. In a moment he was at the first tree; he slung his rifle by its strap over his shoulder and, grasping a bough, took one more glance behind. The Indians' rapid rate of progress had been somewhat decreased by the same obstacles which had retarded him but they were barely seventy yards. Several times, even in the moment that he surveyed them, rifles were pointed but one, who seemed to be the chief, raised his arm and they were again lowered. Their object evidently was to capture him alive: he saw this and holding the bough with fearful tenacity swung himself over the dizzy height.

He felt it but saw it not as he well knew that to look down would unnerve him and then—. He dared not think, but using the greatest caution, though trembling with agitation, swung himself from tree to tree suspended in mid-air. He could see the Indians without turning his head and he distinctly saw them stop and one raise his rifle.

This time the chief shouted no word of command, neither did he raise his arm. Ben's suspense was at that moment fearful. With every muscle almost starting from its place he moved carefully and as rapidly as possible from bough to bough. Still no sound, no flash, no stinging sensation in any portion of his body, the savage evidently determined to make sure. There was now but one tree to pass and he would be for the present safe. To pass this tree he had to swing himself upon a slender branch which upon feeling his weight would undoubtedly bend and safely land him upon the narrow ledge of rock which formed the continuation of the path. There was no other means of reaching it, but for a moment he hesitated. The bough was very small in proportion to those he had passed, it was hardly larger than his wrist. However there was not a moment to lose, he felt his strength gradually failing and in desperation seized it. It bent as he had expected, his feet were within seven feet of the path and he almost fancied his feet touched it. At that moment the savage fired, the report reached Ben's ears and the bullet struck the branch he held at the same moment. Crack, crack went the now weak branch. Half cut in two, it could not withstand his weight, and suddenly snapped. Ben felt himself going, a mist swam before his eyes, and he came upon the ledge with a terrible bump. The blow however had one good effect, it awoke him from the trance in which he had fallen, and he found himself upon his back, his feet and legs up to the knees hanging over the precipice while his head touched the wall of rock which had succeeded to the wood. Slowly he dragged his legs up and, having at length done so, arose. The path of rock upon which he stood was barely four feet wide. He carefully walked along, thus bringing himself full in the sight of the Indians as the cliff, as before stated, turned sharp out into the river forming a point, and then as sharply turned back again. They were within forty yards of the spur of the wood as he came into view. A yell of disappointment mingled with rage arose and four rifles were immediately discharged. Owing however to the haste with which the Indians fired, he escaped with a terrible fright as each bullet struck the rock near and fell flattened on the path. He rushed forward to pass the point and as he did so five more bullets went whistling past.

Ben felt that he must go on, to go back would be to run the gauntlet twice over, he therefore walked as swift as he dared forward, for the path was narrow and he could not help seeing the fearful depth below. In a few moments he gained the point; but how to pass it was the question which immediately arose. It would have been comparatively easy had the ledge continued the same breadth, but it did not: at the extreme point it was barely eighteen inches wide. Ben took a glance behind, the chief was kneeling, his rifle rested on a rock, evidently he was taking good aim. Ben made his resolution at once and, grasping what he could of the rock, suddenly swung himself round. At the same moment the chief fired and the ball went through the edge of his coat as he disappeared behind the cliff. Once round, the path widened again and to his great joy, at about a mile ahead, he saw that the cliffs went down and gave place to the rolling prairie, whose tall grass—such is the power of fancy—he would have sworn he saw waving. At this joyful sight his heart expanded and he uttered an exclamation of thankfulness.

As for the Indians, losing all control over their usual calm temper, they indulged in the most frantic gestures of rage and disappointment. They advanced right up to the spur of wood but not one was hardy enough to attempt the passage. They then turned to the chief who, unlike the rest, stood perfectly calm, and commenced upbraiding him for not allowing them to fire before it was too late, and even offered to use violence. But the chief was deaf to their abusing and merely saying, "He cannot even now escape us, what is the use of this exhibition of passion?" led the way with a firm step back to their encampment.

Ben walked slowly forward for the ledge was as yet but narrow and his agitation had not entirely subsided. Gradually however the path broadened until at the distance of three hundred yards it was ten or twelve yards wide and he then stepped rapidly forward. The wall of rock too, which had formerly risen steep and inaccessible above him, now lost its severe and rugged aspect. Half a mile further it had almost disappeared while in its place rose a sloping bank of green turf here and there covered with clumps of trees. Here Ben flung himself down to rest for he felt terribly exhausted. His stomach also renewed its reminders of its want of food but he felt it impossible to proceed in quest of game before having a roll upon the greensward. While he lay a sense of extreme happiness came over him, which, conjoined with the beauties of the scenery, made him reluctant to move. Far beneath him he could see the winding blue river clothed on each side by a narrow strip of wood succeeded by the boundless rolling prairie extending to the far-off horizon. Ahead he could see those abrupt hills that had caused him and his two companions to take the narrow path by the river. A few of these he saw he must pass before he felt the delightful turf of the prairie beneath his feet.

All appeared so still, so calm, so luxuriant under the hot beams of the midday sun as to almost make him forget the awkward situation he was in. For although he was in no immediate danger yet he well knew that there was but little chance of his ultimate escape. Thus he lay ruminating, chewing the cud of contemplation until the demands of hunger disturbed his reveries and he arose and walked forward. At first his legs almost refused their office but, after a few hundred yards were past, they recovered something of their old litheness and he walked rapidly forward. On he went with joyful thoughts of presently meeting deer, and soon reached those broken hills before mentioned and, carefully ascending each one, peeped over into the valley below, hoping to see game. But none appeared, and having passed the last hill he, to his delight, entered the rolling prairie and, keeping near the wood which skirted the river, moved forward with rifle cocked in momentary expectation of deer. But mile after mile was thus passed—still no signs of any description of quadruped and he began to think he should lose his dinner. The sun too began to decline and, feeling that it was useless to continue his present course although loath to leave the river, he struck boldly out into the prairie towards the glorious luminary.

On he moved, surmounting small eminences and traversing the valleys between, still no signs of game save two or three turkeys far out of range and several immense condors high above his head. It was very strange, at all other times he had observed numbers of buffaloes, now there was not a single one to be seen. The sun now began to cast his beams in a much more horizontal direction and Ben, on mounting a small eminence, beheld apparently two or three miles off a dark strip, which experience told him must be a wood. To reach this wood 'ere night set in was now his main object as he thought it probable that the buffalo, being incommoded by the heat of the sun, had retired to its shelter. Nor was he wrong, they had done so in whole herds, but even had they not he would have found none. The explanation is he had had the wind, such as it was, right in his *back*, and buffalo have particularly sharp noses. They had been feeding towards the wood before but, now smelling him, rushed away at full speed and never halted until they gained its shelter. Thus Ben on arriving at the wood, which was mainly composed of a short scrubby species of evergreen oak, did not find a single animal. They had of course retreated further in. His disappointment was extreme, and he began to feel anxious not only about his dinner, but his supper, his breakfast, in short Ben began to think it probable he should starve. However it was no use thinking and grumbling, the sun had set, night had come, and seating himself, back to a tree, he composed him for sleep.

Sleep. In five minutes he found it would be impossible to do such a thing. Sleep indeed, sleep with a gradually collapsing stomach, the thing was not to be thought of. Ben uttered an inelegant expression between a grunt and a groan and, falling back against the tree with a bump, made several horrible grimaces. It was now perfectly dark as the sky was covered with clouds and a low wind began to sough mournfully through the forest. Ben listened to the sound feeling anything but comfortable for it boded a drenching rain, and then uttered the same questionable ejaculation. Suddenly he sprang to his feet with finger upon trigger and head bent forward. His heart beat quick and he resolved to sell his life dearly. Cracking sounds mingled with a tramp as of many men moving swiftly forward fell upon his ear. He thought of the pursuing Comanches and set his teeth firm together. A low muttered ejaculation or two reached him while the cracking continued on his right and finally died away in front. Ben sat down again and collected his thoughts. He was terribly hungry—eaten up by hunger—and knew not what to do with himself. His head was bent upon his breast and he remained perfectly still. A pattering of raindrops around foretold the coming of the storm, the wind increased in violence, a branch was snapped off, it fell upon him and he looked up. Again he started to his feet and, glancing in the direction the cracking had gone, tried to pierce the gloom.

Ben thought that he had seen a light, and a few moments convinced him, it was a light seemingly of a large fire and at a short distance. He formed his resolution in a moment, he would walk forward and reconnoitre. Slowly and stealthily he advanced, using every tree and moving with the greatest caution lest it be Indians. At last he arrived behind a large hollow oak and, taking his stand there, surveyed the party before him. An immense fire burnt brightly, resisting the efforts of the now fast falling rain to extinguish it, and around it sat with its glow full upon then—joy of joys—fifteen white men. They were smoking in silence while another prepared some deer's meat. Ben smacked his lips as beheld this latter article, and putting his rifle in the hollow of his arm he walked boldly to the fire.

The cook immediately noticed him and uttered an exclamation of alarm. In a moment every man was on his feet, rifle in hand, while lowering, suspicious glances were cast upon the intruder. One who appeared to have authority approached him and asked him who he was, and what he wanted. To the first of these questions Ben replied that he was one of a party of three, two of whom had been lately captured by the Indians, and to the other he confessed he was dying of hunger. The man in authority, whom the others addressed as Pierre, now advanced still nearer and, after gazing at Ben for half a minute, gave him a cordial welcome and asked to hear his adventures. All the other sixteen joined in this request and seating himself Ben commenced the detail of his misfortunes and remarkable escape. Ejaculations of astonishment burst from one or two as he went on and as he concluded each man shook him by the hand and expressed his admiration of his conduct. As the deer's meat was now done Pierre offered him something more substantial than mere words, and as may be imagined Ben was not long in cramming down his voracious throat enough to have killed an ordinary person, in ordinary circumstances. But Ben was not an ordinary person, neither was he in ordinary circumstances. Therefore he ate extraordinarily. Upon finishing, he with some timidity brought forward the position his friends were in, and finally requested them to aid him in rescuing them. A profound silence ensued, everyone seemed to be weighing the project in his mind, but presently every one swore by the thunderbolts of Jupiter to help him. Ben eagerly commenced to thank them, but one stopped him by saying that nothing was done yet. This truism set Ben upon another tack, he now enquired whether it was probable that his friends had been tortured.

Pierre answered with a decided negative and said he, "Ef this rain falls longish ther won't be a mighty lot o' yer trail for 'em to ris."

The fact was that the storm had now burst, the rain poured down with fury and the fire was quickly extinguished. For a few minutes they sat in darkness and silence but the man, a long thin man, who had uttered the truism, observing, "Neow I shall snore," they all, except a couple of sentinels, rolled upon the damp ground and slept. Upon awakening the next morning Ben found all the others as the thin man said "cheowin'" and he soon began the same operation.

The meal was soon over and, seizing their rifles, the party arose and, emerging from the forest, stood upon the prairie. It was a beautiful morn, almost all traces of the evening's rain had disappeared save a few pools which had not yet been evaporated by the powerful sun. They now set out at a rapid pace for the river and after a three hours' journey stood upon its banks. Here they halted for a few moments and the following conversation ensued.

"Shall us follow the creek up?" said Pierre, leaning upon his rifle and gazing at the peaceful river.

"Us mou't, moutn't us," was the laconic answer he got.

"Wal, I kalkilate we mout," remarked he, and putting himself at the head of the troop he led the way at a rapid rate.

Ben kept up with them how he might, now talking to the long thin man with whom he had struck up a sort of friendship, now trudging on in silence. As for the rest but few words passed between them. It was evident that they were men of action and consequently could not waste time in idle talking. Thus on they went for another hour when the cliffs became apparent and they soon stood at their bases.

Here the men spread and examined the ground with great care. In a few minutes one uttered a low ejaculation and called his comrades to him. Ben went with the rest and saw where the man pointed the impress of a horse's foot deep in the turf. A slight search for more was immediately successful and a broad trail was shortly discovered. Having taken a good survey of all the marks Pierre shook his head. Ben rushed up to him and with an anxious expression of countenance asked what was the matter.

"Why youngster, I'm most afeared thurs too many. Neow don't look queer—cos we'll foller 'em an' see," answered the addressed party, thereby somewhat reassuring Ben, who was afraid that they intended to abandon the attempt. After a short consultation with his men Pierre again started forward, following the trail with his eyes bent upon the ground. All that afternoon they followed it until, as the sun commenced to sink, they halted at the edge of a forest through which the Indians had passed by a buffalo path. Here they bivouacked but Pierre would allow of no fire as it was extremely probable that several Indians had been left behind to scout the prairie in search of Ben. They consequently had to "cheow" dried meat and after appointing this time three sentinels all turned over and slept.

Ben at first could scarcely close his eyes for thinking of Ned to whom, notwithstanding his somewhat fierce nature, he was deeply attached. Nor did he forget Finnikin who had been very kind to him but was evidently more partial to Ned. He could not help fancying them tied to the stake undergoing the dreadful torture of being roasted alive by a slow fire, while their sufferings were mocked at by the surrounding Indians. These thoughts kept him awake far into the night and when he did sleep it was a troubled slumber. Consequently, when awakened in the morning, he felt not the slightest refreshed but rather tired.

After making a slight breakfast the troop started and walked forward with a firm steady step, Pierre at their head and apparently utterly regardless of distance and dinner. On they went, never stopping a single moment, until they emerged from the gloomy forest and beheld the sun's disk touching the horizon. Ben was extremely gratified on beholding the glorious luminary so near being put out because he knew that they would halt and he should be allowed to cram as much as he liked. Which they accordingly did, and he at last, being perfectly unable to eat more, leaned back and listened to a conversation between the tall thin man who was denominated Abe and the guide Pierre. The purport of which conversation was that he, Pierre, the guide, having as he remarked with extreme modesty, traversed the prairies and woods of Mexico for the lengthy period of thirty-seven years, gave it as his opinion, confidential and decided opinion, that they were within half a day's march of a Comanche village. It was impossible, he expressed, to explain why he held that opinion, but he did and had moreover determined upon sending forth that very night a small reconnoitring party. To this communication Abe listened with exemplary patience and, upon its conclusion, with the like modesty, "kalkilated" that nowhere could be found a better man than himself to be put in command of the proposed party. Pierre signified that such had been his original intention and then raising his voice called upon those individuals who respectively answered to the denominations of Bill Johnson, Jose and one who he called Don Luis, all of whom shortly appeared. Don Luis was a Mexican who, having come into possession of an immense fortune at the early age of twenty-two, had, with that generosity which generally characterizes the Mexicans, squandered it in the short period of five years, so that having nothing to leave his relations he was now on his way to California in the hopes of being there enabled, by dying with a few thousands, to leave a good name behind. He was a short, fiercely moustachioed, strongly-built man, and advanced with a haughty stride as if spurning the very earth that bore him. From constant intercourse with Americans he could speak English or rather American with tolerable fluency, but always ejaculated in Spanish.

These three, having received their orders, departed with Abe at their head, and in ten minutes afterwards all the rest were sleeping save three sentinels. As for Ben this night he made up for the last and slept, snored and dreamed all sorts of rubbish, unconnected and unintelligible, until as morning drew on he fancied that an Indian with a tremendous flourish was scalping him, when just as he gave a fearful tug at the refractory cutaneous covering, Ben awoke and found Pierre pulling his hair. He had hardly ever felt such an agreeable reversion of feeling—it almost reconciled him to the pain of having a handful of hair pulled out. As he ate his breakfast too, he remembered that as dreams always go by contraries, they would now be certain of killing the greater number of the Indians.

"But," said he aloud, "I don't know—"

At that moment Abe and Don Luis entered the circle and, overcoming his reluctance to bestir himself, he actually opened his mouth and enquired what everybody else did—what they had found. Abe, upon being thus interrogated, replied that about midnight they stumbled upon an Indian village of no less than fifty wigwams, each doubtless containing a warrior, his wife and a few imps. He also informed Ben that he had seen the prisoners confined in an hut, but that they could not rescue them because of no less than six Indians being in it. Ben uttered his usual exclamation of satisfaction—"Jolly"—, and a few minutes afterwards was with the rest of the party trudging forward.

Chapter 12

Slowly they wound along following the trail across the broad prairie in the direction of a considerable elevation, the other side of which, said Abe, the Comanches were encamped upon the banks of a small stream. The long tall grass rising above their heads perfectly shielded them from view but it also prevented their seeing any great distance. But when they arrived, which they did at midday, at the base of the elevation the grass decreased so much in height as to barely reach above the knee. They would have gone around the hill but on one side there was a large matted forest, on the other no vegetation at all, nothing but a bare sandy desert, seemingly boundless. There was, consequently, no other mode of proceeding than that of crawling upon all fours over the hill, which Pierre immediately began to do. The rest followed in single file and after some quarter of an hour's toil, arrived at the summit, which was hollowed and leaving a sort of bowl wherein they quickly established themselves. By peeping over the edge of the hollow the wigwams of the Comanches could be seen far below and occasionally a dusky form appeared, to disappear the next moment. As Abe had said, the huts were all built upon the banks of a small stream, by following the windings of which Ben saw that it entered the forest. Having taken a good look at all the leading features of the scene Ben returned to the centre of the hollow where he found the whole party seated upon the ground and smoking.

"Yer sed, Abe, didn't yer, that 'urn wur alright when yer seed 'um?" quoth Pierre.

The addressed party merely nodded and remained silent.

"Neow wur did yer leave Bill an' Jose?" asked Pierre.

"Cum 'long and I'll sheow yer," said Abe, and he crept to the edge of the hollow closely followed by Pierre. "Neow," said Abe, "yer sees that thicket by the creek?"

"Wal?" said Pierre.

"Wal, I tells yer thats war I left 'em to watch whats up. Too-rul-loo-rul-loo-looky, neow," continued Abe in a considerably raised voice and he pointed with his long thin arm at the apparently boundless plain of sand. Pierre following with his eye the finger post discovered at what appeared a mile or so distant upon the desert a cloud of dust which rapidly approached the Indian village. The two men eyed it attentively and both uttered a prolonged Whew! as a large body of horses appeared through the cloud galloping, apparently without a rider, straight towards the Comanche wigwams. The rest of the party, hearing the suppressed whistle, came forward and each uttered the same note of surprise. Ben also came and saw what had attracted their attention, and he was somewhat startled when Pierre, who had been muttering figures, almost shouted "One hundred an' eighty, that'll do—cum on." Whereupon he crawled over the ledge of the hollow and, then rising to a stooping posture, began to rapidly descend the hill. All the party did the same and Ben, not exactly relishing the idea of being left alone, followed, though what upon earth they were up to he could not imagine. By tremendous exertion he managed to keep up with Abe who, with his body bent forward, was clearing the ground with immense strides close behind Pierre.

"Wha—What's up?" he presently jerked out enquiringly.

"Apaches," laconically answered his long friend as coolly and with as little exertion as if he had been seated.

Ben was as much in the dark as before, but he was not long suffered to remain so, for a terrific yell burst upon his ear and raising his head, he beheld, not as he imagined a body of riderless horses but a charge of Indians. The next moment a rapid discharge of firearms told that the attack had commenced, and now the party strode or rather leapt along at such a rate that he was left behind to follow at a reasonable pace.

The attacking Apaches had all disappeared in the trees which grew upon the banks of the stream, but the discharge of rifles, the cloud of smoke that arose and hung over the place, and the yells which reached him showed that a savage battle raged. Pierre and his men had disappeared and Ben followed as he might. He now saw their plan, which was in the confusion that would ensue on the Apaches' attack to rush in, and carry off the prisoners as quietly as possible. As this idea struck him Ben quickened his pace and ran down the hill at a rapid rate. Upon arriving at the bottom, although he could see nothing from the tall grass and numerous trees, yet the firing directed his steps and, crashing through briers regardless of tears or scratches, he rapidly drew near the scene of conflict. Shouts of victory, of rage, the sharp crack of rifles, and the groans of the wounded now struck upon his ear. Bullets also whistled occasionally through the air, sometimes striking trees near him. But Ben, in the hope of bearing a part in rescuing his friends, rushed on regardless of danger, and in ten minutes suddenly emerged upon the bank of the stream almost running against a wigwam. On the opposite side of the river he could see arms flashing and men entwined within each other's arms engaged in fierce combat, while ever and anon the peculiar sharp crack of a rifle told that a bullet had sped upon its deadly mission. For a moment he surveyed the scene from behind the hut, and then rushed round it to find the opening. A few steps brought him to it and, dashing down a blanket which performed the part of a door, he entered.

At first sight he could see nothing but looking again beheld in the furthest corner an old hag who, head between knees, was uttering dismal groans. Seeing that it held nothing else Ben rushed out and ran along the bank of the stream to another. As he did so he came in full view of the combatants on the opposite bank and a bullet or two went whistling by—merely causing him to quicken his pace and, in another moment, he was before the wigwam. Again he dashed down the blanket and entered, the smoke for a moment obscured his sight, the next he beheld standing at the further end a young female Indian whose flashing eyes were turned upon him. In her right hand she held a long dagger ready in a moment to perform its deadly office should it be necessary. But Ben seeing no one else within turned on his heel and left her to herself. Again he rushed along the banks of the stream and was about to enter another hut when he fancied he saw a white man disappear to the left. Ben shouted but obtaining no answer was about to follow, when a Comanche Indian stepped from the hut near and, uttering the war cry, rushed towards him, bowie knife in hand. Ben was standing within five yards of the wigwam when the yell smote upon his ear and turning he beheld the advancing Indian's demoniacal countenance. He saw there was not a moment to be lost and raised his rifle. A loud laugh greeted the action, it was wrested from him 'ere he could press the trigger and dashed upon the ground. In a moment his bowie knife was out, the next the Indian's grasp upon his wrist and he could see a bluish flash as the knife of the Comanche passed through the air. With a sudden backward spring Ben released himself, stumbled and fell to the earth. In a moment the Indian was upon him. Ben struck his bowie knife in his shoulder, a terrible yell for vengeance was the only result and looking up he saw the Indian's knife rapidly descending. He shuddered and shut his eyes, the next moment the crack of a rifle sounded in his ears, the bowie knife grazed his cheek and the Indian fell dead upon him. Ben rolled from beneath him and arising to his feet beheld Don Luis reloading his rifle with the greatest sang-froid. Ben ran to him and commenced giving earnest thanks but the Mexican slightly smiled and turned away.

"Wurs Pierre—the prisoners?" shouted Ben, following him.

"Alright—cum on," laconically answered the Don and he dived into the prairie leaving the sounds of the combat behind.

Ben walked by his side and endeavoured to engage him in conversation, but to each of his queries the Mexican smiled a cynical smile and stepped forward. On he went straight towards the hill until out of range from the Comanche village and then turned sharp to the left

and made for the forest. In about ten minutes they arrived at its edge, and followed it until the stream stopped further progress. The Mexican then uttered an unearthly sound that apparently came from his inside and then listened. In a few minutes the cry of a crow answered, seemingly deep in the forest; the Don then turned to the right and, following the banks of the stream, dived into its recesses. Ben followed in his wake continually bumping himself against trees, squeezing through others, then having the great felicity to scratch himself with brambles which caused him to groan. At which the Don laughed aloud as if gratified extremely. Thus they moved along for some time in perfect silence, but Ben was never able to keep his tongue from going for any lengthy period of time therefore he presently shouted as if to compel a reply:
"Wur be we goin?" To which elegant enquiry the Don vouchsafed no answer but again laughed aloud. Ben thought to himself that he was a precious queer customer. And he *was* a queer customer.

All Mexicans are peculiar but Don Luis was peculiarly peculiar. The fact was, he had not only recklessly spent a large fortune but had been jilted or rather crossed in love. Now the Mexicans are a very hot-headed, ferocious set of people and suppose you don't exactly please them—why an ounce of lead is a very handy article. So the Don, being particularly hot-headed, on finding he had a rival, drew his sabre and vowed vengeance on its blade. Which vow he fulfilled. He called out his rival, fought for two hours and finally ran the sabre through his heart—to his extreme satisfaction. And then to crown all, she for whom he had risked his life, she for whom he had had his arm almost chopped in two, she quietly cut his acquaintance and would have no more to do with him. Thereupon Don Luis cast a look of rage upon her, drew his cloak around him and departed. From that day he had turned misanthrope.

The two continued the pleasant exercise of being squeezed to atoms until, as they were up to the point of vanishing, they suddenly emerged upon the rolling prairie, and Ben beheld before him his two ancient comrades cramming deer's meat down their delighted throats. Ben ran forward, Ned arose and ran forward; of course their foreheads projected considerably and of course came into friendly collision—at which the Mexican smiled. Down they went and rolled about in ecstatic joy at meeting once more alive and kicking, and better still with whole skins. Having punched one another to their extreme satisfaction and the Don's,

Ben advanced and shook hands with Finnikin who grinned considerably and ate more. Thus it was a happy meeting. As for the rest of the party, they smoked in silence, their hearts doubtless bursting with sympathy, until Pierre "kalkilated" it was time to proceed. Whereupon all arose and followed him in the direction of the setting sun—for Calfornia.

On they went until the sun's disk touched the horizon when they halted and cooking commenced. All watched the operation with hungry eyes and upon its being pronounced done, each man's portion quickly disappeared. After which sentinels were appointed and, rolling themselves in their blankets, the others soon entered the regions of Morpheus.

Early the next morning, after making a hearty meal, they put their best feet forward and marched all day over hills, through valleys, occasionally entering a forest but never for long traversing its welcome shades. Both Ben and Ned found the exercise very fatiguing after being accustomed to jog easily along upon horseback, but there was no help for it and they strode valiantly forward.

Thus day after day passed without any particular incident occurring, until at noon of the eighth day, after the encounter with the Indians, they suddenly came upon a desert waste of sand which barred further forward progress. This somewhat damped the spirits of the party and some grumbled loudly—at which the Mexican laughed. It was of course impossible to cross a glowing desert of sand. They were therefore obliged the remaining portion of that day to skirt it, going northerly until evening. Remarkably, they had as yet escaped the Indians, for not a sign of one had been seen since the rescue of Ned and Finnikin, but nevertheless Pierre kept a good watch at night and his eyes open in the day. That evening the men sat longer than usual around the fire discussing their prospects and smoking. As for the Don he kept aloof from the greater number only making himself agreeable to a select few among whom were Pierre and Finnikin. These three looked into the fire for some time but feeling rather tired Pierre and the Don said goodnight and, wrapping themselves in their blankets, were soon in a comfortable slumber, while Finnikin took his rifle and walked fifty yards to windward—he being one of the three sentinels appointed for that night. The other two, at much the same distance from the sleepers, were stationed one to the north, the other to the south. Finnikin leant against a tree and at intervals hummed his favourite verse seemingly with great enjoyment. Thus the night with him passed on and he began to think about calling his nominated successor when, casting a glance up into the sky to read permission there, he found that some clouds to windward looked singularly red. He stared at them as if trying to look through them. Yes, they certainly were very red, glowing. "Hum," muttered Finnikin, "what's the row?" At that moment something went crashing by, startling him, and passed on to leeward. Finnikin listened. He could not exactly understand it although he began to suspect. He had seen nothing but certainly something had passed by. Whew! whistled he as a tremendous gust of wind almost blew him down. He was standing in a sort of coppice and consequently could not see far, but now feeling alarmed he stepped out of it and looking to windward hardly suppressed a shout. A fiery glow low down upon the horizon, but evidently rapidly rising, was all that was apparent but to Finnikin that was enough. His worst fears were in a moment confirmed, and taking one glance he rushed to the sleepers and awoke Pierre.

"The prairie's on fire," he shouted in a hoarse voice.

Pierre started to his feet, perfectly awake, and asked where. Finnikin answered not but pointed in the direction of the rapidly advancing, devouring flames. Though the trees obstructed direct vision yet the glowing sky would allow of no doubt and they hastened to awake the rest. Just then the other two sentinels came rushing in, they had also observed the fire and had immediately rushed to communicate the startling intelligence. In a few minutes every man was wide awake and upon his feet, including the Mexican who smiled his cynical smile. Both the youths were terribly frightened and, keeping near Finnikin, they ran out into the sandy desert along with the rest of the party. Occasionally they cast a glance behind at the tongues of flame which could be now seen darting high in sky. The earth shook with the tramp of animals flying before the dreadful destroyer, the wind blew high whirling clouds of sand before it, and Pierre, shouting "on, on," now ran forward at a rapid rate. Their great danger was being trampled underfoot by the immense herds of frightened animals whose advance made the earth to shake. Along went the whole party helter-skelter sinking often ankle deep in the sand, which fearfully retarded their progress. If they could but get a mile or two out into the desert before the fire had burnt to the edge of the prairie all might be well as the animals would greatly spread. A hot wind rushed past parching up their lips and reducing the strength of the little party. The two youths now lagged sensibly behind but contrived to drag themselves a few yards more and then fell to the earth exhausted.

Finnikin immediately missed them from his side and, by the light of the prairie, discovered them lying on the ground. He stopped and shouting "Cum on," picked both up. They declared it was impossible to move further but Finnikin would hear of no such thing and linking their arms in his literally dragged them forward in the direction he fancied his mates were gone. But it was dreadful hard work for him and he uttered a heart-felt exclamation of thankfulness as about fifty yards ahead he discovered, by the bright glow of the burning prairie, a huge boulder rearing its gigantic proportions. To gain this was now all his object, he strained every muscle, but still they seemed no nearer while the hot wind again rushed past filling his mouth with sand and almost entirely prostrating his strength. Loud bellowings behind indicated the rapid approach of the still flying animals and one or two dashed frantically past. Finnikin toiled and toiled, there was but twenty yards, twenty miles it seemed to him, as with the heavy weight on each arm he staggered forward with staring eyes bent upon the sky. At last he gained it, turned round behind and laying his charges on the ground leant against it and panted for breath. They had arrived but just in time, the next moment thousands and thousands of buffaloes, wild horses and deer rushed past in an intermingled herd going they knew not whither and caring but to escape the dreadful death by fire. Finnikin felt the huge boulder actually shake and tremble as buffalo after buffalo was hurled with tremendous force against it. None took the slightest notice of the three human beings, neither the puma, the grisly bear, nor the wolf, all with tongues hanging from their foaming mouths rushing headlong onwards. Finnikin thought of his companions and blessed himself for staying behind to help the youths, which meritorious action had in all probability saved his life. The animals kept continually passing for a quarter of an hour by which time but few remained and he then looked from behind the boulder in the direction of the prairie. The tongues of flame no longer shot up high in the air, nothing but a glowing low line of fire showed where they had passed. As he turned round the boulder the hot wind again rushed by almost suffocating him, so charged was it with small particles of burnt wood and sand. He staggered back to the shelter of the boulder and found both the youths arisen and leaning against it. Both immediately poured forth their thanks for his tremendous exertions in their behalf and only wished they could reward him with something more than mere words. But Finnikin stopped his ears that he might hear no "sich rubbish" as he was pleased to term it. He had, he said, by saving them saved himself; consequently nothing was due to him. This silenced if it did not convince them and Finnikin then stated his fears of the fate of their former companions. Both the youths agreed with him and proposed making a search upon the first glimpse of daylight. To this proposal he assented and they waited impatiently for the dawn.

At last it appeared and the sun arose over the burnt prairie. No sooner did his beams light up the melancholy waste of sand, displaying to view here and there the carcass of dead animals, and causing the burnt prairie to appear as a black spot from which arose a continual smoke than the three set upon their search. Finnikin pointed to the smoke and likened it to that which may reasonably be supposed to arise from a certain hot place which all orthodox Christians hold in detestation. The youths agreed with him and turning their backs on the desolate prairie set out at a gentle pace.

"They couldn't have gone far," said Ben after an unavailing search of half an hour.

"No, guess they didn't—but looky yonder," said Finnikin and he pointed to an upright object at some distance.

"By jingo it's somebody—cum on," shouted the youths and away they ran. Finnikin followed at a more sedate pace and upon arriving found it was the Mexican.

"Air yer much hurt?" enquired he.

"Guess rather," laconically answered the Don, striving to rise but falling back with a suppressed groan.

"Wur do it hurt?" said Finnikin. The Mexican touched his ankles. "Oho," quoth Finnikin, "oho," and stooping he examined the articles of locomotion. "Yer'll do—it's only sprained," said he.

"Help me up," asked the Don, and by the assistance of Finnikin, the youths having gone in search of others, he was soon upon his feet. The youths now returned looking pale and startled and in answer to Finnikin's "Yer skeared," acquainted him with the melancholy news that all the rest had perished, and were lying about the neighbourhood in various attitudes. On the receipt of this intelligence Finnikin drew the back of his rough hand across his eyes, but the Mexican laughed and this time it sounded as the laugh of a fiend. Finnikin looked savage at him and the youths astonished, but Don Luis laughed again and said he was hungry. Ben said he felt much the same, so taking Finnikin's arm the Mexican began to slowly move towards the boulder, behind which Finnikin knew there was enough meat to last them a year, did the sun not spoil it. In little less than an hour they arrived at the immense stone, and Finnikin drawing his bowie knife commenced to cut the tongue from a buffalo's mouth, which had by some good luck remained open, else the united strength of all four would not have sufficed to open its colossal jaws. Ben walked round to watch the operation and he uttered an exclamation of surprise at the heaps of buffalo piled upon each other in all imaginable forms, some with tongues protruding, others with eyes starting from their sockets, and all showing that they had died in terror. Finnikin, having severed the tongue, and spread a large quantity of flakes of meat to dry upon the boulder, advised advancing to the burnt prairie that they might roast or rather bake the tongue on the hot ashes. To this all acceded and the Don this time laying his hand on Finnikin's shoulder they started at a slow pace.

It took more than half an hour to cover the half mile which lay between the boulder and the prairie, but they at last arrived and commenced cooking operations. The air in such close proximity to the ashes was of course very warm, in fact according to Finnikin it resembled the atmosphere of a before mentioned hot place. He did not say he had visited it though and consequently could not speak from personal experience. In a few minutes the tongue was cooked and four knives aided by a proportionate number of grinders soon demolished it. After a little rest Finnikin arose and said he should fetch the meat he had left to dry upon the boulder and that on his return they had better move forward. Ben timidly suggested the idea of burying the unfortunates, but on being asked what they were to do it with was silenced. Finnikin however visited the bodies and took from them one man's ammunition, a flint and steel and a small hatchet. They were a fearful sight, trampled upon and mangled to almost shapeless forms and he stopped no longer than necessary. Upon his return with the dried flakes of meat the load was equally divided, as the Don insisted upon carrying his proper share although he could scarcely stumble along, even with the help of Finnikin's shoulder. He did however and that without a murmur and as the sun's disk touched the horizon they calculated having made six or seven miles.

Still the prairie was burnt right to the very edge of the desert and presented the same smoking aspect where they halted as at the place whence they had come. This circumstance conjoined with the fact that since yesterday they had touched nothing in the way of drink, save a slight, a very slight, sip of whisky, a bottle of which to be ready for emergencies Finnikin carried, served to depress the spirits of the party, and gloomy thoughts reigned supreme.

Don Luis bowed his head upon his hand and spoke not a word but, with him, such a proceeding was usual. But Finnikin, Martin Finnikin, even he looked and felt precious glum. He did not even produce the remarkable pipe but remained stretched upon the ground and gazing at the sky, which now twinkled with stars. Ben felt he did not know how and at intervals rolled over and uttered dismal groans. Ned did the same and all spent a gloomy evening. When however the moon arose and shed her silver light upon the dreary sand, upon the carcasses of dead buffaloes, upon the gloomy desolate burnt prairie, while ever and anon came the howl of gorging wolves, all felt doubly wretched and Finnikin proposed that all save him should sleep. All acceded and he alone was left awake to listen to that dreary howl, to gaze upon the melancholy scene.

About midnight he awoke Ben and, charging him not to sleep upon the watch, laid himself down to take that rest he so much needed. Ben promised as desired, and for once kept his word, but it was tremendously difficult and he had to walk about towards morn. However he did and upon the first glimpse of the sun was rewarded by having the pleasure of pulling Finnikin's hair as a slight punishment for having "once upon a time" fired close by his ear. Up jumped Mr Finnikin staring as if electrified. Presently he came to himself and the others having been awakened all partook of a little creature comfort although sadly feeling the want of water.

The Don's ankles were considerably improved and, upon starting, he found himself able to walk slowly without the aid of Finnikin's shoulder. As the sun climbed high in the heavens and proportionate heat ensued the travellers' thirst grew stronger, until as he arrived overhead they could hardly move. Finnikin again produced the whisky but instead of allaying it increased their thirst, which was now all but intolerable. Their lips were parched and even the power of speech had nearly departed, but still no signs of water, still the black and now rapidly becoming offensive prairie on their right, whilst the boundless sandy desert continued on the left. All now began to feel excessively weak, so much so that they could hardly draw their feet from the sand and stagger along. Neither thought of food, it would have choked them, their throats were burning—nothing but water could satisfy them. Their eyes became fixed—staring forward; the veins seemed bursting from their foreheads; truly they were in a wretched state. The Mexican at intervals uttered an inhuman sound meant for a laugh, but which sounded as the growl of a fiend. He staggered along evidently near exhausted, and in fact all but Finnikin were in much the same state. He had been more accustomed to privation, to long abstinence from the necessaries of life and consequently could bear more than they. But even he could now barely move, his muscles almost refused their office and were rapidly giving way. Thus they struggled on an hour longer, when the sun nearly touched the horizon and Don Luis fell to the earth with a groan. In a few minutes more the youths followed him, but they did not groan, they had not even strength for that.

Finnikin stopped and cast one look of tenderness at them, in his heart he half resolved to lay with them. But he was as yet conscious, he could as yet feel intolerable thirst and turning he again toiled forward foot by foot. At last he too could not walk but dropped upon his knees and crept. The very elements seemed against him: as the sun went down the wind arose and now dashed the sand in his nose and eyes. Finnikin felt fearfully weak, he was nearly exhausted but still slowly dragged himself along. At last his limbs also refused their office and he fell back all but insensible. He felt that his last hour had arrived but could not pray. He could do nothing but think of water and continually repeated the word to himself, fancying he shouted it. Suddenly, as if with the last effort of expiring nature, he arose upon his knees trembling with excitement. Was it true? That ice-cold drop upon his forehead. Finnikin bent his head back and looked up at the sky. He could see nothing, no moon, no stars. Evidently they were obscured by clouds. At that moment a flash of blue lightning illumined the sandy desert, the next it vanished and a peal of thunder rolled over his head. It ceased, and pattering drops of heavy rain fell upon the hot burning sand and the scarcely less hot face of Finnikin. They increased in number, in size, and in another minute literally poured bucketfuls upon the desert plain, whilst the lightning flashed and the thunder growled continually above, around. Finnikin leapt to his feet and tearing the blanket which hung at his back from the strap spread it to the rain. In a moment it was saturated, and he squeezed the welcome drops into his mouth. He repeated the process again and again, he seemed perfectly insatiable. Meanwhile the storm increased in fury until it seemed one continuous flash, one never-ending roar. On one side he could plainly discern the black burnt prairie, on the other the sandy desert. Still he squeezed the blanket incessantly, thinking of nothing else, wishing for nothing else. Suddenly a ball of fire appeared nearly overhead, it approached the earth rapidly, sending forth on either side bright yellow lightnings in deep contrast to the other which was blue. Thunders of tremendous intensity heralded its approach, the clouds opened, the heaven was one blaze of blinding light. Finnikin stood amazed. He forgot to squeeze the blanket, his whole soul staring from his eyes upon the dreadful meteor. Rapidly it approached the earth, yet he moved not, he breathed not.

It touched the ground but fifty yards distant and burst into sparks while a heavier peal than ever of thunder rent the skies and rolled along the arch of heaven. Gradually its intensity decreased, while the lightning almost discontinued its blinding awful glare. The storm had exhausted its fury and nought but the pouring rain remained. Suddenly a thought struck Finnikin. His friends. He ran guided by the wind towards where he had left them, shouting their names. He knew that he had not progressed far before he had fallen, so after running a few hundred yards he halted and shouted loud and long. A low hail answered at a short distance and guided by it he presently stumbled on a person seated upon the ground. It was Ben, the cold rain had somewhat revived him but he was still very weak. Finnikin spread the blanket, let it soak and then squeezed the welcome drops in Ben's mouth. It strengthened him greatly, and on the process being repeated a few more times he unrolled his own blanket while Finnikin went in search of Don Luis and Ned. He soon found them and by squeezing the blanket restored them to consciousness and strength just in time, as the rain soon ceased and the pale moon cast a mournful light over the scene. By her light Finnikin, who had recovered more than the rest, made a meal of the dried meat, but the others refused it, saying it would choke them. They felt tired and in spite of the dampness of the sand laid down and slept, while Finnikin, leaning his head upon his arm, gazed at the moon whose light shone upon the numerous small puddles around. Thus the night wore away and the sun rose upon the desolate scene looking watery and sullen.

Shortly the three sleepers awoke and they now ate heartily. As they ate, strength returned, and in an hour's time from rising they notified their willingness to start to Finnikin who was laying full length on the ground. But he immediately arose and, taking a draught of water from a small pool, started at a moderate pace. Ben examined the powder in his horn and to his great delight found it uninjured. This considerably added to the spirits of the party and with lighter hearts, though slower footsteps than yesterday morn, they moved along. Finnikin in particular experienced a joyful sensation and joked the others continuously on their "drowned rat" appearance, whereupon Ben reminded him that he was in the same plight. Finnikin winked wisely and, producing his remarkable pipe upon which he cast a glance of considerable affection, proceeded to fill its capacious bowl.

Whilst thus occupied the Mexican suddenly uttered a Spanish ejaculation and seeing all eyes upon him pointed forward. Upon following with their eyes the direction in which he pointed all three simultaneously shouted "Too rul loo rul loo!" and flung their caps sailor fashion high in the air. Indeed the sight which burst upon the delighted travellers' gaze was enough to gladden their hearts and eyes, so long accustomed to the hue of death upon one side and that of desolation upon the other. Right ahead, far in the distance, they beheld a slight eminence clothed in green and upon it a herd of deer, their forms distinctly apparent against the sky. No wonder then that they uttered such an exclamation, no wonder that the exuberance of joyful feeling should cause their caps to soar in blue ether, no wonder that the Don blessed the Virgin Mary in Spanish and laughed. Laughed not his old demoniacal laugh but one diametrically opposed to it—a laugh that indicated pleasure.

On they walked at a rapid rate the green hill acting as a magnet, and to Ben's intense mortification off walked the deer—probably they smelled his murderous intentions. Shortly they arrived and had once more the pleasure of feeling green turf beneath their feet, of having green grass around them, of feeling a balmy wind in opposition to the hot air of the burnt prairie. They had also the great satisfaction to find that the desert here made a bend and thus allowed them once more to follow the direct track for the goldfields.

All that afternoon they trudged merrily forward until the sun's disk touched the horizon when they halted by the side of a large pool. Here after supper Finnikin again produced his exceedingly remarkable pipe which he smoked with great gravity, at times removing it to joke or tell the most enormous bouncers that ever issued from the mouth of man. Even the Mexican somewhat relaxed his stern features at Finnkin's dry sayings and, producing a pipe, blew a cloud with great complacency. Thus the evening passed away and as the fire went out all save the Don, who kept the first watch, rolled over and enjoyed refreshing slumbers.

Chapter 13

On the evening of the seventh day after the events detailed in the preceding chapter, the four travellers stood before the first house of the town of Christobal. It was evidently uninhabited as the door was open and swung about from side to side with every breath of wind while part of the roof had fallen in. Passing on, they presently halted before another but it was in much the same state and would not have afforded the slightest shelter. "Hum," muttered Finnikin and they again moved forward. In a few minutes they entered a sort of street with houses on each side but on examination they were all found tenantless and falling to pieces. The place seemed deserted, the light too, which they had observed half a mile back, had vanished. At last they reached the termination of the melancholy street and turning to the left beheld a small square from which came a red flickering light. A sigh of satisfaction escaped Finnikin—they had at last found an inhabited place. But inhabited with what? Spirits probably for although they battered at the door making noise enough to have attracted the attention of a mortal ear yet no stir could be heard within.

"Burst the door," quoth Ben lifting his foot in a threatening attitude.

"No, no, the shutter," said Finnikin, and he dealt it a fearful blow with the butt of his rifle. It being perfectly rotten the stock went clean through, knocking out a large piece which fell in with a terrific crash. A groan ensued, followed by a Spanish ejaculation of rage. Finnikin by standing on tiptoe managed to peep in and beheld a man sitting on a bedstead rubbing his eyes. He was evidently past the prime of life and contemplated the wreck of his crockery, upon which the piece of shutter had fallen, with a mournful gaze.

"Hulloa," shouted Finnikin. Up jumped the Mexican and looked around with an expression of alarm upon his meagre features. Finnikin, having grown tired of exercising his toes, had dropped down and consequently no one was to be seen. To be prepared for any emergency, however, the Mexican took a machete or short sword from a nail and listened attentively. At that moment Ben, tired of waiting, applied his foot to the door in anything but a gentle manner, making the whole mud structure shake. The Mexican immediately advanced to the door and enquired who they were and what they wanted in bad Spanish. Don Luis being the only man who understood him answered that they were hunters and wanted a night's shelter. To this the polite Mexican answered that if they were hunters they could sleep on the ground.

"Ah, but we want a guide over the mountains and will pay well," said Don Luis. The word "pay" produced the requisite effect as the door flew open with a fearful creak, discovering the Mexican, who now the very essence of politeness bowed and led the way to his only apartment. Motioning them to be seated, the Mexican first carefully bolted the door and then propped up as he might the fallen shutter, groaning at the sight of his smashed crockery. He then advanced, threw an armful of wood upon the fire and seated himself upon the bed, or rather bedstead as no covering of any description was visible.

Don Luis now requested supper to which the meagre man replied that he had none and his appearance fully corroborated his words. They therefore had to cook some deer's meat, or rather Finnikin did, whilst Don Luis drew from the meagre man, who called himself Jose, the reason of the place being deserted. He was informed that the inhabitants had been seized with the gold fever and that man, woman and child had all disappeared months ago for California. Why he had remained was not forthcoming save some muttering of "unable to, too old," which anybody could see was rubbish as he looked all bone and sinew. However as it was no matter to him Don Luis asked no more questions on the subject but passed it over and enquired how far it was to the mountains. Hereupon Jose very wisely scratched his head and informed him that it was two days' sharp travelling, supposing they escaped the Indians whom he said lived in swarms in the neighbourhood. Don Luis then wished to know whether they could pass the mountains without a guide. Jose appeared astonished at the idea.

"Pass without a guide?" he exclaimed. "Impossible, you would be ten times lost."

"Lost?" echoed Don Luis with a sneer. "However, as we wish to get on we will employ you—name your price."

Jose grinned and twisted his fingers into indescribable contortions from which he extricated them with a snap and jerked out, "Five piastres."

"Agreed," said Don Luis and he adjourned to supper, which Ben at that moment announced. When the meal was concluded Don Luis communicated the intelligence he had gained to Finnikin and the youths, who discussed it and the probable character of Jose until the topics were exhausted, when all rolled themselves in blankets and laid upon the ground, feet to the fire. Jose offered his bedstead but no one would receive it and he therefore rolled upon it himself. Then arose various nasal sounds apparently indicating that all the party were asleep.

But Finnikin, probably being a suspicious character himself, suspected others and just then entertained an idea that Jose was hardly to be trusted. He consequently remained awake although with eyes all but shut and uttering with open mouth sleepy tones. He found it very difficult to restrain himself from yielding to the soft influence of sleep as he had walked far that day, and the flickering light of the expiring fire threw at intervals a dreamy supernatural kind of glare upon the sleepers beside him and the heavy bedstead. He reasoned with himself upon the stupidity of denying himself the natural repose of man, and tried to convince himself that there was nothing to suspect in the sinister twinkling eyes and meagre form of Jose. But it was no use: something would whisper "keep awake" in spite of all his endeavours to close his ears. Thus he lay to all appearance firm asleep, but in reality wide awake with eyes fixed upon the bedstead, for what appeared to him two hours but was twenty minutes, when it suddenly struck him that the noise within the room had unaccountedly dimished. To make sure he lowered the scale of his own guttural utterances and then discovered it to be a fact. He could plainly hear Don Luis's low hard breathing, Ben's snore and Ned's ditto but the bedstead's snuffle had ceased. "Hmm," quoth Finnikin to himself and stared with his half closed eyes at the article.

Whew! He very nearly whistled but very readily disguised it in a prolonged groan. Jose was sitting up with twinkling eyes surveying his guests. Apparently satisfied that they were all in a firm slumber he quietly got out and on tiptoe reached down his machete. He felt its edge and point with a light touch of affection and then stealthily and slowly approached Don Luis. Finnikin watched his proceedings with horrified glance, hand upon bowie knife and ready to start up the moment it was necessary. Slowly Jose drew near, he stood over the Don, he poised the machete, his eyes glittering in the uncertain light of the fire which glanced with a red light upon the blade—soon, thought Finnikin, to be stained with a deeper, more lasting colour. Finnikin raised his head, he was about to spring to his feet when Jose uttered a short low demoniacal laugh and returned the machete to his girdle. He then again slowly moved forward, this time for the door, which he soon reached and made his exit drawing it close together after him. Finnikin's heart, in spite of his usual calmness, beat fast, he essayed to rise but could not, the vision of Jose, machete in hand, standing over Don Luis was ever present to him, and he could not move.

Slowly the moments wore away, he thought of Jose's intentions, he had probably gone in search of confederates, but why? To murder them in the mountains and thus take the actual stain of blood from his hands, while he would receive a share in the booty as an informer? Or more horrible still, did he intend to engage Indians, to inform them of the white men's presence and thus get the whole booty as the Indians would be content with the prisoners themselves. This seemed to Finnikin the only reasonable explanation of his conduct, and he began to revolve in his mind schemes to prevent its accomplishment. He determined, on the slightest appearance of treachery of that sort, to shoot him down as a dog. Hardly had he made this resolve when the door slightly creaked and was slowly opened by Jose who peeped in before he inserted his lengthy carcase. All were apparently sleeping and the meagre man having shut the door wriggled to the bedstead and rolled in or rather on it. Soon snuffling sounds proclaimed that he was firm asleep and Finnikin wondered to himself how a man with such dark intentions should be able to do so. Wondering how others could sleep made him doubly sleepy, and notwithstanding that he made a resolution every five minutes to remain awake and watch all night, his head presently drooped back while natural nasal sounds proclaimed that he had followed Jose's example.

The next morning the sun's bright beams shining in at the broken shutter rested on the meagre man's eyelids and awoke him and he aroused the others. Finnikin finding himself alive inwardly thanked God while the rest, being ignorant of what he had seen, grumbled exceedingly. Jose now in contradiction to what he had said about supper produced some excellent viands and spread them upon a table. Finnikin could hardly bring himself to eat any fearing that it was poisoned, but he saw the necessity of appearing unsuspicious and made a slight repast. The meal being finished Jose arose and from out of a corner brought a couple of paddles, he then signed them to follow and led the way from the dreary tenantless town of Christobal.

Shortly they arrived upon the banks of the Rio Bravo del Norte and crossed its broad waters in a wooden canoe that Jose paddled with great dexterity. Upon arriving on the opposite bank the canoe was hauled up and hid among the bushes, and putting himself five yards in front away marched the meagre man. Then by dinted whispers Finnikin contrived to convey to the Don what he had seen the preceding night. In spite of himself the Don started and shuddered when informed of the imminent danger he had been in. Soon his alarm turned to rage, all his Mexican fierceness returned and in a hoarse whisper he expressed his determination to blow the scoundrel's brains out on the slightest pretext. Finnikin even had great difficulty in preventing him doing so at once, but at last he brought him to see that it would be worse than useless, as they would be entrapped exactly the same and would moreover lose a guide, who at all events was leading them to the nearest road to the mountains.

"Wal," said Don Luis, "I won't yet, but—", and he shook his fist at the thin form of Jose in front, "presently."

All that day they walked stoutly forward, Finnikin and Don Luis keeping a good look out upon all sides, and as the sun's red ball touched the western horizon they halted upon the banks of a small stream. Here they bivouacked and passed the night, Finnikin watching the first half, the Don the remaining. But nothing suspicious occurred, no sound broke upon the silence of the night save the distant howl of the coyote or the hoot of the owl. The stars rose and set with their accustomed regularity and presently Aurora's rosy cheeks began to blush heralding the near approach of the dawning sun. Shortly he arose and displayed himself above a bank of ruby clouds, casting disproportionately long shadows upon the ground and dissipating whatsoever mists that had made their appearance during the night.

Don Luis, seeing that it was the sun and no deception, awoke the party who immediately arose and performed their toilets by rolling up the blankets and washing themselves in the gurgling stream. The breakfast was devoured and, having allowed it a few minutes to settle, they again set out upon the journey following the banks of the stream in an opposite direction to its current. Towards midday Jose, who was ahead, suddenly stopped and, pointing forward with his long thin arm, shouted "Volcano." All rushed tumultuously to his side expecting to see an active one, but to their disappointment beheld only a long low range of what appeared mole hills and one a little higher than the rest rising in the form of a cone. That, said Jose, was the Volcano, and in answer to Don Luis's query of whether it was extinct, answered that it had not been in action since the memory of three generations and that a few trees grew at the summit. Then, having communicated all he knew of the matter, he again commenced to clear the ground with a long swinging stride. All that day they neared the mountains which perpetually appeared to grow higher, until as the sun began to rapidly decline they seemed to pierce the clouds, to hang almost overhead. The Volcano stood out boldly from the rest, towering above and clothed to within apparently a few yards of its summit with dark impenetrable forests, which extended on either side seeming to block all passage. When they halted for the night, still upon the banks of the stream, which had decreased to a mere brook to be crossed by a bound, the tall sugar-loafed mountain seemed to rise beside them and to almost overhang. That night diligent watch was kept by Finnikin and Don Luis but it again passed quietly and they arose the next morn refreshed, and ready to begin the toilsome ascent.

Both the youths expressed a great desire to ascend the extinct Volcano, and even Finnikin and Don Luis felt enough curiosity to make the latter enquire of Jose whether it was possible. He was informed that it would be an arduous undertaking but perfectly possible and as they would pass close beneath it not much out of the way.

"Hum," quoth Finnikin on being made to understand, "S'pose we do."

"Wal," replied Don Luis and the thing was settled to the great delight of the youths.

Jose now said that if that was their intention they had better start at once and all being ready he took the lead. In less than an hour trees began to thicken around them and soon increased in number to such a degree as to materially retard their progress by causing them to make continuous turns. They now commenced ascending while the stream had entirely disappeared but the gully from which it had issued continued and up this the travellers panted, stopping every ten minutes to recover breath. Each side rose the impenetrable woods interlaced and bound together by creepers and underwood. The path grew rugged and all but inaccessible, while the travellers struggled forward following Jose who by the aid of a stout stick scrambled on. Thus they gradually ascended and the air grew colder, while the woods on either side thinned giving place to rugged rocks which had fallen ages past from the mountains above and now seemed tottering on their insecure resting places. Now the high conical mountain was seen towering high above them with almost perpendicular sides and apparently unscalable. The forest grew to within one hundred feet of the summit upon either side save that which now presented itself to them and was rocky and rugged. Jose now stopped and approached the side of the gully, he then by the aid of a few trees raised himself and stood upon the edge. The travellers followed him as quickly as possible by slinging their rifles upon their shoulders.

Seeing them arrived safely Jose began to ascend the Volcano by the edge of the forest in much the same manner as he had the gully. The travellers followed him making use of every bough and of every indentation that afforded a safe step. Soon the forest grew thinner and the toil of ascending increased in proportionate ratio. However they struggled on and presently arrived at the most difficult part—where there were no trees.

Jose went first on hands and knees, crawling with his body almost trailing upon the ground and using every small projection. Slowly he moved up closely followed by Ben until within five feet of the summit. Here he by some oversight caught hold of the root of a small dead cactus and bore his whole weight upon it. In a moment the frail thing snapped, he grasped at a projecting stone but it also gave way, and Jose with a yell fell back and rolled down, upsetting Ben who also began to roll at a frightful velocity down the almost perpendicular side. Finnikin, by tremendous exertions, managed to save Ben by catching his coat as head over heels he went by. But Jose, having no friend, rolled over and over yelling with fear while the others above watched his awful descent. Just as his body was about to strike with fearful force the first tree, a Red Man, yes a veritable Indian, emerged from behind in time to save his life. A shout arose from the four travellers above of indescribable meaning and with terrific efforts they scrambled up the remaining distance and rolled over into the crater. Once within that there was no present danger as on three sides at least they were unapproachable but the future, the future. The crater was a hollow bowl-like place and affording then fifty or sixty square feet to sit in, they could even stand in the centre without fear of the Indians should they fire. For although but one Indian had as yet been seen yet neither doubted there being a legion hid among the trees. A couple of moderate sized firs grew in the crater whilst quantities of stones were scattered around. Finnikin picked up a few of these and by exercising patience built a small breastwork at the scalable place, behind which one could watch all the proceedings below without the slightest danger to himself.

Here Ned was established and the rest, retiring to the centre of the crater, produced all the provision they had about them. To their extreme consternation there was hardly sufficient to furnish two meals even with the greatest economy—not enough for one at an ordinary time.

Finnikin growled. "The tarnation d—ls, they've catched us at last," he muttered and seating himself upon the ground appeared absorbed in thought.

Don Luis called upon the Virgin Mary in Spanish while Ben stared at him speechless. However the natural buoyancy of his temper soon lifted him from the Slough of Despond and he asked Finnikin if there was any possible means of escape.

"No, not as I kneows on," was the dismally sententious answer he received. But Ben unheeding him said that there was another side to the one they had come up, probably unwatched, might not they by joining the lassos escape by it under cover of night? Finnikin however merely shook his head, and Ben finding it useless to talk to him at present crawled to Ned and passed the time in watching the trees below.

No Indian could be seen, all was apparently still. Not even a breath of air stirred the branches of the trees, nothing save the shadows moved.

The youths conversed in low tones but Finnikin and Don Luis remained perfectly silent chewing the bitter cud of contemplation. Thus the day wore on, and after what seemed an interminable period of time the sun began to rapidly decline to the great delight of Ben who under cover of night proposed ascertaining if his project was practicable.

Slowly the glorious luminary descended until his lower edge touched the line of forest in the distance, when he apparently waited a moment that he might be certain his bed was ready, when with a sudden bound he vanished and darkness crept over the land. Yet hardly darkness as the moon shortly shed her pale white light over the scene, casting the accessible side of the mountain in deep shadow while on the other every projection, every stone was plainly perceivable.

During the day Ben had communicated his plan to Ned, who expressed great reliance upon it, and now that they would not be seen by the Indians below he proposed taking a survey of the place. Accordingly, leaving Ned to watch the accessible place, Ben crawled until about opposite and looked down. The height was tremendous and made his brain swim, however it soon wore off and he was then enabled to form some idea of the difficulty of descending. It was about one hundred and fifty feet he calculated to the forest below, and rather more than halfway down was a small tree scarcely the size of his leg. On this tree, thought Ben, depended their hope of escape. If it would bear a man's weight they could join the two lassos they possessed and fastening one end to the fir trees in the crater slide down to it. Once there it appeared that a bold active man might make the forest without danger. Ben having noticed this crawled to Finnikin who still sat in the centre of the crater and in a low voice communicated his project. Finnikin took but little notice of him at first but as Ben concluded he arose and requested to be shown the place. Ben pointed it out and anxiously watched the expression of Finnikin's features which to say the least were anything but encouraging.

"It looks ugly," said he. "Don, cum here."

Don Luis arose and on having the plan communicated to him by Finnikin he laughed, smacked Ben on the shoulder and said he was a "cute lad." Then unwinding his lasso he fastened it securely to Finnikin's and then tied one end to the two fir trees while the other end hung over the crater. Now the question of who was to make the attempt arose. Finnikin claimed it on account of being a good climber, Ben as he was a lighter weight, and the controversy ran high. However Don Luis quickly solved the difficulty by tearing a piece of paper into lots, which were then well shaken in his cap and drawn. To his great delight Ben drew the deciding one and immediately commenced preparations by slinging the rifle over his shoulder and giving a fantastic spring into the air probably for the purpose of stretching his muscles. He then caught hold of the lasso rope and, grasping it with tenacity, rolled over the edge of the crater while Finnikin held the upper end of it and watched his proceedings.

Slowly Ben descended grasping the rope with all the strength he could muster and planting his feet firmly as possible on the all but perpendicular side. In a few minutes he had arrived half the distance to the tree and stood upon a small ledge to recover breath. Having waited what he considered long enough Ben slung himself off and again moved slowly downwards with every muscle strained to the utmost. He was as yet ten feet above the tree when to his surprise and chagrin he found he had arrived at the extreme end of the lassos. He knew he could not ascend, he was already much too tired for that, even had he wished to. He was standing on a small projection, to the tree it was ten feet of perpendicular and beneath it but little difference. Ben looked up, and beheld Finnikin's face in the moonlight intent upon his proceedings. He felt it useless to remain where he was, unable to ascend, afraid to spring and catch the tree as he fell. Ben summoned up courage, of which article he had a considerable quantity, and determined to make the latter attempt. He steadied himself and marked in his mind's eye the place he must come upon. Then he left hold of the lasso and with staring eyes fixed upon the tree sprung from his position. He felt himself falling through the air for a moment, the next his feet struck the earth beside the tree and with a convulsive grasp he caught a small branch. It bent, cracked and Ben finding it would not bear his weight fell upon all fours and scrambled for a safer bough. For a moment he barely prevented himself from rolling head over heels down the mountain, but the next he ascended a few feet and, by a spring into which he threw all his remaining strength, managed to grasp a large bough, which although it bent gave no signs of breaking. Holding the bough with fearful tenacity he then flung himself upon the mountainside at full length that he might recover breath. His heart beat fast and he panted with the exertion while thought for the present was impossible. Here he lay for several minutes until he thought himself strong enough and then by slow degrees climbed up and sat astride the tree. He now considered in what manner he should descend the remaining distance to the dark line of forest below. As he looked upon it he shuddered, what if Indians were concealed there? His hand involuntarily sought his bowie knife giving evidence of deadly intentions. But a little reflection convinced him that it was extremely improbable for Indians to be there as they would of course know or think it unscalable. He therefore commenced the descent slowly and with great caution on all fours using every projection, every slight indentation. Soon he arrived halfway, here he would have rested but it was impossible and he continued the descent. When within twenty feet of the forest the perpendicularity of the side considerably decreased and he then seated himself, surveying with scrutinising glance the dark trees whose shadow fell to his feet. But he could perceive no gleaming rifle barrel, no dusky form hid among the underwood waiting until he came within reach, and he therefore continued the descent at a rapid rate down the now grassy slope. In another minute he arrived at the first tree and hardly suppressed a shout of joy as he touched the welcome trunk and felt himself safe. For a moment the contemplation of his own happiness took away all thoughts of others and he hugged the tree in excess of jollity.

Soon however he remembered his companions cooped up in the crater, and the perilous descent they would have to make before they could experience the same delightful sensation. As he thought of them he looked up and by the light of the moon could indistinctly perceive one roll over the edge of the crater, and as he rapidly descended by the lassos he saw it was Finnikin. When he arrived at the termination of the lassos Ben almost fancied he could see an anxious expression on his countenance as he looked at the tree beneath. Finnikin however did not keep him long in suspense as after a good look at it he boldly sprang from above and in another moment was seated astride. Ben breathed freer when he saw this as he now had no doubt that Finnikin would arrive safe beside him. Nor was he wrong, as after allowing himself a few moments' rest Finnikin left the tree and by springing, rolling and crawling, quite a contrast to Ben's slow movements, soon stood beside him, panting with the exertion. When he recovered breath enough to speak Finnikin gasped out "Ugly place—lookey neow," and pointed up. By looking in the designated direction Ben perceived the lithe form of

Ned slipping down the lasso at a rate much resembling Finnikin's. He quickly brought up at the end and looked dismally below as if afraid to spring. Twice he left hold of the lasso and appeared to leap but as many times recoiled. The third time he advanced too far and although he tried to recover his balance lost it and fell through the air. The next moment he struck the tree and grasped it with one hand while his body swung below. But he could not hold and fell, throwing up his arms in despair. Head over heels his body came rolling down the mountain, bounding occasionally several feet into the air to fall again with a heavy thud.

Ben groaned aloud, and clasped his hands together. Finnikin ran as far as he could up the side to catch him if possible 'ere he was dashed to pieces against the trees. Ned came on rolling at a fearful rate, his near approach heralded by quantities of stones and clods of earth which he had dislodged in his headlong descent. As he was almost upon him Finnikin caught hold of a small bush and flung himself at full length on the ground with his back a little arched. Ned came bang against him with fearful force and knocked him over but his velocity was checked and he was finally stopped by Ben when within ten feet of the trees. On examining him it was found that although awfully bumped yet luckily no bones were broken, and by the time Don Luis joined them, he having descended in Finnikin's fashion, Ned said that he felt much better and by the aid of Finnikin's arm could limp along.

The method of proceeding which the travellers now decided upon was to walk around the base of the Volcano, keeping well in the shade as far as they could without being seen by the Indians, then to dive into the forest and regain the gully they had originally left in a slanting direction. This they presently did and in spite of the thickness of the trees and the quantity of dead branches on the ground managed to gain the gully undiscovered. All night they then followed the gully which ran straight over the mountains, now ascending, now descending and occasionally crossing small water courses, until as morning broke they found themselves standing upon a slope of green turf, which undulated downwards until it was lost in the rolling prairie far beneath.

Slightly to the right could be seen a winding stream running nearly west and losing itself in the blue distance. This was the Rio Gila that empties itself in the Gulf of California running through a vast extent of prairie country. They would have to follow its turnings until arriving at the coast when they would cross the Rio Colorado and make for the town of San Miguel, there to obtain some information as to the exact whereabouts of the gold diggings.

This they did after a long, tedious, monotonous journey in which they met with no incident worth recording. The sun rose and set, the wind blew with its accustomed irregularity, the stream gurgled placidly over its rocky bed, fish sprung high in the air, buffalo fled at their approach, the night came as of old, the stars twinkled brightly and then grew dim, in short they arrived at San Miguel. It was a sample of most Mexican towns, large palaces jostling insignificant huts, all jumbled together without the slightest order or regularity. Here they made the necessary enquiries and wandered about its dirty streets for two days when, getting tired of houses, they started.

On the evening of the third day, as they were about to bivouac on the banks of a small stream, a red light arose a short distance ahead and at the same time a wild jovial song burst upon their ears, showing that the party ahead were whites and probably upon the same errand as themselves. They immediately packed up traps and walked forward to join the bacchannalians. On emerging into the light of the fire they beheld some dozen men seated around it who all sprung to their feet on seeing them. Imagine the surprise which seized the slim youth Ned when he beheld in one of the men—rifle in hand, bowie knife in girdle—who but the redoubtable Mr Snicks, his own respected and valued father. Mr Snicks in a moment recognised his son and rushing forward with indescribable motions of the arms, meant no doubt to express inexpressible joy folded him to his breast. Ned returned the embrace with vigour and on being released about one thousand questions poured in at his denoted ear. Where had he been, what was he doing, who were these with him, are merely examples. To answer all these at once was clearly impossible. Ned therefore answered one at a time and ended by introducing Ben and his other companions. Mr Snicks offered his paw, bowed with a courtly inclination, but put on a most sorrowful, dolorous tone when he addressed Ben, who eagerly enquired what was the matter.

Now the fact was Mr Snicks had been an auctioneer and consequently accustomed from his youth to tell the most enormous falsehoods, and now, seeing in prospect eighty guineas in his pocket, determined to throw what remained of his conscience to the gentleman in black and by fair means or foul—which to him was much the easiest—inveigle Ben to

England. He, therefore, with many expressions of his immense sorrow, acquainted Ben with the melancholy *fact* that, when he left the white cliffs of Albion in search of his fugitive son, Mrs Tubbs lay at the point, nay the very door, of death.

Ben loved his mother and upon the receipt of this awful intelligence sank to the ground and piteously whined for the space of fourteen minutes. He then arose and before the quarter of an hour had elapsed conveyed to Finnikin, Ned and Mr Snicks, who heard him with great internal joy, his resolution to make all speed for Britain.

Finnikin looked thunderstruck but could not in conscience oppose him, and Ned being now under parental government was silent. The silence was presently broken by Mr Snicks who in a loud firm voice proclaimed it as his intention, wind and weather permitting, to accompany him and take his regained rascally son with him. Finnikin looked awfully savage but of course could not dispute Mr Snicks' right to convey his property wherever his listed, but he passed the greater portion of that night in muttering nobody knew what. However it came to no head and the next day fortnight Ben, Ned, Mr Snicks and Finnikin stood upon the deck of an English vessel bound for London and getting under way.

With every argument they could think of the youths tried to persuade Finnikin to accompany them, but it was useless. He would come and see them at some future period, he promised, and that was all that could be got from him. The anchor was soon up, the sails spread and those who were not passengers were ordered on shore a few minutes afterwards. With a long hearty shake of the hand Finnikin stepped into his boat and was soon lost in the distance, his two men pulling swiftly for shore, while the vessel began to slip through the water. The youths passed a melancholy day and a much more melancholy night as seasickness prostrated them the easier for the excessive sorrow of parting. However in a few days they were well and strutting about the deck in fine style. No particular incident occurred during the voyage, favouring winds bore them swiftly forward, while occasionally a severe gale ruffled the serenity, and while it lasted gave a slight spice of danger, which was quite delightful. At last they arrived in the Channel and soon afterwards entered the noble Thames, which they tided up as the wind, for almost the first time, was unfavourable.

Having but little baggage and Ben a great desire to know if his mother still lived—which desire was only equalled by Mr Snicks's to pocket eighty guineas—they did not stop in the great city but immediately on landing set out for the country. Two days of bumps rapidly passed away and early on the third Ben beheld in the distance the well-remembered house, in which he had passed so many mischievous and consequently happy hours.

In a few minutes the coach stopped and Ben, impatient youth, not waiting for the others sprang out and rushing up the steps to the door banged away furiously with the knocker. Sarah opened it and upon perceiving him shrieked and fell upon her knees.

"Is she—?" said Ben, "is mother—?" but at that moment Mrs Tubbs, having heard the scream and burning with curiosity to know its cause, opened a door and stepped into the passage.

She stared at Ben in unspeakable surprise for half a second and then, shouting at the top of her delighted voice "Beny, Beny," rushed forward and buried him in kisses, dress and her maternal arms. Long did she hug him with tremendous strength making him groan with the excess of her motherly squeezing and he returned the compliment in good style. Smack, smack, smack, went volleys of kisses while the cook having arrived at the scene of action also fell upon her knees and shrieked in despair at seeing that "Young himp" safely returned and luxuriating in his mother's arms. The delighted woman quickly conveyed him to the parlour where a bright fire burned and a table groaned with the weight of eatables. Then, seeing him seated right in front of the fire that he might receive its full benefit, Mrs Tubbs looked to her other guests. She shook hands cordially with auctioneer Snicks who, bowing and smiling, had stood upon the doormat, refusing to come in any further, to the great disgust of Sarah who wished to shut the door.

He could not of course refuse Mrs Tubbs, the "sister in misfortune", who owed him eighty guineas, and Sarah then had the extreme pleasure to slam the door. She had however to open it the next minute as Dr Smales' equipage dashed up and his footman announced him with an aristocratic rat-a-tat-tat. What was his surprise upon seeing Mrs Tubbs, her hair in disorder and her cheeks red as if interrupted in blowing the fire, and his *quondam* pupils discussing a glass of ale, and Mr Snicks bowing with tremendous activity. It was unbounded. What was the youths' consternation when they beheld the Doctor, hat in hand, enter the apartment, bow to Mrs Tubbs and Snicks and cast a lightning glance of thunder at them. It was indescribable.

Mrs Tubbs was in her element: she bustled about, ordered more plates and finally announced dinner. All arose and sat at table when, after a most impressive extempore grace by the Doctor, the viands began to disappear while the table continually groaned as mouthful after mouthful was removed from it and it sprung to its old position.

After dinner the wine was pushed freely about, even the youths on the joyful occasion were allowed by indulgent Mrs Tubbs to have glass upon glass. Soon the article began to rise in their heads and escape in various Masonic nods, winks, and surreptitious conveyances of other people's property. As the afternoon wore on they grew more and more noisy until as tea was being brought in the room was in a perfect uproar and oranges, apples and nuts flew from side to side in great profusion. One of the first mentioned articles happened to light upon Sarah's right eye as she was placing the spoons, causing her to perform various gyrations in a backward direction, and to finally alight in a sitting posture in the coal-box. Shouts of frenzied laughter rang through the room at this successful hit of Ben's while poor Sarah, looking awfully indignant, rose from her position and rushed out slamming the door behind her.

"My coal, my coal, my carpet," sung Mrs Tubbs half angry, and she poured out tea. Its soothing influence somewhat abated the roistering mirth of the youths but when the card-table was presently produced it awoke with redoubled fury. Mrs Tubbs would allow them no more wine upon which Ben arose and, followed by Ned, descended to the cellar in spite of cook and Sarah, who vanished upon the rattling together of a poker and tongs with which the assailants were armed. Soon they reappeared in triumphal procession with bottles sticking out of every available pocket and corkscrews in hands. Then there would soon have commenced a terrific guzzling of wine had not the Doctor and Snicks stopped it and a game at Loo[16] commenced. Presently Ben said he was sure Ned had a card in his pocket. That young gentleman scouted the idea and returned the compliment. Up jumped Ben, up jumped Ned and

---

[16] A trick-taking card-game popular in the eighteenth and nineteenth centuries. Wordsworth refers to playing Loo as a boy in Book I of his autobiographical poem, *The Prelude*.

in attempting to walk through the table upset it and, both losing their balance, rolled upon the ground in utter confusion. Both were too lazy to rise so there lay until Mrs Tubbs, deafened with their roaring, requested the two gentlemen to help her upstairs with them. "Decidedly," said they and in ten minutes, as the youths being in the act of falling asleep made no resistance, they were popped into bed.

"Nice pair," said the Doctor as he pulled down a counterpane and extinguished Mr Ned Nidle and the redoubtable BEN TUBBS.

oooOOOooo

That night Mr Snicks the auctioneer departed for home with eighty guineas in his pocket, while Doctor Smales returned to Chilton and detailed the youths' return to his mother who threw up her arms, exclaimed, "Goodness gracious!" and fell to darning stockings.